PRETEND I'M DEAD

- A Novel -

JEN BEAGIN

SCRIBNER

New York   London   Toronto   Sydney   New Delhi

Scribner
An Imprint of Simon & Schuster, Inc.
1230 Avenue of the Americas
New York, NY 10020

First Scribner hardcover edition May 2018
Previously published in 2015 by TriQuarterly Press

For information about special discounts for bulk purchases,
please contact Simon & Schuster Special Sales at 1-866-506-1949 or
business@simonandschuster.com.

The Simon & Schuster Speakers Bureau can bring authors to your live event.
For more information or to book an event, contact the Simon & Schuster Speakers
Bureau at 1-866-248-3049 or visit our website at www.simonspeakers.com.

Interior design by Alexis Minieri

Manufactured in the United States of America

1   3   5   7   9   10   8   6   4   2

Library of Congress Cataloging-in-Publication Data is available.

ISBN 978-1-5011-8393-5
ISBN 978-1-5011-8394-2 (ebook)

For Heffo

CONTENTS

HOLE

FOR MONTHS HE WAS JUST A NUMBER TO HER: SHE COUNTED HIS dirties, he dropped them in the bucket, she recorded the number on the clipboard, and he moved down the line. Another pelican mired in oil, worn to the stump and nodding to his own ruin. A goner like the rest of them.

Then, after switching to the needle station—instead of counting, she handed out clean rigs—she noticed that he was the only exchanger carrying library books. Biographies, mostly, and crime fiction. She dubbed him Mr. Disgusting on account of his looks and dirty clothes. His hair was a long angry scribble in need of hot oil treatment, his face an overworked drawing with too many wrinkles, but he was tall and broad shouldered and could carry her around the block or up a flight of stairs if he ever needed or wanted to, a quality she'd found lacking in her previous boyfriends, and she was pretty much in love with his eyes, which were dark, frank in their expression, and seemed to say, You Are Here.

It was supposed to rain that night, the night of their first conversation. Half of the exchangers stood under a tarp; half were exposed to the stiff gray sky. The exposed ones looked sodden and miserable, even though it wasn't raining yet. Mr. Disgusting stood toward the end of the line. Unlike the others, he looked perfectly at ease, a book shielding his face. She squinted at the title: *Straight Life, the Story of Art Pepper*—whoever that was. She was already anticipating the somatic effect his presence had on her: when he was within five feet she'd suddenly lose her peripheral vision along with all the saliva in her mouth, and her heart would beat as if being hunted. Seeing him was the highlight of her two-hour commitment and tonight she'd made adjustments to her wardrobe, ditching her high-tops and hooded sweatshirt for ballet flats and a vintage leopard-print cape. She was even wearing blush and a padded bra.

The line shuffled forward and soon he stood before her, smiling faintly. He was wearing the leather jacket she liked—once white, now scuffed and weatherworn, with a cryptic tire mark running directly up the back. There was a dead leaf in his hair she didn't have the nerve to pluck out. She decided to stick to the script.

"How many?" she asked.

She expected the usual four clipped syllables: "Twenty-two, please." Instead he replied, "I was fleeced last week." He smiled with one side of his mouth. "Flimflammed," he said.

It was her turn to say something, but she was too startled by his voice, which was distinct enough to be its own creature. It had a spine and sharp little teeth.

"Actually, the cops took them," he said. "I just like saying flimflam."

She smiled. "Where?"

"Couple blocks from here."

The needle exchange was nothing more than supplies set up on roll-away carts, situated at the end of a little-known alley wedged between an abandoned convent and a Laotian bakery in what was called The Acre, a largely Cambodian neighborhood in Lowell. They'd been here five months but now it was October and soon they'd have to move indoors, somewhere under the radar.

"Must have been a rookie," she said.

Their tacit understanding with the cops was that they could operate the exchange in peace, so long as the exchangers didn't do anything stupid, such as sell needles for money or dope, or shoot up on the sidewalk, but occasionally the wrong cop wandered by and busted some hapless exchanger for possession and paraphernalia.

She shook out a paper bag and dropped in a starter kit. Technically, it was a one-for-one exchange, but if someone showed up empty-handed she gave them a bag of ten points and a small bottle of bleach.

"Thanks," he said. "I appreciate it. But I don't need the bleach."

No bleach meant he didn't clean his needles, which meant he probably didn't share them. She took this to mean he was single and unattached. She handed him the bag with what she hoped was an easygoing smile. In fact she felt queasy. It was always over too soon, and now she'd have to wait another week. He mumbled thank you and she watched him walk down the alley. He never looked back at her.

HE BECAME A FURTIVE PRESENCE IN HER LIFE. SHE FANTA-sized about him every other day, usually while vacuuming. She made her living as a cleaning lady and daydreaming was a vital part of her happiness on the job. Knowing nothing but his taste in drugs and library books, the daydreams were loose and freewheeling. She gave him a Spanish accent, a pilot's license, a way with words. She dressed him in various costumes—UPS uniform, lab coat, motorcycle leathers—and invented interesting monologues for him.

They had their second conversation three weeks later. The site had moved into the dingy waiting room of a free clinic two blocks south. She was working the supply table, handing out cotton balls, bleach, alcohol swabs, condoms, and donuts donated from the Lao bakery around the corner, perhaps in gratitude for moving out of their alleyway. The fluorescent lighting made her feel like she was in high school again, back when the medication had made her skin green and her nickname was Witchy. He asked for cotton and alcohol swabs. In an effort to prolong their encounter, she offered a handful of condoms—black, their most popular color—even though she suspected he didn't need or want any, as he wasn't a sex worker and his libido was likely a distant memory. He let out a sad laugh.

"What's funny?" she asked, playing dumb.

"Oh, nothing," he said, and shook his head. "It's just that I have little use for condoms except as water balloons, which I also have little use for."

He looked at the floor, seemingly searching for words. She grasped for something to fill the growing silence, but she was too captivated by his voice.

"Sorry," he said. "I've made you uncomfortable with my creepy honesty." He shook his head again.

"Not at all," she said. "I'm actually a fan of creepy honesty."

He made tentative eye contact. His eyes made her feel all gooey and exceptional, but the tension in his jaw told her he hadn't fixed that day, and she wondered how far from the site he lived. Was he able to wait until he got home, or was he like some of the other exchangers, who spiked themselves in public?

"Would you care for a bear claw?" she asked.

He nodded.

"Take two," she said, breaking the one-per-person rule.

He gave her a wide smile and she took a quick inventory of his teeth: all there, reasonably white, and sturdy enough to tear linoleum. A minor miracle.

"You're very kind," he said in an oddly deliberate way, as though speaking in code. She watched him turn abruptly, cross the street, and disappear around a corner.

HE VANISHED FOR MOST OF THE WINTER. SHE FIGURED HE was either in rehab, prison, or the ground. In his absence she grew listless and bored and almost quit, but what the hell else was she going to do on Tuesday nights? She lived alone, sans television. Her only friend was attending college in another state. She had more in common with the exchangers than anyone she knew. They were both invisible to the rest of society—they by their status as junkies, she by her status as maid—and they'd both eat pretty much anything covered in frosting. Spending time with her fellow volunteers was just as edifying. No do-gooders, no show-offs, no save-the-children types. They chain-smoked and ate nachos and hot dogs from 7-Eleven—she admired that.

Mr. Disgusting reappeared one afternoon in early spring, looking like an out-of-work character actor. He wore a seven-day beard, old sunglasses with amber lenses, a long-sleeved, forest-green button-up, some extra weight around his middle. He shuffled up and asked to speak to her alone. Excusing herself, she walked to the corner, stopping before a boarded-up tanning salon called Darque Tan II. She was going to say "It's good to see you," then opted for something more neutral. "I haven't seen you in a while."

"Rehab."

"I was hoping that's where you were."

"So you thought about me, then," he said, removing his glasses.

"Are you okay?"

He put his sunglasses back on. "I'm not very good at this."

"Good at what?"

He did some aggressive throat clearing. "I came here to give you something." He handed her a shard of broken mirror the size of her palm. It was thick and sail shaped and worn smooth around the edges. She looked at it briefly and mumbled thank you.

"Turn it over," he said impatiently.

He'd scrawled his name and phone number on the back in bright-pink crayon.

"I thought I'd put my number on a mirror so you can check yourself out while we're talking on the phone." He smiled.

She could tell he'd practiced the delivery of that line and she meant to reassure him, but was thrown off by the advice written on the wall behind him: "If God gives you lemons, find a new God."

"That is, if you feel like talking," he said.

She nodded slowly. In fact, she suddenly wasn't sure about any of it—him, herself, herself with him. In her fantasies they never bothered with phone numbers. He just showed up, wordlessly threw her over his shoulder, and then he carried her down a different alley, where they did some violent making out against a brick wall.

"Do you even know my name?" she asked.

He blushed. "I'm convinced it starts with *K*," he said.

"*M*," she said. "It starts with *M*."

"Mommy?"

She laughed. "Mona."

"Hm," he said. "Can I call you Mommy instead?"

"Maybe." Turning away, she nodded toward the mouth of the alley, where one of her fellow volunteers was talking on a cell phone and openly staring at them. "Look, Big Brother's watching."

"You care what they think," he said. "That's why you won't look at me?"

"I'm looking at you," she said, then looked at the ground.

"Well, call me if you feel like it."

She watched him walk away and thought back to the weekend of volunteer training mandated by the organization that ran the needle exchange. She and the other volunteers had role-played various hypothetical situations, such as what to do in the event that an exchanger inadvertently, or perhaps purposely, stuck you with a dirty needle. They never went over what to do if the exchanger handed you a broken mirror and asked you to call him sometime.

MOST DAYS SHE WORKED ALONE, IN THE FANCY PART OF town, where many of the houses still had servants' quarters left over from the last century. Her contact with the homeowners was limited, but when they discovered that English wasn't her second language, they treated her warily, as if she were mentally ill, learning disabled, or an ex-con. They assumed she was sullied somehow. Disgraced. The fact that she was white, managed to graduate from a decent parochial high school, and yet chose to clean houses seemed beyond their comprehension.

———

Right now she was cleaning the Stones' place with Sheila, her employer and legal guardian. The Stones lived in a sprawling Tudor mansion with a fireplace in every room, including the kitchen, which they were cleaning now. Sheila stood at the sink, rinsing dishes, and Mona was on her knees with her head in the oven, removing grease loosened with half a bottle of Easy-Off. Consequently, her skin was tingling and imaginary bionic noises accompanied the movement of her arms. Usually she enjoyed a good oven cleaner buzz, but just then she wanted to pull a Sylvia Plath. Sheila must have intuited as much, because she suddenly shut off the kitchen faucet and asked Mona if she was still taking her meds.

"Nope," she said. "Been drug free for three weeks now."

"How's Dr. Tattleman?"

"I quit her, too."

To Mona's surprise, Sheila seemed unconcerned. Nonchalant, even. "Well, how're you feeling?" she asked.

"Not as, uh, neutral as I'd like, but okay."

"You don't need to be any more neutral, honey," she said, and sniffed.

Mona waited for the inevitable barrage of AA slogans. Sheila could string two hundred together in one sentence.

"I'm going to miss you," Sheila said instead. "I miss you already."

In four days Sheila was fucking off to Florida. For good. She'd sold her house and the business and had just closed on a condo in God's waiting room, as she called it, where she planned to join a book club and take up golf.

"I wish you'd try group therapy," Sheila said.

"I'm tired of talking."

"Individual counseling promotes self-pity. There's less wallowing in group, and you don't have to talk if you don't want to. You can

---

8

share your pain and then just . . . turn it over, listen to someone else's problems."

"Turn it over?"

"To God," she said. "You know, let go and let God?"

Let go and let God? Let go and let God. Let go, let God! Let go! Let God! Let go!

Lately phrases got stuck in her head and tumbled around for days. They made a terrible racket, like loose change in a dryer. Last week it was "Get bent, you stupid bitch," which she'd heard someone shout from the open window of a pickup truck.

"You're not even here," Sheila said. "Where are you right now?"

"I'm here, I'm here." It was only noon and already she was bone-tired. Sheila, on the other hand, was just getting warmed up—she made cleaning look like swing dancing. Right now she was loading a dozen cereal bowls into the dishwasher. Cereal was all Mr. Stone seemed to eat, and he left milky bowls in every room.

"The man has serious Mommy issues," Mona said.

"Who?" Sheila said.

"Daddy Stone. The cereal bowls are like lactating boobs. He cradles them in his hand, shovels the cereal into his mouth, the milk dribbles down his chin, and it's like he's . . . nursing. He's probably all pacified and drowsy afterward, which is why he can't be bothered to bring the bowls to the kitchen."

"Stop," Sheila said. "He seems nice."

"Did you see the bidet they installed in the master bath? They can't even wipe their own asses."

Sheila frowned. "I agree it was an interesting choice."

Mona rolled her eyes. No matter how much Mona goaded her, Sheila refused to talk shit about their clients. "I'm sweating my balls off," Mona said. "Will you scratch my back?"

Sheila dried her hands and leaned over to scratch Mona's back. "Higher," she ordered.

"Maybe it's time you got a dog."

Mona laughed. "Why?"

"When you're forced to do things that take you *out* of yourself— like picking up dog poop—that's when you *find* yourself."

"You hate your dog," Mona reminded her. "He shits in your shoes, remember?"

"Go to the pound," Sheila said. "Adopt another terrier."

She'd grown up with two Jack Russells. This was back in Torrance, California. She'd named them Spoon and Fork. Spoon ran in circles, Fork in figure eights. They'd been loving and affectionate killing machines, and she'd loved them more than anyone, including her parents, but they'd been indomitable and were eventually sent to a farm in Idaho, or so she was told, and then her parents got wild, too, and divorced each other and shacked up with new people, and a year later, when she was twelve, she was sent to live with Sheila, her father's first cousin. Sheila was single, childless, and sober with a capital S, and she agreed to take Mona in without ever having met her. It was supposed to be just for a summer. She'd heard of Massachusetts, but for all she knew, New England was attached to England, or, if not attached, then possibly connected by a system of underground tunnels. Lowell and London, she imagined, were affiliated, and she envisioned herself walking along cobblestone streets in the fog, wearing a trench coat with the collar turned up, and living in a turret covered in ivy, images she'd culled from various movies and postcards.

"Service to others," Sheila said now, snatching the dirty sponge from Mona's hands and rinsing it in the sink. "It'll take your focus off your own problems." She squeezed water from the sponge and handed it back.

"Service to others," Mona repeated.

"It leads to greatness, sweetie."

"But I'm already a servant."

"Doesn't count," she said. "You make money."

"And I already volunteer, remember?"

"Yeah, but why'd you have to pick *that*? I mean, running abscesses? *Barf.*"

Mona shrugged and got to her feet. "What's for lunch?"

"Leftover Chinese."

Sheila nuked their lunch in the microwave. Crab rangoons, green beans, pork lo mein. They sat on stools in the butler's pantry and looked out the arched window. The Stones' garden was customarily pristine, but someone had maniacally hacked at all of their hydrangea bushes.

"Disgruntled gardener," Mona said, pointing. "Or maybe Mrs. Stone lost her mind."

Sheila nodded vaguely. "You know," she said. "The summers are hotter than Haiti in Florida, so maybe I'll spend part of August up here with you."

"Hades," Mona said.

"What?"

"Hades. Hotter than Hades."

"Hai-ti," Sheila said. "There's no *s* on the end."

"Hades is the underworld, Sheila. From Greek mythology? It's another term for hell. Haiti, on the other hand, is a country."

"You're upset."

"I'm fine," she said, and shrugged. "My correcting you is a sign of respect."

"You respect me?" Sheila asked, surprised. "As a person?"

"No, as a pigeon."

———

"Remember that first day, when I picked you up from the airport and you asked me if I masturbated?"

Mona rolled her eyes and bit into a crab rangoon.

"You were only twelve. That's when I knew you were special," Sheila said. "What's that word? Begins with a *p*."

"Precocious."

Sheila snapped her fingers. "Right."

"These crab rangoons are precocious," Mona said, chewing. "You should eat one."

Sheila cleared her throat. "You know, when I decided to sell the business and retire, my first thought was that I needed you to come with me. I even looked into colleges for you down there. But you're almost twenty-four now. I shouldn't be trying to caretake you. My sponsor says it's instinctive, deeply ingrained behavior, a result of my overattachment to you, and that I'm in danger of preventing you from taking the falls necessary for your personal growth."

"More falls?" She coughed. "That's what I need?"

"What you need is for me to let you make your own decisions and mistakes. Our relationship is very co- and always has been."

"Co-" was Sheila's shorthand for "codependent."

"Yeah, well, your lunch is getting co-," Mona said.

"I'm not very hungry, for some reason."

"Why didn't you just give the business to me?"

"Because then you'd stay in Lowell forever," Sheila said. "Which would depress the fuck out of me. And I can't just give it to you— I need the money, silly."

The buyer was some chick named Judy, who owned another cleaning business in Andover.

"So presumably I start working for this Judy person next week?"

"You won't even notice. Your schedule will be the same, and she'll cut you a check every two weeks."

"Fuck," Mona said. "So I have to start paying taxes."

"That's the only difference."

"Well, it's a pretty big difference."

"I think it's a good thing," Sheila said. "Maybe now you'll realize you need to do something else for a living."

Mona felt a twinge near the bottom of her spine. The pain shot down to her toes, which, as usual, were partially numb. If she made any sudden movements, her back would go out completely. This would include coughing or sneezing. Even whistling would be dangerous. But crying—crying would be worst of all.

"Who's going to be my emergency contact? Who will I not celebrate the holidays with?"

"You'll meet someone," Sheila assured her. "Trust me. He's going to sweep you off your feet and you'll forget all about me. Just promise me you'll stay in school."

SHE WAITED THREE DAYS BEFORE DIALING HIS NUMBER. IT rang five times and then his machine picked up. "Leave a message or not, I don't give a—" The beep came sooner than expected.

"Uhh, I'm calling you." Before hanging up, she added lamely, "It's Saturday." Realizing she forgot to leave her name and number, she waited a minute and tried again.

This time he answered on the first ring. "I was worried you wouldn't call back," he said, winded. "I forgot to change my voicemail recording."

"It's a little intimidating," she admitted. "I got flustered and forgot to say my name. How'd you know it was me?"

"You have this weird nonaccent," he said.

"I'm from Los Angeles," she explained. "Originally, I mean."

"You must be homesick."

"Nah," she said. "Lowell's gotten under my skin. I don't think I could live without all this brick and repression."

He asked why here, of all places.

"Oh, I was shipped here," she said. "When I was twelve. I've been here ever since."

"Must have been quite a shock, landing in this dump. You're probably still recovering."

"It took some getting used to," she admitted. "There's stuff here I'd never been exposed to in L.A."

"Such as?"

"Snow, wool, guilt."

He laughed. "You're probably saving your pennies to get out of here."

"I'm not a saver," she said. "And I have zero ambition."

There was a silence.

"What do you say we get together tomorrow?" he asked.

"Sure," she said. "Where?"

"My place," he said. "I want to get that out of the way—my living situation, I mean. Besides, it'll be good for you to see how the other half lives." He waited a beat. "You'll probably run away, screaming."

"Do you live in a commune or something?"

"No," he said.

"Projects?"

"No."

"Because I've seen projects before."

"It's worse than that," he said.

"You live in a Dumpster," she said. "Which is fine. I've been in Dumpsters before."

He snorted. "Just remember to bring your ID," he said. "They won't let you into the building without it."

"So it's like a nightclub, then," she said.

HE LIVED DOWNTOWN, IN A RESIDENTIAL HOTEL CALLED the Hawthorne, a six-story brick building sandwiched between a dry-cleaning plant and a Cambodian restaurant. When she arrived, three Cambodian gang members were loitering in front of the restaurant. It was broad daylight and she felt overdressed in her black kimono shirt and slacks. She also felt whiter and richer than she was. The sixty bucks in her pocket felt like six hundred.

The lobby had the charm of a check-cashing kiosk. A security guard stood at the door and a pasty fat man sat in a booth behind thick, wavy bulletproof glass. Mona slipped her ID through the slot.

"Who you here to see?"

She gave him Mr. Disgusting's name.

"Really?" he asked, looking her up and down.

"Yeah, really," she answered.

Mr. Disgusting came down a few minutes later, wearing gray postal-worker pants and a green T-shirt that said "Lowell Sucks."

"You look nice," she said.

"I scraped my face for you." He took her hand and brought it to his bare cheek and then clumsily kissed the tip of her thumb. She blushed, glanced at the fat man behind the desk, who studied them with open disgust. "You get your ID back when you leave the building," he said into his microphone.

They shared the elevator with a couple of crackheads she recognized from the neighborhood. Mr. Disgusting kept beaming at her as if he'd just won the lottery. For the first time in years, she felt beautiful, like a real prize. They got off on the third floor.

"It's quiet right now, but this place is a total nuthouse," he said.

"Doesn't seem so bad," she lied.

"Wait until dark," he said, pulling out his keys.

His room smelled like coffee, cough drops, and Old Spice. All she saw was dirt at first, one of the main hazards of her occupation. She spotted grime on the windowsill and blinds, dust on the television screen, a streaked mirror over a yellowed porcelain sink. The fake Oriental rug needed vacuuming, along with the green corduroy easy chair he directed her to sit in.

Once seated, she switched off her dirt radar and took in the rest of the room. She'd expected something bare and cell-like, but the room was large, warm, and carefully decorated. He had good taste in lamps. Real paintings rather than prints hung on the walls; an Indian textile covered the double bed. He owned a cappuccino machine, an antique typewriter, a sturdy wooden desk, and a couple of bookcases filled with mostly existential and Russian novels, some textbooks, and what looked like an extensive collection of foreign dictionaries.

"Are you a linguist or something?" she asked.

"No, I just like dictionaries." He sat directly across from her, on the edge of the bed, and crossed his legs. "I find them comforting, I guess. Most of these I found on the street."

"You mean in the trash?"

He shrugged. "I'm a slut for garbage."

"Your vocabulary must be pretty impressive," she said. "Do you have a favorite word?"

He thought about it for a second. "I've always liked the word 'cleave' because it has two opposite meanings: to split or divide and to adhere or cling. Those two tendencies have been operating in me simultaneously for as long as I can remember. In fact, I can feel a battle raging right now." He clutched his stomach theatrically.

She smiled. It was rare for her to find someone attractive physically and also to like what came out of their mouth.

"What's your *least* favorite word?" he asked.

"'Mucous,'" she said.

He nodded and scratched his chin.

"I wasn't born like this," he said suddenly. "Moving into this hellhole did quite a number on me—you know, spiritually or whatever. I haven't felt like myself in a long time."

He'd lived there seven years. Before that, he owned a house in Lower Belvidere, near that guns and ammo joint. He'd had it all: a garage, a couple of cats, houseplants. She asked what happened.

"I was living in New York, trying to make it as an artist," he said. "I had a couple shows, sold a few paintings, was on my way up. During the day I worked as a roofer in Queens." He stopped, ran his fingers through his hair. "One night I was on my way home from a bar and I was shit-faced, literally stumbling down the sidewalk, and out of nowhere, two entire stories of scaffolding collapsed on top of me, pinning me to the concrete. A delivery guy found me three hours later. Broke my clavicle, left arm, four ribs, both my legs. Bruised my spleen. My fucking teeth were toast.

"After I got out of the hospital, I couldn't exactly lump shingles as a roofer, so I crawled back to Lowell. Then I got this big settlement and was able to buy a run-down house, but one thing led to the other." He pointed to his arm. "I pissed it away, made some bad decisions. I've been living in a state of slow panic ever since."

"Sounds like you're lucky to be alive."

He shrugged. "Am I?"

She felt her scalp tingle. For as long as she could remember, she'd had a death wish, which she pictured as a rope permanently tied around her ankle. The rope was often slack and inanimate, trailing along behind her or sitting in a loose pile at her feet, but occasionally it came alive with its own single-minded purpose, coiling itself tightly around her torso or neck, or tethering her to something dangerous, like a bridge or a moving vehicle.

Mr. Disgusting plucked a German pocket dictionary off the shelf and leafed through it. He was certainly a far cry from the last guy she dated, some edgeless dude from the next town over whose bookshelves had been lined with CliffsNotes and whose heaviest cross to bear had been teenage acne.

"Do you know any German words, Mona?" he asked, startling her. It was only the second time he'd said her name.

"Only one," she said. "But I don't know how to pronounce it."

"What's it mean?"

"World-weariness."

"Ah, *Weltschmerz*," he said, smiling. "You have that word written all over you."

"Thanks."

He was beaming at her again. Where had he come from? He was too open and unguarded to be a native New Englander. She asked him where he was born.

"Germany," he said.

According to his adoption papers, his birth mother was a French teenage prostitute living in Berlin. An elderly American couple adopted him as a toddler and brought him to their dairy farm in New Hampshire.

"They would've been better off adopting a donkey," he said. "My mother was a drunk and my father danced on my head every other day."

18

He ran away with the circus when he was seventeen. Got a job shoveling animal shit and worked his way up to drug procurer. It wasn't your ordinary circus, though. It had all the usual circusy stuff, but everyone was gay: the owner, all the performers and clowns, the entire crew. Even the elephants were gay.

"What about you?" she asked.

"Straight as an arrow," he said. After a short silence he asked, "Why, are you?"

She made a so-so motion with her hand.

"Wishy-washy," he said. "You really are from L.A."

She laughed.

"Well, I'm glad we got our sexual orientation cleared up," he said. "Listen, there's something else I need to get out of the way. Our future together depends on your reaction to this." He smiled nervously.

"Fire away."

She was 90 percent certain he was about to tell her he was positive.

But he didn't say anything, just continued smiling at her, his upper lip twitching with the effort. She smiled back.

"What is this—a smiling contest?" she asked.

"Sort of," he said.

"You win," she said.

"Take a good look," he said.

"Yeah, I'm looking. I don't see anything."

He walked over to the sink and filled a glass with water, and then he removed his teeth and dropped them into the glass.

"I've read Plato, Euripides, and Socrates, but nothing could have prepared me for the Teeth Police," he said.

He held up the glass. The teeth had settled into an uneven and disquieting smile. She felt a sudden rawness in her throat, as if she'd been screaming all night.

"They're grotesque—don't think I'm not aware of that. I call the top set the Cathedral of Notre Dame. Notice the massive dome and flying buttresses."

She smiled. The lump in her throat had shrunk, allowing her to swallow.

"What I really need to do is have the roof cut out of the damn thing. There's this weird suction thing going on whenever I wear it."

"It *cleaves* to the roof of your mouth," she managed, and held her hand up for a high five.

"Precisely," he said, slapping her hand. "Very uncomfortable."

He set the glass on the sink and sat on the bed again, gazing distractedly out the window. She realized he was giving her a chance to study his face. He looked better without the teeth—more relaxed, more like himself somehow.

"Well," she said. "It's not like I've never seen false teeth before."

"Yeah, but have you been in love with someone who has them?"

She felt her eyes widen involuntarily. "Who says we're in love?"

"I do," he said.

For the first time since setting foot in the building, she felt a twinge of fear. She imagined him throwing her onto the bed, gagging her with one of his socks.

"I'm kidding," he said.

"How old are you?" she asked, changing the subject.

"Forty-four," he said.

"I might be too young for you," she said. "I'm only twenty-three."

"That isn't too young for me," he said seriously.

"Of course it isn't," she said, and laughed. "What I'm trying to say is that *you* might be too old for *me*."

He frowned. "I had a feeling the dentures would be a deal breaker."

"It's not that," she said quickly. Or was it? She imagined him suck-

---

ing on her nipples like a newborn, and then waited for a wave of repulsion to wash over her. Instead, she felt oddly pacified and comforted by the image, as if she were the one being breast-fed. "I'm thirsty," she said.

He made Mexican hot chocolate with a shot of espresso. They sat side by side on his bed, sipping in silence. She noticed a notebook lying on the bed and resisted the urge to pick it up. He saw her looking at it. "That's the notebook I write snatches of poetry and ridiculous ideas in," he said.

"Good to know."

"Do you have anything embarrassing you want to show me? A bad tattoo, perhaps?"

"My parents gave me away to a practical stranger, so my fear of abandonment feels sort of like a tattoo," she said. "On my brain."

He smiled. "You visit them?"

"Dad, never. Mom, rarely."

Rather than a photo, Mona kept a list of her mother's phobias in her wallet. She was afraid of the usual stuff—death, beatings, rape, Satan—but these commonplace fears were complemented by generalized anxiety over robbers, Russians, mirrors, beards, blood, ruin, vomiting, being alone, and new ideas. She was also afraid of fear, the technical term for which was 'phobophobia,' a word Mona liked to repeat to herself, like a hip-hop lyric. Whenever Mona longed for her, or felt like paying her a visit, she glanced at that list, and then thought of all the pills and what happened to her mother when she took too many, and the feeling usually passed.

"My parents are addicts," she said, and yawned. "But I shouldn't talk—I've been on my share of drugs. Psychiatric."

"Antipsychotics?"

She laughed. "Antidepressants."

"No shame in that," he said. "I'm on 400 grams of Mellaril. My doctor said I could develop something called rabbit syndrome, which is involuntary movements of the mouth." He twitched his mouth like a rabbit, and she laughed.

"What're you taking it for?" she asked.

"Opiate withdrawal," he said. "But they usually give it to schizophrenics."

She nodded, unsure of what to say. He grinned at her and suddenly lifted his T-shirt with both hands. On his chest, a large, intricate, black-and-gray tattoo of an old-fashioned wooden ship with five windblown sails. The *Mayflower*, maybe, minus the crew. Above the ship, under his collarbone, a banner read "Homeward Bound" in Gothic script.

"Wow," she said.

"One of the many useless things I purchased with my insurance money," he said.

"Well, this is kind of embarrassing," she said, "but I have some pretty big muscles. My biceps and calves are totally jacked. When I wear a dress—which is never—I look and feel like a drag queen."

"Let's see," he said.

She hesitated and then pushed up her sleeve and made a muscle.

"What are these?"

He was pointing to the scars on her upper arm. They were so old she didn't even see them anymore, but she looked at them now. There were four in that spot, about two inches long each. The cutting had started her sophomore year, immediately following her first dose of rejection by a boy she'd met at a Circle Jerks show.

"Teenage angst," she said.

"Ah."

"Maybe that's more embarrassing than the muscles."

He made a sympathetic noise and traced one with his finger. Usually she flinched whenever someone touched her arm, but she liked the feel of his hand. She felt something shift inside her—a gentle leveling, as if she'd been slightly out of plumb her whole life without knowing it.

He squeezed her bicep. "Are you a gym rat, love?"

"God, no." She laughed. "I vacuum. I'm a cleaning lady."

He blinked at her. "What—like a janitor?"

"Residential."

"So you clean . . . houses."

"Two or three a day," she said. "In Belvidere, mostly."

"You clean for a bunch of rich turds," he said, finally wrapping his head around it.

"Basically," she said. "Why the surprise?"

"I just think you're a little above that kind of thing. Seems like a waste."

She shrugged. "I've always felt a weird affinity for monotony and repetition."

In fact, vacuuming was among her favorite activities. On applications she listed it as one of her hobbies. Even as a child she preferred vacuuming over things like volleyball and doll play. Her classmates had been forced to learn the cello and violin, but her instrument, and strictly by choice, had been a Hoover Aero-Dyne Model 51.

As a teenager she developed a preference for vintage Eurekas. Now she owned four: models 2087, 1458, an Electrolux canister vacuum, and a bright-red, mint-condition Hot Shot 1423, which she christened Gertrude. She'd found Gertrude in a thrift store. Love at first sight.

"Anyway, I'd much rather push Gertrude around someone's house than sit in a generic office all day. I've always felt very relaxed in other people's homes, and I like the intimacy involved, even though it's not shared—these people don't know the first thing about me. But yes, the rich turds, as you call them, can be a bitch to work for—it's true. I think many of them struggle with the, uh, intimacy."

"Why—are you sleeping with them?"

"Of course not." She laughed. "I never see them. Many of them I've never met in person. But I know as much as a lover might—more, maybe—and they seem to resent me for that."

"Ah," he said. "You're a snoop."

"I'm thorough," she said. "And . . . observant. You learn a lot about a person by cleaning their house. What they eat, what they read on the toilet, what pills they swallow at night. What they hold on to, what they hide, what they throw away. I know about the booze, the porn, the stupid dildo under the bed. I know how empty their lives are."

"How do you know they resent you? Do they leave turds in the toilet?"

"They leave notes," she said. "To keep me in my place. Funny you mention toilets—yesterday a client left me a note that said, 'Can you make sure to scrub under the toilet rim? I noticed some buildup.' And I was like, Oh wait a minute, are you suggesting I clean *toilets* for a living? Because *I'd totally forgotten*—thanks."

He scowled. "I'm glad I don't have to work for assholes."

"Why don't you?" she asked.

He smiled and told her he made his living as a thief.

Awesome, she thought. Well, he lived in a hotel so he was definitely small-time. She pictured him running through the streets, snatching purses.

"You don't take advantage of old ladies, do you?" she thought to ask.

"I do, in a way," he said matter-of-factly. "I mean, sometimes I do."

"Well, are you going to elaborate, or do I have to guess?"

"I work for a flower distributor," he said. "I supply him with pilfered flowers."

"You're a *flower* thief?" Now it was her turn to be baffled.

"That's right. It's seasonal work."

Well, it explained the dirt under his fingernails and the scratches on his hands and arms.

"It's hard work," he said. "There's a lot of driving and sneaking around. And I have to work the graveyard shift, obviously."

"What kind of flowers do you steal?"

"Hydrangeas, mostly. Blue hydrangeas."

"You just wander into people's yards?"

He nodded. "Just me and my clippers! I can wipe out a whole neighborhood in under an hour," he said, clearly pleased with himself.

She thought of the hacked bushes she'd seen in the Stones' yard last week. "I think I'm familiar with your work, actually," she said. "So what do you steal in the winter?"

"Why not ask me in December?" He winked.

"How's the pay?"

"The guy I work for is a friend of mine. He pays me under the table for the hydrangeas, but he also keeps me on the payroll so I get benefits. It's like a real job. Anyway, don't look so upset. It's not like I'm stealing money. They grow back."

Against her better judgment, which had left the room hours ago and was probably on its way to the airport, she hung around. They continued talking and swapping war stories, sitting side by side on the bed. By the time the streetlights came on, he took the liberty of leaning in for their first kiss. It was just as she'd imagined it all those months—dry, sweet, a little on the solemn side.

IT WAS LIKE DATING A RECENT IMMIGRANT FROM A DEVEL-
oping nation, or someone who'd just gotten out of jail. They went
out for dinner and a movie, usually a weekly occurrence for her, but
Disgusting's first time in over a decade. The last movie he'd seen in
the theater was *The Deer Hunter*. At the supermarket she steered him
away from the no-frills section and introduced him to real maple
syrup, fresh fruit, vegetables not in a can, and brand-name cigarettes.
He showed his thanks by silently climbing the fire escape at dawn,
after his flower deliveries, and decorating her apartment with stolen
hydrangeas while she slept. Easily the most romantic thing anyone
had done for her, ever.

Besides the flowers, his first significant gift was a series of drawings he found in the basement of a condemned house. There were
seven in total, about five by seven inches each, loosely strung together
in the upper-left corner with magenta acrylic yarn. They were crudely
drawn in black and red crayon, seemingly by a child. She liked them
instantly but was much more fascinated with the captions scrawled
across the top of each one. The captions read:

There was a house
A little girl
Two dogs
One Fat Fuck
It was a nice skirt
Fat Fuck was found with no hands
Fat Fuck is dead

He thought the best place to display them was the bathroom.
"It'll give us something to contemplate on the can," he said. "We can
come up with Fat Fuck theories."

They decided to hang them side by side above the towel rack, and she stood in the doorway, watching him tap nails into the wall. She'd never been in a relationship with someone who owned a hammer. He was wearing a pair of checkered boxers and his Jack Kerouac T-shirt, which had a picture of Kerouac's mug on the front, along with the caption "Spontaneous Crap." He'd made the shirt himself and usually wore it during the annual Kerouac Festival, when Kerouac's annoying friends and fans descended upon Hole to pontificate about the Beat Generation. He called himself president of the I-Hate-Jack-Kerouac Fan Club.

His teeth, she noticed, were resting on top of the toilet tank. As usual, the sight of them produced a buzzing in her brain, like several voices talking over one another. She wanted to put them back in his mouth, or in a jar, the medicine cabinet, a drawer. They needed some kind of enclosure.

"Ever been with a fat guy?" he asked.

She told him yeah, she'd gone to the prom with a fatty named Marty, a funny and friendless guy she knew from art class. He'd been a couple years older than her and, at age seventeen, had already been to rehab twice. Since his license was suspended, his mother had driven them to the prom in her Oldsmobile, and they'd sat in the backseat as if it were a limo.

"Did you wear a dress?" he asked.

"I did," she said. "It was black and made of Spanish lace. I found it in a thrift store. It came with a veil, but Sheila wouldn't let me wear that. In fact, she insisted I wear this really gay red flower in my hair."

"I bet you looked like a hot tamale," he said.

"I've always wanted to be more Spanish," she admitted.

"How Spanish are you?"

"A quarter."

"How was it, being with a fat guy?" he asked. "Were you on top?"
She rolled her eyes. "Never happened."

"Did you get loaded?"

"We split half a gallon of chocolate milk on the way there. Then he had a panic attack, so I fed him some of my Klonopin."

He scratched his beard. "We should start a band called Klonopin."

She brushed by him and retrieved an old canning jar from under the bathroom sink. She filled it with water and then dropped the dentures into the jar and placed it on the counter, next to her toothbrush. When she looked at him she was startled to see tears in his eyes.

"What's wrong?"

"Nothing," he said.

"It's just a jar."

He shook his head. "You're the first woman to touch my teeth without wincing."

"I clean toilets for a living," she reminded him. "It's hard to make me queasy."

"Makes me want to marry you."

She laughed. He'd been saying that a lot lately.

IF ONLY THEIR SEX LIFE WERE LESS DIFFICULT. HE REFERRED to his organ as either "a vestigial, functionless appendage" or "the saddest member of the family." As for hers, he paid it a lot of attention and talked about it as if it were his new favorite painting—how young and fresh; what extraordinary color and composition. "You have the most beautiful pussy I've ever seen in person," he marveled. "And I've seen dozens. You can't imagine the shapes they come in." Since he'd taken care to qualify the compliment with "in person"—obviously, he'd seen more beautiful pussies in print or on film—she thought it must be true, and it popped into her mind randomly and without warning, while cleaning out someone's refrigerator or vacuuming under a bed.

He made love to her primarily with his hands and mouth—like a woman would, he said—and also with his voice. She wasn't read to as a child, which he considered an outrage, and so, after sex—or sometimes before—he read to her from Kipling's *The Jungle Book* (his choice), which suited his voice perfectly, because if wolves could talk they would sound just like him, and then short stories by Hemingway, whom he called Uncle Hem, and Flannery O'Connor and Chekhov and some other people she'd never heard of.

On Sundays they climbed the fire escapes of the abandoned mills downtown—their version of hiking—and rolled around on the rooftops. If the weather was nice they smoked cigarettes and took black-and-white photographs of each other with her old Nikon. After one such expedition near the end of August, they were walking back to her apartment when Disgusting veered toward a large pile of garbage someone had left on the street.

"Mind if I sift through this stuff?" he asked.

She waited on a nearby stoop. She heard someone exit the building behind her and blindly scooted over to let the person pass.

"Mona," a voice said.

It was Janine Stromboni, an old acquaintance from high school, one of the few girls Mona had liked, even though they'd had zero in common. Janine looked much the same: huge hair, liquid eyeliner, fake nails, tight jeans.

"Wow," Mona said. "You live here?"

"Just moved in," Janine said, and sat down. "You still smoke?"

Mona fished two out of her bag and lit them both before passing one to Janine. They chatted for a few minutes and then Mr. Disgusting waltzed up carrying a green vinyl ottoman.

"A footrest for my footsore princess," he said, and gallantly placed it at her feet.

She introduced Disgusting to Janine. To Mona's relief, he looked good that day, like your average aging hipster. He had a tan, recently dyed black hair, and was sporting a Mexican cowboy mustache. His denim cutoffs were a little on the dirty side, but his shirt was clean, and Janine would never know the shoes he was wearing had been retrieved from a Dumpster.

Janine, however, looked plainly disgusted by Disgusting, and for a split second she saw him through Janine's eyes: an old dude with dirty hair and no teeth, what Janine would refer to as a "total creature."

Janine bolted right after the ciggie. The encounter permanently altered Mona's perception of Disgusting, and from that day forward, depending on the light and her angle of perspective, he alternated between the two versions—aging hipster, total creature, aging hipster, total creature—like one of those postcards that morphs as you turn it in hand.

Her feelings for him, however, didn't change. If anything, she grew more attached. Like cancer, he had a way of trivializing the other aspects of her life. Things that had previously seemed important were now pointless and absurd, her college career in particular. So, when the time came to register for the fall semester, she blew it off. Her major, studio art with a concentration in photography, seemed like a joke now, especially in busted and depressing-as-hell Hole. If she was going to study art, she reasoned, didn't it make more sense to go to a real art school in a city that inspired her?

"Fuck art school altogether," Disgusting said. They were in bed, wearing only their underwear and listening to his collection of psychedelic records, which he'd brought over to her apartment on their fourth date and to which they'd been dancing ever since. Dancing, Disgusting maintained, was the key to salvation.

"I can see going to college for math or science," he said. "But art? Waste of time. All you really need is persistence and good taste, which you already have. The other junk you can pick up from books." He smiled and slipped his hand into the front of her underpants. She was wearing one of her days-of-the-week underwear, the green nylon ones with yellow lace trim, the word "Wednesday" stitched across the front in black cursive. It was Friday.

"You smell different today." He removed his hand and thoughtfully sniffed his fingers. "You smell like . . . hope."

"What do I usually smell like—despair?"

"Like a river," he said. "A little-known river in Latvia."

She pulled at the waistband of his boxers, but he stopped her. "Let's leave my genitals out of this."

"Why?"

"Too sad and disappointing."

"But I like your sad and disappointing genitals," she assured him. "Besides, they wouldn't be so sad if you weren't so mean to them."

He kissed her hand and placed it on his chest and she traced the words "Homeward Bound" with her finger. "Move in with me," she heard herself say.

He was silent for a minute. "I'm pretty high maintenance right now."

"I can handle it."

He cleared his throat. "Let's embrace our lone-wolf status. Few people have what we have, which is true and total freedom. No parents, siblings, spouses. No offspring. Nothing to tie us down. We can roam the earth and never feel guilty for leaving anyone behind, for not living up to someone else's expectations."

———

"Sounds lonely," she said.

"Don't think of loneliness as absence. If you pay attention, it has a presence you can feel in your body, like hunger. Let it keep you company."

"That's not the kind of company I want."

He kissed her mouth. "We're lucky we found each other," he said. "Two orphans."

SHE VISITED HIM IN HIS ROOM AT THE HAWTHORNE TWICE A week. Once, after a reading session, he excused himself to go to the bathroom, located down the hall, and while he was gone she heard someone tap on his door with what sounded like acrylic fingernails.

"It's me," a female voice sang out.

Mona opened the door to a shapely woman with a pretty face and a crazy look in her eye. She looked American Indian—brown skin, tall nose, long black hair parted down the middle—and was wearing a red button-down blouse with open-toed stilettos half a size too small. She'd apparently forgotten to put pants on, but had had the presence of mind to wear underwear. Mona wondered whether she was a prostitute, insane, or both.

"Is he here?" the woman asked.

"He's in the bathroom," Mona said.

"Are you a cop?"

"No." Mona snorted. "Why, do I look like a cop?"

"Sort of."

"Well, I'm not," Mona said.

"Just slumming then, I guess," the woman said, but not unpleasantly.

She shrugged. You may have bigger tits than I do, she thought, but otherwise we're not so different. We both have jobs that require us to work on our knees.

"Well, tell him I came by," the woman said as she walked away.

When Mr. Disgusting came back he launched into a story about his near suicide in Oaxaca, where he'd planned to shoot himself in the head with a gun he'd purchased in Mexico City, but had been too distracted by the scorpion on his pillow—

"Do you have a date tonight?" she interrupted.

"What?"

"Some chick came by looking for you."

"What'd she look like?"

"A pantless Pocahontas."

"Roxy," Disgusting said. "She's a sweetheart. You'd really like her."

"Is she your girlfriend or something?"

"God, no," he said. "I look after her and a couple of her friends."

There was a silence while she turned this over in her mind. "Are you telling me you're a pimp?" she asked. "Because that would be worse than having no teeth. Much worse."

"I prefer 'Gangster of Love,'" he said, somewhat smugly.

"Terrific."

"It's not what you think," he said. "Since I work nights, I let them use my bed, provided they change the sheets. I give them a clean, safe place to conduct business. I consider it an act of kindness."

"What do they give in return?"

"Beer money, actually." He raised his shoulders in a so-sue-me gesture.

"But you're sober now," she reminded him.

"I know," he said. "Look, this isn't *Taxi Driver*, okay? These girls aren't twelve years old. *I'm* not the one turning them out. They'd be doing it anyway, only they'd be out God knows where, in the back of a van—"

"Dating a pimp isn't what I envisioned for myself at this point," she interrupted. "At any point," she corrected herself.

"All I ask is that you try not to judge me."

She sat there for a minute, trying.

"You can leave if you want," he said. "I'm not holding you hostage here. We could end this right now, in fact. But I don't think we're done with each other yet, do you?"

"No," she said morosely.

"Look, I'll start packing tomorrow," he said. "Okay? I'll move in next week."

TWO DAYS LATER, IN THE MIDDLE OF A THURSDAY NIGHT, HE called and said he was having trouble reading the writing on the wall. She knew what he meant, and replied that she, too, couldn't always see what was right in front of her. She needed some distance from it, space—

"No, Mona, there's actual *writing on the wall*, but I can't read it," he interrupted. She heard panic in his voice. "It's only there when I turn the lights off and I hold a flashlight to it."

"What's it look like?" she asked.

"Like a swarm of bees, scribble-scrabbling."

"Scribble-scrabbling?"

"Yeah, like, protecting the queen," he said.

"Are you on mushrooms?"

"It's ballpoint ink, strangely enough," he continued, ignoring her. "Red ballpoint."

"Well, is it cursive, or what?" she asked, at a loss.

"Yeah, only it's swimming backward. It's indescribable, really. Could you come over? Just for five minutes? I'm freaking out."

She sneaked into the back of his building, ran up the stairs, and let herself in with the key he'd given her. He was passed out on his back with his mouth ajar, naked except for a hideous turquoise Speedo, clutching a flashlight against his chest like a rosary. She looked at the walls: nothing there, of course.

She figured he took one Mellaril too many, but in his nightstand drawer she found a dirty set of works surrounded by dirty cotton, and her head started spinning. His arms were bruise free, but his hands and feet were swollen and she saw the beginning of an abscess on his ankle. He must have been putting it in his legs or feet. Fuck!

His notebook was lying open on his pillow and she read the open page:

> I have renewed my travel visa to my favorite island.
> Now I can come and go without being stopped by the
> border police and accused of trespassing. It is pathetic
> how much I've missed this island's scenery, its exotic
> food, its flora and fauna. Tonight I am in my little plane,
> flying around the island's perimeter. To amuse myself,
> I perform tricks: triple corkscrews and low, high-speed
> flybys—my version of a holding pattern. But I'm running
> out of gas. The engine keeps cutting in and out, making
> little gasping noises. I'll probably crash any minute now.

She was offended that she didn't see her name in his diary. She tried nudging him awake, but he was out cold. No point in hanging around. She didn't want to leave, though, without him knowing she'd been there. Rather than write a note, she removed her left shoe and then her purple sock, and slipped the sock over his bare foot. He flinched but never opened his eyes.

———

35

Over a week passed. He didn't call and wouldn't answer his phone. She waited for her back to go out, which was usually how her despair chose to manifest itself, but instead she became suddenly and bizarrely noise sensitive. At the supermarket she was so overwhelmed by the noise she had to clamp her hands over her ears and hum to herself, sometimes abandoning her shopping cart. After an embarrassing incident at Rite Aid, wherein she asked a woman if there was any way the woman could quiet her baby, who wasn't even crying, just cooing, she had the bright idea to purchase earplugs, and took to wearing them whenever she left her apartment.

At work she raided people's refrigerators, often taking breaks in the middle of the day to eat and lounge around in their living rooms, reading magazines or watching television. When there was nothing to eat, she raided medicine cabinets. Xanax, Valium, Vicodin, Darvocet—only one or two of whatever was on the menu, enough to take the edge off and still be able to vacuum. She'd always had a snooping policy—No Letters, No Diaries—but when she was high and itchy she read people's diaries and personal papers. She read them hungrily, even if they were boring. And they were almost always boring. Afterward, she felt nauseated and ashamed, as if she'd eaten an entire birthday cake and then masturbated on their bed.

It was while reading Brenda Hinton's weight-loss diary—full of body measurements, scale readings, and daily calorie intakes—that she finally broke down. That is, she had a coughing attack, which triggered a gripping back spasm, the likes of which she'd never felt before. She fell to her knees and lowered herself the rest of the way to the floor, where she lay for twenty minutes or so, staring at a water stain on the ceiling while Brenda Hinton's dog, a miniature schnauzer with an underbite, calmly licked her elbow. Eventually she reached for the phone and called Sheila in Florida.

"What's the matter?" Sheila asked.

"Back," she said. "Muscle spasm."

"Yoga, honey," Sheila said.

"The downward dog isn't going to help right now." The schnauzer seemed to roll his eyes at her. She decided she didn't like dogs with bangs.

"I never hear from you. What's going on?"

She spilled the beans: she'd fallen for an addict, someone she met at the needle exchange. They were in a relationship. Yes, a romantic one. He'd been sober for six months. Now he wasn't. "Blah, blah," she said. "You've seen the movie a million times."

To her relief, Sheila didn't offer any banal Freudian interpretations.

"Maybe now you've finally hit bottom." Sheila sighed. "I know you won't go to Al-Anon, but it's time to get on your knees and start talking to your H.P."

"What's that again?"

"Higher Power, babe."

"Right," she said. "Small problem: I don't believe in God. As you know."

"What happened to Bob?"

Bob had been her nickname for God when she was a child. She'd talked to Bob like an invisible friend. She'd mentioned this to Sheila in passing once, years ago, and Sheila never forgot it.

"Bob's dead," Mona said. "Prostate cancer."

"He's not dead, sweetie," Sheila said sadly. "But forget about Bob. Your H.P. can be anyone. It can be John Belushi or Joan of Arc or Vincent van Gogh. In fact, Van Gogh might be perfect for you. He was tortured by his emotions, never received positive feedback, and died without selling a single painting. If his spirit is out there, it can relieve you of your suffering. So, start now. Get on your knees and ask Vincent for help."

SHE TOOK THREE DAYS OFF WORK, TWO OF WHICH SHE SPENT resting her back. On the third day she hobbled to the Hawthorne and let herself into his room. He was in the same position as last time, lying diagonally on his bed and wearing only his underwear. His room was trashed: he'd stopped doing laundry, emptying ashtrays, taking out the garbage.

She waved her hand in front of his face, snapped her fingers. He opened his eyes momentarily and whispered, "I'm gonna put my boots on and make something happen." Then he nodded out again. She envied the blankness on his face.

Her presence never fully registered with him and she sat in the corner for twenty minutes, feeling as invisible as a book louse. It was worse than the way she felt at work, passing in and out of rooms, a ghost carrying a cleaning bucket.

Again, she wanted to let him know she'd been there. She removed an earring and placed it on his nightstand, along with some items from the bottom of her purse—a broken pencil, a ticket stub to a Krzysztof Kieślowski film, several sticky pennies.

It became a kind of ritual. Over the next several weeks she visited his room and left behind little tokens of herself: his favorite pair of her underwear, a lock of her hair, a grocery receipt. When she was feeling bold, she tacked a picture of herself onto the wall near his bed. But now he was never there when she was. She figured he was out and about, *making something happen* somewhere. Still, leaving the items made her feel less adrift, less beside the point. In fact, she was amazed by how much a few minutes spent in his room—marking her territory, as it were—seemed to straighten her out.

One day he surprised her by being not only there, but awake and lucid. She hadn't seen him in three weeks and was startled by the amount of weight he'd lost, particularly in his face—his eyes were what they called sunken—and by the fullness of his beard, which he tugged on now as he sat on the edge of his unmade bed.

"Are you here to deliver one of your voodoo objects?"

She shrugged, embarrassed. "I guess I'm worried you'll forget me."

He nodded thoughtfully, as if she'd just said something really interesting. She noticed the loaded syringe parked on his nightstand, waiting for takeoff. "Looks like I'm interrupting your routine," she said.

"I can wait until you leave."

"Pretend I'm not here," she said, and felt her chin tremble. She'd missed his voice, his anecdotes, his eyes on her.

"I have to hop around on one leg to find a vein these days. It's humiliating enough without an audience." Apparently the feeling wasn't mutual; he didn't miss her eyes on him, or anything else about her. In fact, he barely looked at her. She sat down in the armchair.

"Why'd you relapse? Is it because we're moving in together? If it freaks you out that much, we don't have to do it."

He shook his head. "It'll sound stupid to you."

"Try me," she said.

He pursed his lips, shook his head again.

"What's with the sudden reticence?" she asked. "I thought you were the show-and-tell type."

He crossed his legs, lit a cigarette, blew smoke toward the ceiling. If she were one of those willful, high-maintenance girls, she'd be throwing a tantrum right now—stomping her feet, interrogating him, demanding answers. But then, a high-maintenance girl never would have set foot in the building in the first place, wouldn't even be seen in the neighborhood. "You know, you're lucky I'm so easygoing," she said, stupidly.

"It was free," he said after a minute. "And it hadn't been free in twenty years. It's hard to say no when something is free, especially for someone like me."

"That's your excuse?"

"It's really as simple as that," he said. "It has nothing to do with you."

"Is that all you have left?" she asked, nodding toward his night-stand.

"For now," he said.

"If I buy some more, can we do it together?" she asked. "I have a wicked backache."

He studied her face for several seconds, finally acknowledging her, but it was quickly followed by indifference and his gaze returned to the floor.

Since he'd apparently chosen drugs over her, even after everything she'd shared with him—her mattress, her secrets, her so-called beautiful whatsit—it seemed only fair that she know what she'd been up against. She pulled forty dollars from her wallet. "Is this enough?" she asked, placing the money on the bed.

"Cut it out," he said, rolling his eyes.

"I'm serious," she said.

He picked up the syringe and held it in front of her face. "*This is this*," he said emphatically. "It isn't something else. *This is this*."

She blinked at him. "Is that a line from a movie?"

He crossed his arms. "Maybe."

"You're being slightly grandiose," she said. "You know that, right?"

"Yeah, well, you're not taking this shit seriously enough," he said.

TWENTY MINUTES LATER, THEY WERE SITTING ON HIS BED and he was inserting his only clean needle—the loaded one on his nightstand—into her arm. "That syringe looks really . . . full," she said, too late.

"Believe me, it's barely anything," he assured her.

The next thing she knew, she was lying on the floor of a stuffy attic. The air smelled like pencil shavings. A fan, some high-powered industrial thing, was on full blast, making a loud whirring noise and blowing a thousand feathers around. It was like the Blizzard of '78. Then the fan clicked off and she watched the feathers float down, in zigzaggy fashion. They landed on her face and neck and she expected them to be cold but they were as warm as tears, and that's when she realized she was crying and that the feathers were inside her. So was the fan. The fan was her heart. A voice was telling her to breathe. She opened her mouth and felt feathers fly out. There was a rushing noise in her ears, a mounting pressure in her head, a gradual awareness that something was attached to her. A parasite. She was being licked, or sucked on, by a giant tongue, a wet muscle. The sucking sensation was painful and deeply familiar, but there was no comfort in the familiarity, only dread, panic. She felt herself moving, flailing, trying to get away from it.

When she opened her eyes she felt a presence next to her on the bed. An exhausted female presence. She gasped, turned over, and found Mr. Disgusting sitting on the edge of the bed, scribbling in his little notebook.

"Ah, you're back," he said. "You had me worried for a minute."

She tasted blood in her mouth. "Did something . . . happen?"

He closed his notebook, placed his pencil behind his ear. His pupils were pinned. "I lost you for a few minutes."

"I passed out?"

"I think you must be allergic to amphetamines."

"What?"

"You have a cocaine allergy," he said patiently, as if he were a doctor. "You're probably allergic to Novocain, too. And caffeine, maybe. Does coffee make your heart race?"

"I thought we were doing . . . *heroin.*"

"I mix them together," he said. "I mean, nothing major—just a little pinch. It was meant for me, not you, and I'd forgotten about it."

"Where are my boots?" she asked.

"You looked like a half-dead fish lying on the pier, just before it gets clobbered."

"So what," she said. "Who gives a shit?"

"I do," he said. "That's why I took such careful notes. I knew you'd want to know exactly what happened."

"So what if I died while you were taking notes? You're obviously too wasted to take me to the hospital."

"Since when do you care about dying? Besides, I knew you wouldn't *die* die. I was keeping my finger on your pulse the whole time. Your heart stopped beating for about five seconds and then it normalized. Let me ask you something: did you see anything? A white light? A tunnel? Dead people?"

"I was inside a vagina," she said. "A giant vagina, it felt like, but then I realized it was regular sized and I was just really small."

He smiled and nodded, as if he'd been there with her. "Whose was it?"

"My mother's, probably." She shuddered and hugged herself. "Is it cold in here?"

"You have a really weird expression on your face," he said.

"Do you realize how shitty it is to be born?"

He did some slow-motion blinking.

"It's excruciating—physically, I mean. There must be some mechanism in the brain that doesn't allow you to remember, because if you had to live consciously with that memory . . . well, you'd never stop screaming."

"It's called birth trauma," he said, nodding. "But I doubt it compares to other kinds of trauma. You know, like slavery. Or torture." He gave her a significant look, but she was too nauseated to respond. She got out of bed, hobbled down the hall to the bathroom, locked the door behind her. There it was, her stupid face in the mirror.

Where's your lipstick, she heard Sheila's voice say. *You look like hell. Why don't you get on your knees—right here, right now—and talk to your H.P.?*

She was on her knees two minutes later, vomiting into the already-filthy toilet. Puking was easy, almost pleasurable—like sneezing. She flushed, examined the ring around the bowl, imagined herself dumping Comet into it, scrubbing with a brush, spraying the lid with Windex, wiping it clean with toilet paper, moving on to the rest of the toilet—the tank, the trunk, the floor around it—

Detach, she ordered herself. Observe. Observe the dirt.

Someday, hopefully, she'd be able to enter a bathroom, even on drugs, and not envision herself on her hands and knees, scrubbing the baseboards with a damp sponge—

———

And that's when she noticed Mr. Disgusting's handwriting right next to the light switch:

> If we had beans,
> we could make beans and rice,
> if we had rice.

BACK IN HIS ROOM, HE WAS STILL IN BED, PROPPED UP against the filthy wall with a belt around his arm. His body was slack, his eyes half open. She wondered if he'd had more dope all along, or if he'd gotten it from one of his neighbors while she was in the bathroom.

"Sometimes I wish I were made of clay," he mumbled.

He was miles away now, in his little plane, she imagined, flying around his favorite island. She put her boots on and he opened his eyes and said, "No, no, no—stay." He patted the space next to him on the bed. "I'll read you a story. Chekhov. 'The Lady with the Dog.'"

"I'm sick of stories."

In fact she felt a little like Anna Sergeyevna right now, after she and Gurov have sex for the first time. Disgraced, fallen, disgusted with herself. Aware that her life is a joke. Anna gets all moody and dramatic, but Gurov doesn't give a fuck, and just to make it clear how bored he is by her display, the watermelon is mentioned. There it is on the table. He slices off a piece and slowly eats it, and thirty minutes tick by in silence.

Mona laughed.

"What's funny?"

"That's who you remind me of," she said. "Gurov and his watermelon. You don't really care about me. I'm just your boring mistress."

He rolled his eyes. "Aren't you at least a little high?"

"I read your diary," she said.

"Of course you did," he said. "And?"

"I'm not your favorite island."

"There are better places to be sober," he said, as if continuing an old conversation. "In the next life I'll have an Airstream next to the Rio Grande, a silver bullet with yellow curtains. I'll wash my clothes in the river and hang them on a clothesline. I'll have vegetables to tend, books to read, a hammock, a little dog named Chek—"

He nodded off, his mouth still twisted around the word. His voice, she noticed, had lost its teeth. She crept over him on the bed, carefully unbuttoned his pants, worried her hand into his boxers. What the fuck are you doing, she asked herself. He's gone, you fool. It's over.

FOR THE NEXT FEW WEEKS SHE MENTALLY PROJECTED MR. Disgusting's face onto whatever surface she was cleaning, just for the pleasure of scrubbing it off. The procedure worked best on tiled bathroom walls. She lathered the tiles with Ajax, then, covering her mouth with the collar of her T-shirt to guard against bleach throat, she scrubbed out his left eye, obliterated his right with a furious scrib- bling motion, and then expanded her strokes to remove his mock- ing eyebrows and long black hair. She scrubbed vigorously, her hands sweating in the rubber gloves, her breath moistening her T-shirt. When his face was gone at last, she doused the tiles with water from the tap. Her mind often seemed to clear itself of debris, and in its place, she felt the pleasant but slightly irritating sensation of having a word on the tip of her tongue.

A month later her anger suddenly dissipated and was replaced again by longing. So he'd almost killed her and then told her she looked like a fish—big deal, people made mistakes. She was getting over it. Besides, he'd apologized profusely via voicemail, and on her doorstep he'd left a Japanese dictionary in which he'd circled the words for contrite, shame, repentant, confession, apology, remorse, touch, please, help, and telephone. That certainly counted for something.

It was spring now. No more shitty snow. People were pulling their heads out of their asses and checking each other out. Even her mailman, whose beard had been long enough to flap in the wind, was now clean-shaven and winking at her occasionally. Perhaps Mr. Disgusting had gone in for some spring cleaning himself? He'd been in rehab this time last year, and had given her that shard of glass as soon as he'd gotten out, and by the time summer rolled around they were rolling around on rooftops and feeding each other Goobers. Maybe this time she'd convince him to move to California with her and they could avoid another winter in Hole.

She dialed his number but his phone was disconnected. She stopped by the Hawthorne a few times, but he was never in his room. She checked his other haunts—the Owl Diner, the Lowell Public Library, and the Last Safe and Deposit, a bank turned dive bar—all without luck. Since he loved getting mail, she sent him a postcard of a Henry Darger drawing featuring little girls with penises. On the back she wrote, "How's it goin? You're prolly just hanging around, being rad. I miss you a super ton, dude. I'm like totally lost without you. I fully want to make out with you again." He loved it when she wrote in her native tongue.

WEEKS PASSED AND HE DIDN'T CALL. SHE CONSIDERED BURN-ing the Fat Fuck drawings, but fuck it, she liked them too much. She wound up burning herself, instead, with a curling iron belonging to one of her clients. Carrie Dailey, a divorcée in her forties, owner of a hair salon in Andover, lover of spider plants. The curling iron was professional grade, some newfangled thing with multiple temperature settings. She'd been staring at it for weeks without knowing why. Well, now you know why, she thought. Now you know.

It made a ticking noise as it heated up. Where to put it? The crack of her ass came to mind, followed by the backs of her thighs, the inside of her mouth, her scalp. Something along the hairline might be nice.

She spat on it. Four hundred forty degrees, the dial said, though she didn't see how that was possible. Holding it loosely in her hand, she let it hover over her left forearm, felt the familiar giddiness in the pit of her stomach. Then she brought it in for a bumpy landing. It was so hot it felt like ice at first, and she could smell her arm hair burning. She removed it, watched her skin pucker, and then touched down again, closer to her wrist, and counted to three.

Very hot, indeed!

For the sake of symmetry, she switched hands and burned her right arm. Nothing serious, just a few baby burns. There was something missing, though, some satisfaction she used to feel. Maybe it was simply too blunt an instrument. With a razor she could dictate size and shape and depth—she had more control over the outcome. And, because it was more active, and there was actual penetration involved, she'd felt more . . . engaged. Present.

Still, she was satisfied enough to unplug the iron and went back to dusting the living room. She'd been dragging ass before, but now she felt light on her feet, relaxed, expansive. Even the spider plants didn't bother her. "Though I prefer rubber plants," she imagined telling Mr. Disgusting. "The simplicity of their leaves, their shameless way of showing themselves, how they can be pushed only so far before their leaves crack and bleed, how their blood looks like mother's milk—"

That's what was missing, she realized then. Blood.

On the way out she paused at the console table in the entryway, straightened all the magazines and mail, swept the loose change and keys into a drawer. She pocketed the cash Carrie had left for her and glanced at the personalized notepad lying there, the words "Mental Note" printed across the top. If Sheila were here she'd draw a smiley face on the pad, along with something like "Happy Solstice, Carrie! Hope you're well!"

She wrote,

Dear Vincent,

You may have witnessed my little episode. I know you understand, what with that stunt you pulled with your ear. Please relieve me of my suffering.

Pathetic, she thought, and tore off the sheet. She crumpled it up, but she didn't want to throw it away. She smoothed it out on the table, folded it into a small square, and then wandered around Carrie's yard, looking for a rock to put it under.

TWO WEEKS LATER, ON HER TWENTY-FOURTH BIRTHDAY, SHE received a large cardboard box in the mail. No return address, but she recognized Mr. Disgusting's cramped handwriting and felt a flutter in her chest. At last, he'd come to his senses. And, he remembered her birthday. Not bad for an old man. No doubt he sent her something he'd found in the trash, but whatever—she'd take it.

She brought the box to bed and sat with her back against the brick wall. Inside the box were two smaller boxes, one much larger than the other, but each carefully wrapped in wrinkled maps of her native state. Nice touch. With a red Sharpie he'd drawn a heart around her birthplace, Santa Monica, and another around her hometown, Torrance. She wondered what had possessed him; he definitely wasn't the heart-drawing type.

Inside the first box was everything she'd ever given him: love letters; purposely bad cowboy poetry; several drawings of her hands and feet; an eight-inch lock of hair she'd meant to donate to Locks of Love; a deck of hand-illustrated German playing cards; a small lamp made of Japanese silk thread; and a locket with a skeleton keyhole, the doors of which opened to reveal a photograph of her very beautiful left eye.

The other box contained photographs of *her* box, photographs for which she'd reluctantly posed atop his bed at the Hawthorne last summer. He'd never showed them to her, but then she'd never asked to see them, either. She'd examined herself with a hand mirror before, but there was something about the pictures that unsettled and sickened her. It was like looking at graphic photographs of her own internal organs.

Happy birthday to me, she thought. Thanks for negating our entire relationship.

Perhaps she was more sentimental than she was willing to acknowledge. Never in a million years would she send someone a box like this.

Before the package, her plans that evening had been to order pho from the Viet Cafe and watch *Liquid Sky* on VHS. Instead, she opened a bottle of Cabernet, brought it to bed, and emptied the contents of the first box onto the comforter. She picked up a love letter.

Her handwriting looked frumpy and reminded her of uncombed hair. She rummaged through the rest of the contents, and that's when she found the note written on the back of a beaver shot:

My Little Wallaby,

I'm leaving the planet shortly. I apologize for the tragic ending. I always told you I wouldn't make it past fifty. Please don't take my departure personally. You know very well it has nothing to do with you. My pain is ancient and I'm tired of carrying it around. That's all this is.

Enclosed are all the precious gifts you've given me. I only wish I could take them with me. I would have left them here, but I couldn't stand the thought of these vultures picking through it. And I thought it would be nice for you to have both sides of our correspondence. How often does that happen? This way our biographers will have to do less running around.

Please don't despair. I am toothless, dickless, and twice your age—be happy to be rid of me. You need someone younger and more optimistic, who can fuck you properly and perhaps get you pregnant someday.

Some unsolicited advice on my way out: get the hell out of here. You have no real ties here so it's stupid for you to stay. The reason you're so comfortable in other people's homes, Mona, is because you don't have one. Keep searching.

Go to the desert. I've always wanted to live in New Mexico, and I can easily picture you living in Taos, a small town I passed through when I was your age. Why

not move there and start over? Rent an adobe casita.
Paint some pictures. Join a healthy cult of some kind. Get
a guru. Surround yourself with [illegible]. I really want
you to be—

THE SENTENCE ENDED THERE. SHE FLIPPED THE PHOTO-
graph over, hoping he'd finished the thought, but there was only the
graphic image of her vag in all its squishy, purple glory.

She didn't believe he'd actually killed himself. He was too attached to his problems. She'd always maintained that if everyone
were forced to throw their problems in the garbage, each person
would show up at the dump the following day and sift through any
amount of muck to find them again. He'd probably just moved out
of the hotel, gotten his own place like they'd always talked about,
only without her. Maybe he'd taken up with one of his whores. An
addict like him. Someone who accepted him as he was, or whatever
the hell. More likely he was still living at the Hawthorne, not having
the wherewithal to secure real housing, and sending her this box
was just his way of saying goodbye. Moving on.

Well, it would be easy enough to find out. All she had to do was
walk down to the Hawthorne and look up at his window. If his blue
curtains were still hanging, and his plastic goose lamp still visible, that
would tell her something, wouldn't it?

Plus, it was hydrangea season, so presumably he was "working"
again. If she hurried she might catch him leaving. He usually killed
a couple of hours at the Owl Diner before going to work at 1:00
A.M. She pictured him sitting at the counter in his uniform—forest-
green ski cap, matching jumpsuit, oxblood boots with orange laces—
drinking coffee and chatting up the waitress. Perhaps she'd sit next to

him at the counter and order a lemon square. "You don't take pictures of someone's pussy and then send them back, you dumb fuck," she imagined lecturing him. "And you don't fake your own death to avoid seeing them again. I understand the impulse—who doesn't want to start over from scratch? But we can start over together. I still love you. Didn't you get my postcard?"

She fortified herself with two more glasses of Cabernet, retrieved her binoculars from a kitchen drawer, and then slipped into her skunk coat and zippered it to the throat. The coat was calf length and made of synthetic black fur with a jagged white stripe going up the front and down the back. It was one of the few items she had that belonged to her mother, who used to wear it around the house, probably to ward off sexual advances from Mona's father, but now Mona wore it wherever she went. It worked—people generally steered clear.

The coat was too warm for the weather, but she didn't care. She walked down Pawtucket Street, past her favorite pharmacy and the Grotto of Our Lady of Lourdes, past all the funeral homes— O'Donnell, Archambault, Martin, Laurin & Son—before turning down Merrimack Street, crossing the bridge over the canal and cutting through Kerouac Park, where a group of dumbasses were hanging out, passing a bottle.

She could always smell the Hawthorne before she saw it— surrounded on three sides by a dry-cleaning plant, a sausage factory, and a Cambodian restaurant, it smelled like a combination of starch, chorizo, and fish sauce, which for some reason always made her crave donuts with maple frosting. She avoided the lobby, walked to the side of the building, and stood gazing up at his third-story window, where the goose's belly was glowing, its orange beak pointing east, toward the river.

Aha, she thought. He lives.

There was something on his window ledge. A perishable item, probably. Since he didn't have his own refrigerator and hated storing food in the community kitchen, he often kept things like milk and cheese on the ledge, when it was cold enough to keep from spoiling. This was only effective in winter, obviously, and it was now April, so chances were the item had been there for months, long forgotten. She stared at it with her binoculars and saw that it wasn't dairy, but rather meat: a roasted chicken with a syringe stuck in it. She lowered the binoculars, mystified.

She felt eyes on her. After scanning the windows she saw someone staring down from the second floor. A tall, gaunt man. He waved at her. She waved back. Mr. Disgusting! He was probably renting his bed to Roxy, killing time in someone else's room. She trained her binoculars on his face.

Unfortunately, it was only Ray, a deaf crackhead originally from Georgia and an acquaintance of Mr. Disgusting's, who claimed he wandered out of a Carson McCullers novel. Ray accosted her in the lobby once; he'd been broke and base-crazy and handed her a picture of a dollar bill, which was his way of asking for money. When she indicated that she, too, was broke, he karate-chopped her on the shoulder and then ran out of the building, wailing. He later apologized by handing her a drawing of a frowning stick figure holding a gun to its head, with the word "sory" scrawled underneath. She'd framed the note and hung it in her bathroom, next to the toilet.

He was frowning at her now, in fact. She lowered her binoculars and he disappeared from the window. Could be he was coming out to greet her, and she wasn't in the mood for a Ray encounter. She walked to the front of the building and turned south, toward the Owl. If Disgusting wasn't there she'd order a slice of coconut cake to go and call it a night.

The Owl was on Appleton Street, where the hookers sometimes

hung out, but the only people on the sidewalk were two Puerto Rican yo-yos.

"Yo," one of them called out.

"Yo," she replied.

"Yo," the other one said. "What you need?"

"All set," she said.

"You in business?" the other asked, looking her up and down.

She was surprised—she wasn't exactly wearing business attire—and oddly flattered. "I'm closed on Fridays," she said, and quickened her pace.

The neon sign read "ow DINER," the *l* having shorted out over the winter. She smoothed her hair down and entered the lopsided dining car. The booths were empty and there were only two people at the long Formica counter, a drunk with a dented forehead at the far end, and a dark-haired woman wearing bright-blue patent leather stripper shoes at the closest corner. No Disgusting. She wasn't used to seeing the place so deserted. On Monday mornings, which was when she usually ate there, every table was occupied by old folks from the nursing home down the street—the Scrod Squad, she called them, since all they seemed to order was baked scrod.

She took a seat at the middle of the counter, ordered cake from the bored, pear-shaped waitress, and then sat there, stroking the fur on her sleeve and staring at the scratches inscribed in the Formica. The only words she could make out were "4-eva and eva"; the rest was chicken scratch.

"I smell a skunk," the woman at the end said.

Mona raised her head toward the kitchen, where a gray-haired man was scraping the grill with a cigarette in his mouth.

"Seriously," the woman said louder. "Something really reeks."

Mona reluctantly looked in her direction. The woman sat

hunched over a plate of half-eaten pancakes, the contents of her purse scattered all over the counter. Her black hair was teased on one side and she still had baby fat on her arms and neck.

"Roxy," Mona said.

"Maura," Roxy said.

"Mona."

"Right. Sorry." She stood and walked toward Mona, teetering slightly in her platform sandals. She was wearing her signature look— long shirt, no pants. Her hair wasn't teased on purpose, Mona saw now, but rather tangled around a wad of fluorescent green gum, and she appeared to have something in her eye. Both eyes, actually. As she came closer Mona realized she was wearing about eighteen layers of mascara on fake eyelashes, which made her lashes look like furry little critters.

"I'm surprised you remember me," Mona said.

"He had pictures of you all over his wall. I used to stare at them while I was—" She waved her hand and then reached up to straighten one of the critter's legs. Mona noted her use of the past tense and felt her throat close.

"Anyway, you probably heard. He's gone. His body hasn't been found yet, but he always said that's the way he wanted it. He must have crawled into the woods somewhere."

She was struck with a sudden awareness of her nipples. They felt chafed, as if she'd been nursing a bearded man for the past thirty minutes. Then she realized it was loneliness. Which made perfect sense: nothing made her lonelier than a mouth on her nipple.

Loneliness is a presence you can feel in your body, she heard his voice say. She crossed her arms, thrust her hands into her armpits. Her head felt heavy and she considered resting it on the counter.

"You look totally cracked out," Roxy said. "Why you wearing a bathrobe?"

"I'm fat," she said.

"I take it you didn't know," Roxy said. "Must be a shock. I wasn't surprised, though. He was pretty miserable." She tapped her foot.

"Take a load off," Mona said. "You're making me nervous."

She sat down. Her thighs dimpled where they met the stool. Her feet dangled slightly, not quite reaching the floor, and the leather on her shoes was marbled.

"What's with the binoculars?" Roxy asked, pointing to where they sat on the counter.

"Bird-watching," Mona said.

Roxy frowned. "I'm gonna miss the crazy fucker. That crazy voice'a his. Those stories he liked to read. He opened my eyes to a lotta shit. Whole other worlds. He used to read to me from this big fat book on myths? Persephone, Narcissus, Eros."

She winced inwardly. Just another of his whores—that's all Mona had been. She'd fooled herself into thinking they'd had some special bond. She looked over her shoulder toward the exit. Get away, she told herself. Make some excuse. You don't need to hear anything more about it. She swiveled away from the counter and stood up.

"Where you going?"

"I'm cursed," Mona said. "You probably shouldn't be talking to me."

Roxy looked irritated. "Don't be like that," she said seriously.

Mona swallowed and sat down again.

"I was gonna say—about Persephone—you know, I think about her a lot, 'cause I been tricked by pimps like that, but I don't have anyone making deals with the devil for me, you know? I don't have a mother, or anyone in my corner. I gotta look out for myself, not let myself get tricked. I gotta stop eating these pomegranate seeds, you know?" She licked her lips. "I think that's the message."

Mona shook her head. "The message is that you're supposed to spend time in hell every year," she said. "It's, like, necessary."

Roxy snorted. "For what?"

"Growth," she said. "Development. Happiness."

"I don't know about you," Roxy said, "but I live in hell year-round. I'm not some tourist."

"Neither am I," Mona said.

"I eat pancakes to get the taste of come out of my mouth."

"Yeah, well, my mouth gets fucked, too—daily."

Roxy looked at her sideways. "By what?"

"Bleach," Mona said.

"You drink bleach?"

She laughed. "I clean houses. I inhale a lot of toxic fumes. It leaves a residue in my mouth and throat. I call it bleach throat."

"You're a maid? He never told me that."

"He was embarrassed by it, I think," Mona said. "Which is puzzling on a variety of levels."

Roxy petted the critter on her right lid with the top of her forefinger. The gesture seemed to soothe her. Mona suddenly longed for a furry critter of her own. Tugging at the fur on her sleeve didn't make her feel any better. She looked and felt like roadkill.

"Anyway, I saw him a week ago," Roxy said. "I walked into his room and he was in bed with the television going. Old reruns of *Soul Train*—his favorite. He loved jerking off to that show."

"I know," Mona said, though this was the first she'd heard of it. Her eyes filled up. Don't let it out just yet, she ordered herself. But the tears leaked out of her anyway, like sweat, and there was that feeling in her nipples again, the pain tugging from the inside, first one and then the other and then both at once.

Roxy reached over and adjusted the collar of Mona's coat. "My

mother used to wear a fur coat," she said. "Real fur. She wore it while she worked. She'd just lay there on this dirty mattress, in the coat and nothing else, and the men would wait in line."

"Jesus," Mona said.

"Anyway, he wanted people to think he was all tough and stuff, but he was a total softie. He was like me—he felt things," she said. "I can't be in a room and not feel things."

"Really?" Mona asked. "What are you feeling now?"

"Your sadness," she said. Her face suddenly changed expressions— her mouth and chin drooped slightly and her eyes misted over. Then she swallowed hard and blinked several times, fighting back tears. It took Mona a second to realize Roxy was mirroring her expression.

"I feel things!" the drunk at the end shouted.

"Shut it, Carlos," the waitress said.

"I have feelings," he said in a loud whisper.

"I'll give you a feeling if you don't simmer down," the waitress said.

"You think you're better than me," he said, to no one in particular. "But you're no better." He turned and looked at Mona. "You're no better," he repeated.

"Okay," Mona said.

"Guess what, Carlos," the waitress said. "It's sleepy time."

These were magic words, apparently, as he rubbed his eyes with his fists like a child, stood up, put on his coat, and walked to the door. "I've been to Egypt," he murmured on his way out. "Where the fuck have you been?"

"He's very charismatic," Mona said, after he was gone.

"He's Portagee," the waitress explained, and set a plastic container containing the cake on the counter. "It's mangled on one side,

so it's on the house." She disappeared through a set of swinging doors. Mona caught a whiff of marijuana coming from the kitchen.

"Is that why you do drugs—because you feel things?" Mona asked.

"I'm not addicted to drugs. I'm addicted to this." She gestured to her outfit.

"To not wearing pants?"

"Hooking," Roxy said, unfazed. "It's very addicting, believe it or not. I used to go to meetings for it."

"Hookers Anonymous."

"I kept relapsing. It's really hard to work a regular job after you've done this awhile." She reached up and stroked the critter on her left lid. Mona imagined the critters disengaging themselves from her eyelids and walking across Roxy's face in opposite directions, disappearing into the damp jungle of her hair, where they'd eventually meet one another, embrace, and start mating.

"What's your D.O.C.?" Roxy asked.

"Pardon?"

"Drug of choice."

"Rubber cement," Mona said. "And Liquid Paper."

"For reals?"

"I was hooked on that stuff in elementary school. The glue was like coke, and the Liquid Paper was like crack."

"You musta killed a lotta brain cells."

"I never thought about it that way."

"So what's your D.O.C. now?" Roxy asked, swinging her legs slightly.

"I don't have one."

"There's gotta be something," she said. "And don't say something retarded, like ice cream."

Mona thought about it briefly and decided to be candid. "My smell," she said. She wished she were in her apartment now, lying on the couch in front of the television with her hand down her pants, alternately touching herself and sniffing her fingers. "You know, down there."

Roxy laughed. "You must really like yourself."

"Yeah, you'd think so," Mona said. "Actually, I've been something of a panty sniffer my whole life." She routinely sniffed the underwear of her female clients; she didn't go rummaging through the hamper, but if it was on the floor and she had to pick it up, she usually gave it a tentative sniff before throwing it in the laundry basket. "I've never told anyone that, by the way."

"You shouldn't," Roxy said.

Mona shrugged. She expected to feel exposed, but didn't.

Roxy leaned toward her and lowered her voice. "Do you, like, get off on it, or what?"

"Well, no. But it definitely alters my brain chemistry. It sort of stimulates and tranquilizes me at the same time."

"Like a speedball?"

"Not as intense, obviously, and minus the, uh, life-threatening element."

"I heard about your close call," she said, and looked at the counter. "He felt bad about it."

"Well, good, he should have. I was flopping around like a possessed person and he was all cavalier about it afterward."

"He said you had a religious experience or something like that."

"I was born again," she said. "Literally."

Roxy pointed to the cake. "You have a sweet tooth, like him."

"It's my birthday."

"Aw," Roxy said. "And here you are, all alone." She reached over and touched Mona's sleeve. Mona felt like punching her in the throat suddenly.

"I'm not alone," Mona said.

They sat for a minute in silence, during which the words "I'm not alone" echoed in Mona's head. She felt pain in her nipples again.

"Listen," Mona said. "I'm thinking of leaving Lowell and moving to the desert."

"To live?"

"No, to die," she said. "Of course to live. Anyway, you can come with me, if you want. We can clean houses there. Start a business."

"Thanks, but I wouldn't last five minutes. I can barely wash my own hair." She fingered the knot in her hair.

"Peanut butter might get that out," Mona said.

"I'll give you my underwear to sniff, if you're jonesing," Roxy said. "Might make you feel better."

Mona laughed. "Enabler."

"I'm serious."

"It doesn't work that way. It's sort of a private thing—"

But Roxy slipped off the stool and strode toward the bathroom.

Mona swiveled toward Roxy's backside, baffled. Did she really think Mona wanted her crusty underwear?

Time to go, she told herself. Sleepy time! She placed a few singles on the counter, grabbed the cake, and left before Roxy came back.

THE "DEAR VINCENT" LETTERS WERE BECOMING A HABIT. She wrote them in people's kitchens. They were quick and dirty, whatever popped into her head, even if it was just a string of unrelated words. Often it was a question: *Why do I feel the desire to perform minor surgery on myself? Should I go back on my meds? Why am I here?*

She sealed the notes in ziplock bags and left them in people's yards. Under the porch, usually, or under a big rock. She liked the idea of someone finding them years from now, wondering who wrote them, how they got there. Although, she was beginning to feel a little like Emily Dickinson.

But now that was over, too. Judy, her new boss, hired a bunch of Colombians and made everyone work in teams. The main client, it turned out, was the Massachusetts Department of Public Health, which required cleaning houses condemned for unsanitary conditions. Hence the shit heap in Pawtucketville last week. Its windows and light fixtures had been coated with what looked like honey but was actually nicotine, and so Mona and the Colombians—Judy of course wasn't there—had been forced to clean in this weird brown darkness. Mona had opted for the kitchen, which she'd estimated would take a solid sixteen hours. The counters were littered with rotting garbage and unopened mail from the seventies, and for some reason there was dry dog food all over the floor, and not just a few cups but pounds and pounds of it, far too much to sweep or vacuum. The only thing to do was to shovel it into a trash can, which she began doing in earnest, and that's when she noticed that it was alive and moving.

She dropped the shovel and called Judy. "Maggots" was all she could say.

"Pretend it's white rice," Judy said.

Thanks, Coach.

She'd continued shoveling in the dark, muttering to herself and listening to the Colombians laughing and singing in various parts of the house, and she must have shoveled herself into some kind of trance, because the old thoughts were coming back, telling her to fill her coat pockets with rocks and walk into the Merrimack River.

Later, when Mona was at home and in bed, Judy called and said, "I'm sorry, Mona, but I'm going to have to let you go."

"Let me go?" Mona asked. "Where?"

"You're burned out," Judy said. "I need someone who can put their hustle pants on."

"Hustle pants?"

"It's not personal," she said. "I have to think of my business right now."

"You mean immigrant pants, right?"

"Don't worry, I'll still give you a good reference."

Mona hung up and stared at Disgusting's suicide note next to the alarm clock. She read the last paragraph as she did every night before turning off the lamp. "Go to the desert. I've always wanted to live in New Mexico, and I can easily picture you living in Taos, a small town I passed through when I was your age. Why not move there and start over? Rent an adobe casita. Paint some pictures. Join a healthy cult of some kind. Get a guru . . ."

A WEEK LATER SHE KNOCKED ON HER LANDLORD'S DOOR. HE answered wearing a sweater vest and reading glasses and holding a bowl of what looked like soggy Apple Jacks.

"I'm moving out, Mr. Lim."

"When?"

"Next week."

"Your eyes is confuse," he said.

She didn't know what to say. "Yeah." She nodded. "Hey, you want to buy my bed? It's only a few months old and it was really expensive. I'll give you a discount."

"Your *bed*?"

"Yep."

"*Your* bed."

He had a habit of repeating whatever she said, placing the emphasis on different words.

"Yes."

"How much?"

"Five hundred," she said. "Cash only."

He clucked his tongue.

"It's a good deal."

He wound up buying it for one of his nephews. He was also kind enough to help her drag most of her belongings out of the apartment. They arranged it all on the sidewalk: couch, armchair, kitchen table, nightstand, lamps. She decorated the tree in the courtyard with her winter clothes and shoes, which seemed to delight Mr. Lim, as he took pictures of the tree with a disposable camera. Aside from a holey blanket, some old canvases, and a frying pan, it was all gone three hours later.

The only items she had trouble parting with were her books, knickknacks, and Eurekas. The books and knickknacks would fit in the bed of her truck, no problem, but not the vacuums.

She abandoned three at the curb, but spent one last evening with Gertrude, her baby. She pushed her around the empty apartment and then parked her in the kitchen and stared at her while she drank too much wine. Unable to bear the thought of someone else's hands on her, she considered drowning Gertrude in the Merrimack, but wound up carrying her down an alley instead. It was after midnight and the alley was empty and smelled of ripe garbage.

First she tried bludgeoning Gertrude with a brick, but the only damage she did was to her own ring finger, so she picked Gertrude up by the handle and smashed the vacuum against the pavement over and over like a guitar. It felt good to put her whole body into something and she worked up a nice rhythm.

Before long the bottom plate flew off, and then the belt and brush roll. She splintered the red plastic, put a few dings in the metal hood, and, after several minutes, heard a loud crack—the motor. By then she was panting and her legs and feet were tingling and she could feel her heart beating in her entire face. Who knew it could be so gratifying—so exhilarating—to destroy something you love, to ruin it for anyone else?

YOKO AND YOKO

SHE PULLED WHAT THE 12-STEPPERS CALLED A GEOGRAPHIC: she moved to a new town in another state without telling anyone. Once settled, she wrote to Sheila and her parents, closing each letter with a borrowed line from a short story of Hem's: *I am utterly unable to resign myself.*

An adobe casita in Taos, Disgusting had said. Clearly, he'd never been to Taos, because adobe casitas were way out of her price range—twelve hundred dollars a month, minimum—and so she settled for Valdez, ten or so miles north of Taos proper, a small valley at the foot of the skiing mountain. A handful of Spanish farmers lived here, along with a small population of Anglos, which was what white people were called. Her fellow Anglos consisted of ski bums, assorted artist and bohemian types, oil-rich Texans, and one psychiatrist.

She rented the smaller half of an adobe house on the valley's edge, near a stand of sturdy juniper trees growing along an unused trench. Built from mud and brick, the house leaned to one side in what seemed like shame or disappointment. Inside, it was cavelike and comfortable, with eighteen-inch-thick walls and low, flat ceilings supported by long, rough-hewn timbers hauled from the surrounding forests generations ago. The timbers were uneven, echoing the pitch of the roof, and the well-worn wooden floors groaned underfoot.

The original kitchen in Mona's half of the house emptied into a spacious living room. One of the walls was marked by a wide arched doorway, now thickly bricked up, that once led into her neighbor's half of the house. She lived on the north side of the property, which would make her place cold and dark in winter. Her front door was actually the back door.

At least the place was furnished. There was a double bed, a night-stand, kitchen table and chairs, several decent bookshelves, and a hundred other odds and ends: dishes, silverware, coffeemaker, phone, clock, trash can. In the living room, a set of matching orange leather sofas clashed wildly with the hand-finished plaster walls painted a color somewhere between asparagus, celery, and sage.

First she unpacked her clothes, then several boxes of cherished possessions, including her collection of airline barf bags, which she found aesthetically pleasing, and art by developmentally disabled adults, poorly executed portraits, doodles done by strangers, doodles done by her clients. The main things to unpack, however, were her books, which she arranged according to the color of their spines: red to green to orange to blue to pink to brown, with a fade to black.

"The white spines don't belong," Disgusting would have said. "Obviously."

She agreed. They made her think of cement, classrooms, the sluggish ticking of a clock. She hid them in the closet.

Now her symptoms were returning. The Xanax was wearing off. She kept it in the sock drawer, right next to the Holy Dirt, her other medicine. The Xanax she'd stolen from a former client in Lowell, the Holy Dirt from El Santuario de Chimayo, a small adobe church she'd visited on her way into Taos. At the back of the church was a little room with a hole in the ground. The hole was filled with Holy Dirt, and the walls of the room were lined with pictures of various saints and the discarded crutches of formerly crippled people. They'd been healed, so the story went, on account of the dirt, and now thousands of people made pilgrimages to the church every year just to get their hands on it. Or legs, rather.

She'd waited for the little room to empty of people before reaching down into the hole and grabbing a handful. It was red and clay-like and she liked the feel of it in her hand. She'd made sure no one was looking and then tried filling an empty water bottle with it, but the mouth of the bottle was too small. She deposited several handfuls onto the front of her oversized T-shirt and then hurried out of the church, clutching the dirt to her stomach.

In her truck in the parking lot, she'd transferred the dirt to a Tupperware container she found under the driver's seat. During her first days in Taos she'd rubbed a bit of the dirt on her wrist whenever she felt anxious. It had felt silly initially, but before long she was rubbing it on other parts of her body for good measure—arms, neck, stomach—and not bothering to wash it off when she went out in public.

Her bedroom window was small and too high for her to look out of without standing. Right now she could see the sky, which was currently a blithe, concentrated blue, the color of Windex. A few flimsy clouds clung to the mountains like discarded paper towels. The house had a yard: a large, scrubby field dotted with what looked like scouring pads—dry green shrubs with pale-yellow flowers. Between two cottonwood trees sat an abandoned 1969 Dodge Charger, formerly red, now freckled with rust and ringed by shattered beer bottles. The neighborhood dogs roamed free and traveled in surly packs, often stopping in the field to relieve themselves. Right now they were taking turns pissing on the Charger's cracked flat tires before rolling languidly in the dirt. They didn't seem bothered by broken glass.

She heard something break—a dish, perhaps—in the other, sunnier half of the house, which was rented by an older married couple. Nigel was a tall, malnourished-looking Englishman in his late forties. His wife, Shiori, was Japanese and looked twenty years younger. But they seemed like twins to Mona, perhaps because she'd never seen them in anything other than matching pajamas. They bowed to her whenever they saw her, which she found endearing and sort of flattering at first, then downright irritating. But it seemed in character—they told her they'd met in India, where they'd meditated on eternal mysteries for twelve whole years. They had a studied and deliberate calm about them that struck Mona as affected. She could easily picture them out of their minds, chain-smoking and wandering around town in their pajamas.

That morning they'd invited her for dinner, and she'd instinctively blown them off—an old reflex—claiming she already had plans. Now it dawned on her that the nearest grocery store was closed on Sundays and that eating would require a trip to the bigger store twelve miles away, and that the only people she regularly talked to were herself and Mr. Disgusting, who wasn't even alive. Maybe she could bring herself to knock on their door, even if it made her feel like she had so often in her life: empty-handed and at the mercy of others, a pathetic orphan in a children's novel.

IT SEEMED THEY'D ANTICIPATED HER CHANGE OF MIND: SHE could see a tea set for three on a low table in the living room. They bowed deeply in her direction. Oh what the hell. She started to bend forward, then felt ridiculous and called the gesture off.

"Would you mind removing your shoes?" Nigel asked.

She shook off her slippers, exposing her dirty feet. She was startled by their living room furniture, which consisted solely of a large modular wooden platform roughly three feet off the ground. It was sturdily built and had a light walnut stain. Unlike Mona's, their walls were painted stark white and decorated with Japanese prints of desolate winter scenes.

They motioned for her to sit on the platform. She obeyed, feeling like a large dog scrambling onto the dinner table. Shiori offered a pillow for her behind and she sat facing the large picture window, her legs folded awkwardly to the side. She'd always found sitting cross-legged unnatural. It also made her feel fatter and more out of shape than she actually was. Nigel and Shiori both arranged themselves in an effortless half-lotus position with their backs to the window.

Shiori served tea while Nigel told Mona what he'd learned of the house's history. Built in 1902, it belonged to a large family of piñon farmers by the name of Martinez. It had been passed down through the generations, and then, in the 1980s, there'd been a falling out among the remaining siblings and the house became divided against itself, both literally and figuratively. Now aging Californians owned it and rented it out as an income property. Mona waited for the story to get interesting—no rape? incest? murder?—but it never did. Instead she focused on Nigel's mouth, a crowded elevator—too many teeth crammed into too small a space. His manner of speaking was puzzling yet oddly fluid and mesmerizing. He spoke slowly, carefully weighing each word or phrase, and had a habit of pausing, sometimes mid-sentence, to collect his thoughts. The pauses lasted from a couple of seconds to what seemed to be whole minutes.

Shiori, on the other hand, rarely spoke and had the spaced-out gaze of a Manson chick. Her sleepy eyes were at odds with her short, spiky hair, and there was something . . . supernatural about her. Her skin. Pale and supple, it was utterly lacking in pores, blemishes, or identifying marks of any kind. She had a habit of keeping her thumbs hidden in her fists. Mona kept watch, hoping to get a glimpse of these mysterious thumbs, but it was useless—the fists remained closed.

After Nigel finished his lengthy monologue, she tried to draw Shiori out by asking what her name meant in Japanese.

"Bookmark," Shiori replied softly.

Mona nodded slowly, waiting for her to say something more.

"Oh. Bookmark. Like an actual . . . bookmark?" she asked.

"More like a guide," Nigel interjected. "A guide that keeps you in place and lets you know where you need to be." He gave Shiori a look of such naked devotion that Mona had to avert her eyes.

"Do you know what your name means, Mona?" Nigel asked.

"Cardboard," Mona said.

Blank looks.

"I'm kidding," she said. "I don't know what it means. Probably nothing."

"Well, in Sanskrit mona means 'alone,'" Nigel said.

"Get out!" she said.

He shrugged.

"Is that where the word 'monastery' comes from?"

"Yes," he said. "It means 'alone-place.'"

"Well, the name definitely fits," she said, "as I often feel like an island in a sea of retards."

She instantly regretted "retard," a bad habit left over from her years in Massachusetts, where it was an accepted part of the vernacular. "Present company excepted, of course," she added. "What about your name, Nigel?"

"It's an Irish name, I believe, meaning 'champion,'" he said.

"Everyone loves a winner," she said.

He gave her his crowded smile. "How are you adjusting to the climate?"

"It's extremely dry," she said, and coughed. "I feel like my personality's evaporating along with all the water in my body."

"It's the altitude," he said. "We're at 7,300 feet—"

"Do you like it here?" Shiori interrupted.

"I'm not sure yet." She shrugged. "Not much going on around here but the rent, it seems, and a lot of intense-looking Spanish dudes."

"So you've noticed the racial tension," Nigel said.

"I haven't experienced anything firsthand, but I imagine the Spanish and Native Americans fight over land—and water, probably? The white people just seem to grow beards. But everyone—and I mean *everyone*—seems united in one thing, at least."

"What's that?" Nigel asked.

"Scratch Ticket Fever," she said. "Everywhere I look, people are scratching scratch tickets. Nurses, waitresses, dishwashers, librarians, postal workers, coffee shop owners. Young, old, white, black, brown. On the sidewalk, on the hoods of cars, on dashboards, in stores, restaurants, parking lots, Laundromats, waiting in line at the bank. I've never seen anything like it. Scratching styles vary—some scratch slowly and seem to relish it, some are bored and detached, others look like they're scratching out the eyes of their enemies or, like, beating off or something—"

Nigel frowned.

"Have you caught the Fever?" Mona asked.

He tilted his head at her. "We've been spared," he said.

———

"The other crazy thing about this place is the wind. It's like the town bully and molester. I've seen it try to undress people as they walk down the street. Sometimes I imagine the wind is blowing scratch ticket dust around, and that's how people get the Fever. The dust gets in their eyes and turns them into zombies—"

"It's wind season," Shiori interrupted. "It'll die down in a month."

"Wind gets its own season?"

Shiori nodded. "So does mud."

"Yikes," Mona said.

"You don't care for wind," Nigel declared. "Why?"

"I don't know—because it's invisible? I don't like being pushed around by something I can't see."

"I find it soothing," Nigel said, "and spiritual. It can't be captured or contained—it can only be *felt*. It's invisible, yes, but it has the power to *move*, to *alter*—"

"Something's burning," Mona said quickly. "In the kitchen."

He and Shiori climbed off the platform and disappeared into the kitchen. Mona stared out the window. It was dusk and the magpies were having a party outside, singing loudly and darting in and out of the bushes.

Magpies and cottonwoods make me think of country music, she imagined telling Mr. Disgusting.

THE FOOD WAS SIMPLE AND DELICIOUS—SOME SORT OF macrobiotic glop with tofu and yams. They offered Mona silverware, which she accepted, but they ate with their hands, a custom she assumed they picked up in India. She could now see why Shiori kept her thumbs hidden—unlike the rest of her fingers, they were short and oddly toelike, with slightly misshapen nails. Mona glanced at

Shiori's feet, half expecting to see thumblike big toes, but no, her toes were regular looking. Perfect, in fact.

The walls were lined with books. Hundreds, about half in Japanese.

"I see you like to read," she said.

"Yes. We both read quite a lot," Nigel answered. "You?"

"Sure," she said.

"What are you reading now?"

"A Victorian homoerotic thriller called *The Fingersmith*," she said. "It's set in your native country. I can't put it down." She smiled, anticipating a long pause.

"Are you a lesbian?" he asked finally.

"No," Mona said with her mouth full. "I think I'm probably . . . three-quarters straight and one-quarter fruit? Or maybe it's the opposite." She visualized herself wrestling him to the floor and trimming his caterpillar eyebrows. He would put up a struggle. She looked at Shiori, who was blushing. "I'm sorry." She set her empty bowl on the platform. "I'm just joking around. It's a defense mechanism. I hope I haven't offended you guys."

"Are you well?" he asked suddenly.

"Sorry?"

"Are you well?" he asked again.

"You mean, do I have cancer?"

"Up here," he said, pointing knowingly to his head. "Are you well up here?" He tapped his temple with his forefinger.

She laughed and instantly relaxed. Now they could dispense with the small talk and have a real conversation. But they're your neighbors, she reminded herself. Go easy on the candor. Don't tell them about all the Xanax you're eating, or about the Holy Dirt you've rubbed all over yourself, and, whatever you do, don't mention Mr. Disgusting.

"Well, I've had kind of a crazy year, to be honest," Mona said. "I stopped taking my meds and overdosed on some other drugs—"

"Good grief," Nigel said. "When did you . . . overdose?"

Mechanically, like an idiot, she looked at her watch. "Little over a month ago."

"Which drugs?" he asked.

"Speedball," Mona said.

"What's that?" Shiori asked.

"Sort of like an extreme sport," Mona said.

"Are you a drug dealer?" Nigel asked seriously.

She laughed. "Sort of. I'm a cleaning lady."

Nigel looked mystified. "What do you clean? Hotels?"

"Houses," she said. "I'm, like, tormented by dirt. When I walk into a room—any room—dirt's the first thing I see."

"Do you see dirt in here?" Shiori asked.

"Sure," Mona said.

She watched Shiori scan the room in confusion. "Where?"

"Ask the dust," she whispered, "on the lampshades."

"Are you an addict?" Nigel asked suddenly.

She shook her head. "I have an off switch, thankfully. I'd never sell my mattress for drugs. Or, like, my refrigerator. Or my body. Well, maybe—" She paused. Nigel was looking at the ceiling with his head thrown back, apparently stretching his neck. "Am I boring you?"

"You are your conversation," he said to the ceiling.

"Pardon?"

He looked at her. "You are what you talk about."

"Hm, that explains why I always feel so . . . freakish."

He sniffed. "Feelings are just stories, Mona. They have a beginning and an end. In my view it's best to observe them silently, without judgment, and then let them go. Don't get too invested."

"Feelings are just stories," she repeated slowly. "And who's writing these stories?"

"Well, you are, naturally," Nigel said brightly. "You're the author."

Another pause. She decided to wait it out and not say anything. She could tell by the look on his face that he had another pearl in the oven. He was probably full of them. So full, in fact, that he couldn't help but deposit the pearls everywhere, uncontrollably and without aim, like rabbit poop.

"You're offended," he said solemnly, his eyes seeking hers. "Don't look for occasions to be offended, Mona. I'm only trying to help you. You seem . . . *unwell.*"

Her feet were asleep. "Do you mind if I stretch out?" she asked suddenly. "Would that be weird?"

"Of course not," Nigel said. "Make yourself at home. Would you care for another pillow?"

Before she could answer, he reached under the platform and handed her a green velvet pillow. It smelled like lavender. She lay on her side, cradling her head in the palm of her hand. Shiori returned carrying a tray of tea and biscuits. She poured Mona a cup, arranged a couple of biscuits on the saucer. The biscuits looked dry and inedible, but Mona ate them anyway, filling the silent room with the sound of her chewing.

"Why did you move here?" Nigel finally asked.

"I'm not exactly sure," she said. "Someone told me I might like it here."

"Well, what I do find interesting, Mona, is that you created an entirely new option. You made a truly creative choice. Now you are free of your past and can be whoever you want." He looked at her expectantly, his eyes wide and smiling. "What will be your conversation?"

"I was thinking of starting a cleaning business, actually, since that's what I did in Massachu—"

He and Shiori exchanged frowns.

"You were hoping I planned to do something . . . else?"

Nigel shrugged. "Just because you cleaned houses in the past doesn't mean you have to do that here. You're free to do whatever you want."

"Except I have to make a living—you know, *pay the rent*? I don't have the luxury of loafing around all day, making a new conversation or whatever."

"I'm not proposing you loaf around," Nigel said.

"How do you two make ends meet?" she asked, changing the subject.

"We live very frugally and have for the last dozen years," Nigel answered.

Not exactly a straight answer, which meant they were living off an inheritance of some kind. She wondered if it was his or Shiori's. Maybe they both had one. In any case, she'd been working for people like Nigel and Shiori for years, people who thought rising above one's circumstances was simply a matter of "working smart, not hard" and having a "positive attitude." She was making do on her savings, but working smart would have her broke in less than three months.

"You guys are artists of some kind, I take it," Mona guessed.

"We make music," Shiori said, nodding.

"What do you play?"

"Well, Shiori plays the piano and is a wonderful cellist. I can play guitar and flute. But together we play instruments that we make by hand."

"Oh," Mona said.

"Shi, why don't we bring out a couple things to show Mona?"

They disappeared into the back of the house. She directed a prayer at the ceiling: Please don't let them be flutelike instruments. Whenever she saw someone playing the flute she felt like snatching it out of their hands and bludgeoning them with it.

Thankfully, the instruments seemed to be in the cello family. Fucked-up cousins of the cello, it looked like. One was six feet long, the other four or five, and they each had only a single string. Nigel and Shiori laid them flat on the ground next to the platform.

"We wanted to make something we could play sitting down," Shiori said bashfully.

"Right." Mona nodded. "Okay."

"How long did we spend making these two, Shi?" Nigel asked. "A year?"

"Nine months," Shiori said.

"Will you play something?" Mona asked out of politeness.

"We don't believe in live performance," Nigel said.

"Ah, stage fright," Mona said, nodding. "I get the same thing. Not that I've ever been on stage."

"No, it's not that. We just find live performance artificial. And it doesn't do our music justice. But we'll play something for you, since you're a special guest. You've never heard anything like it, I promise you. First things first, though." He removed a joint from his pajama pocket and placed it between his lips. Mona was startled and relieved.

After she took only two hits, her relief turned into low-grade paranoia.

"This piece we're going to play is somewhat medieval," Nigel announced with a straight face.

Mona braced herself. They each gripped a bow and began sawing away at their solitary strings. After a few minutes, Nigel started singing. His voice was low-pitched, guttural, and way off-key. He was right; she'd never heard anything like it. She spent several minutes deciding whether it was medieval, as Nigel claimed, or *just plain evil.*

They struck her as the type who actually made eye contact during intercourse, who remained present throughout the whole affair and didn't have to think of other people to get off. She flashed to her fantasy that morning of the postman, a huge, Samoan-looking guy. He had her in the back of his mail truck, facedown on a pile of unopened Easter cards, while her former landlord, Mr. Lim, observed the scene from a nearby bush, and Mr. Disgusting, who was in the driver's seat, supervised and gave orders: *faster, slower, harder, stop talking, hurry, the dogs are coming.*

When the song ended, eighteen minutes later, Nigel and Shiori gave each other a private look and then closed their eyes and breathed deeply through their noses for several seconds. "Part of our process," Nigel whispered.

She tried to come up with something to say. Under different circumstances, Nigel and Shiori could have reminded her of John and Yoko, but the truth was, they were more like Yoko and Yoko. But then she'd always had a secret weakness for Yoko.

When they opened their eyes, she said, "It sounded like the music of aliens or highly intelligent wild animals. Have you guys thought about writing for film?"

They looked confused.

"You know, making movie soundtracks. I could easily hear that song in the background of, like, a David Lynch film or something." It was higher praise than she meant to give, and Nigel looked dubious. She had a habit of overshooting.

"Who is David Lynch?" Nigel asked.

"Uh, *The Elephant Man, Eraserhead, Blue Velvet, Mulholland Drive...*"

Nigel shrugged, apparently at a loss.

"Come on, Nigel. You've seen *Blue Velvet*. Dennis Hopper? The oxygen mask?" She attempted a Dennis-Hopper-as-Frank-Booth impersonation. "I'll send you a love letter, straight from my heart, fucker! You know what a love letter is? It's a bullet from a fucking gun, fucker!" She paused, noticing Nigel's blank look. "Are you telling me you don't even know who Dennis Hopper is? *Easy Rider, Apocalypse Now* . . . ring any bells?" She wondered if they were putting her on, if this was part of their shtick.

"Mona, I haven't been to the movies since I was a child, and I don't think I'm missing much, frankly."

"Well, I'm not sure we can really be friends," she said seriously.

"Have you read Homer's *The Odyssey*?" Nigel asked out of nowhere.

"Is that the one with the wine-dark sea?"

"Yes."

"Never read it."

"Well, allow me to get it for you," he said, and climbed off the platform. Mona and Shiori smiled patiently at each other. When Nigel returned, he ceremoniously handed her the book while bowing slightly.

"I strongly urge you to read this," he said. "Its message may have something for you."

When Mona got back to her side of the house, she tossed *The Odyssey* on the floor next to her bed, then picked up *The Fingersmith* and rapidly read fifty pages before falling asleep.

SHE SPENT HER AFTERNOONS DRIVING AROUND THE wealthier neighborhoods of Taos, hanging flyers from people's doorknobs. The flyers were homemade; she designed them herself. They were long and skinny and she fastened them to doorknobs with rubber bands. Her new company name and tagline—Bee's Knees Housekeeping, Clean Like You've Never Seen, Honey!— was printed at the top. Below that, she'd made a compelling line drawing of a lady bee wearing an apron, a bottle of Windex in one spindly arm and a vacuum in the other. Her phone number and fake business license were printed near the bottom. She'd taken out a classified in the *Taos News* as well, but hadn't gotten any calls so far. Hanging flyers, she reasoned, while exhausting and time-consuming, certainly couldn't hurt, and she had nothing better to do. She parked her truck roadside, filled her messenger bag with flyers, and hoofed it up one side of a street and then back down the other. On her third day she was surprised to find herself talking to Bob, her old nickname for God. She hadn't spoken to him in fifteen years. She wasn't sure why now, but suspected it had to do with the landscape. The sky, in particular, seemed to naturally inspire Bob thoughts. The light had a quality of being everywhere at once, even in the shadows, and she felt suspended by it as if by an enormous hand. The Hand of Bob. When the sun was out, the hand held its sweaty palm wide open, and she often imagined she was traveling along the dust in one of its creases.

"I hate happy people," she said, trudging up a newer road of vacation homes, thinking of Yoko and Yoko. She stood before a stone house marked with a large wooden plaque hanging over the front door. The words "Angel House," along with a simple rendering of an angel wearing wings and a halo, were neatly engraved in turquoise paint.

"Looks like we got some Bob lovers here, Bob," she said, pulling a flyer from her messenger bag. "Or angel lovers, anyway." Reaching to fasten the flyer to the doorknob, she was startled when a woman suddenly opened the door.

She froze, flyer in hand. No one ever opened the door.

"You're probably wondering what I'm doing here," she said quickly, laughing nervously. "I was about to leave you this flyer."

The woman had a small glob of grape jelly near the corner of her mouth and hadn't brushed her hair. The entryway was dark, but she could see a chandelier made of bleached deer antlers hanging from the ceiling.

The woman took the flyer from Mona's outstretched hand. Mona was about to deliver her spiel—"I'm new in town, but I'm the best in the business and my rates are super reasonable, so if you're sick of scouring your own bathtub, give me a call!"—but the woman merely glanced at the flyer, said thank you, and shut the door. Mona lingered on the porch for several minutes and pictured herself collecting cans on a dusty road, wearing a flannel shirt with a floppy straw hat. The door cracked open and a wide eye peered at her from the dark.

"Sorry," Mona said. "Still here. If you don't mind my asking, why is your house called Angel House?"

The woman looked distracted, irritated. "I'm a collector," she said.

"You collect angels?"

"Angel paraphernalia," the woman said.

She imagined bongs with pictures of angels glued to them. "Okay," she said.

"It's just a hobby," the woman said, softening.

"I could use one of those."

The woman smiled and slowly closed the door. Mona walked back down the long driveway.

"I'm scared, Bob," she said.

"What're you scared of, Mona?"

"I'm going to end up collecting cans."

"You're safe," he said. "You're in the palm of my hand."

"Then why do I feel like hanging myself?"

"You have to trust me," Bob said.

On the drive home she thought of the Holy Dirt sitting in her sock drawer. Maybe she'd make a mud bath for herself when she got home. A miracle mud bath. She felt momentarily buoyed by the idea. Who knows, it might even have a nice effect on her skin.

She made dinner instead, ginger pancakes, breakfast-for-dinner comfort food. What she called making an effort. Couldn't bring herself to set the table, though. She ate the pancakes out of the pan, standing up, and then guzzled orange juice from the carton. From her kitchen window she could see Yoko and Yoko amble into the side yard, as they did every evening just before dusk, and spread a blanket on the ground. They usually sat side by side and stared at the horizon for a solid hour, sometimes longer. She enjoyed spying on them. At first she thought they were looking for UFOs, but it wasn't dark enough for that, so she figured they must be meditating with their eyes open. Took her a few days to realize they were simply admiring the sunset. Granted, in these parts, sunsets were something to behold, no question, but night after night? Sometimes she squinted at their faces from the window, searching for signs of boredom, but they seemed fully absorbed, and maintained a reverent silence throughout the whole thing. When the sun finally departed, they stood up, folded their blanket, said a few words Mona could never catch, and went back inside.

Tonight she walked over to their yard and plopped down next to them on their blanket. "You guys really need a television," she said.

Nigel smiled. "We'd much rather be here, in this moment."

"I'd rather be inside, watching *Law & Order* reruns."

"Have you had a chance to read Homer?" Nigel asked.

"Not yet. Still reading the lezzie novel."

"I think you will appreciate the lotus-eaters," he said.

"Is that, like, a euphemism?"

He laughed. "No."

"The lotus-eaters are a race of people who live on an island," Shiori explained. "Odysseus sends some of his men to this island to see what's there, to see if it might be a good place to rest, and the lotus-eaters are very friendly and give his men lotus flowers to eat, and soon the men forget what their mission is. The lotus makes them forget about home, and they no longer care where they came from or where they're going. "

"Wow," Mona said. "I need to get my hands on some of that. Do they sell it at the health food store?"

"You're not a lotus-eater, Mona," Nigel said patiently. "Not anymore. You're back on the boat, heading home. It's time you sat orderly upon the bench and smote the gray sea with your oars. Row hard and don't look back."

"Sounds like a lot of work," she said.

"We want to invite you for dinner," Shiori said suddenly, exchanging a look with Nigel that Mona couldn't read.

"Sure, okay," she said. Then she remembered the wooden platform, how numb her ass and feet had gotten from sitting on it for two hours, how she'd been forced to lie down like a weirdo. "Except, how about we do it at my place this time? That way I can cook and play hostess." They exchanged another cryptic look. "Don't worry, I'll make something vegetarian," she assured them.

"Make whatever you like," Nigel said. "We're not particular."

They set a date for the following night and then continued staring at the horizon. Only the sun's forehead was visible, but a couple of its arms were still raised, reaching up to brush the undersides of the clouds, which looked swollen and bruised, and not at all in the mood to be touched. She glanced at Shiori and wondered if she was in the mood to be touched. Look at those perfect little ears hidden under that blue-black hair, those less-than-perfect thumbs hidden in those fists, that perfectly red tongue—

"What do you think, Mona?" Nigel asked.

It took her a minute to realize what he was referring to. She looked at the sky and said, "Good stuff. A little over-the-top, maybe."

THE NEXT EVENING SHE PUT SOME THOUGHT INTO HER OUT-fit for a change. After tearing apart her closet, she settled on a black silk muumuu embroidered with a life-size silver crane. The crane looked as though it was pecking her left breast. Whenever she wore it she felt like a deranged Marlon Brando, minus the bald head and huge gut, which was probably why she didn't wear it often. Still, she didn't want to overdress, as Yoko and Yoko would likely be in pajamas. She tied her long black hair in a knot and painted her lips a raisin color.

They weren't wearing pajamas. Nigel wore a crisp white button-down and a faded pair of jeans; Shiori a fitted halter dress that showed off her chest and shoulders. "You guys look stunning," she said, as she opened the door for them. "And more awake, somehow."

"Thank you," Nigel said, bowing slightly.

Shiori smiled and handed Mona a bunch of weeds. "We found these wildflowers on our hike today," she said.

"Sweet," Mona said. She pretended to search for a vase even though she knew she didn't have one, and ended up sticking the weeds in an orange Tupperware cup, which she left next to the sink.

They sat at her kitchen table, which was rectangular and a little too big for the room. Nigel sat at the head of the table, Mona at the other end, and Shiori in between. While Mona poured herself wine—she offered them some, but they declined—she watched as they examined the art on her walls. They both had their eyes fixed on the Fat Fuck drawings.

"May I ask who Fat Fuck is?" Nigel asked.

"I wish I knew. These drawings were found in the trash," she explained. "But he's dead, apparently. Found with no hands. I imagine he died of blood loss."

Nigel sipped his water.

"Who are they?" Shiori asked, pointing to the large black-and-white photograph on the opposite wall. It was a portrait of an Asian family, circa 1960-something, sitting on a modern and expensive-looking white leather couch. The mother wore a white Chanel-type suit with three-quarter sleeves and a matching pillbox hat, the father a tailored black business suit. Their small daughter wore a plaid dress and sat between them with a finger in her mouth and her eyes on the floor. Mom and Dad were both wearing dark sunglasses and holding cigarettes, but they seemed to be looking at the camera. No one was smiling.

"Those are my parents," Mona said. "I was adopted, obviously." She waited a beat, but it was pointless. They never laughed at her jokes. "I'm kidding," she said at last. "I found it at a thrift store."

"I like the frame," Shiori said politely.

"Are your parents alive, Mona?" Nigel asked.

"Oh yeah," she said. "They're alive and leading miserable lives in California."

"That's sad," Nigel said.

Mona shrugged. "Whatareyougonnado."

"I bet they'd like to hear from you."

"I sent them a letter with my phone number. The ball's in their court." The ball's in their court, she repeated to herself. She'd never used that expression before and made a mental note never to use it again. "Besides, don't be so sure they want to hear from me. I could've been the nightmare of their lives. Maybe I killed their pets."

"Did you?" Nigel asked.

"No," Mona said. "More like the other way around."

"Your parents killed your pets?"

"So to speak," she said. "They sent them to a farm in Idaho."

They were silent for a minute. Mona glanced at Shiori's chest. She was surprisingly stacked, for an Asian woman.

They didn't eat with their hands this time. Granted, they didn't have much of a choice since the main course was soup. Hominy, tomatoes, and Hatch green chilies she bought from a Spanish man roasting them on the side of the road. She'd meant to make stew, but hadn't let it stew long enough. They kept pausing between bites to mop their foreheads with their napkins.

"You're sweating like a couple of alcoholics." She put down her spoon. "Should I turn on the fan?"

"It's a little spicy," Shiori said meekly.

"Sorry," Mona said. "I have beer—that might help."

"Shi, would you like to share a beer?" Nigel asked.

Shiori nodded.

Pussies, Mona thought. Who splits a beer?

After they finished eating, Nigel directed his gaze at Mona. "I've noticed something about you, Mona."

"Uh-oh," Mona said.

"Now, don't be alarmed, but are you aware that you're *sanpaku*?" he asked.

"Sand-packed-who?"

"*San-pak-u,*" he repeated. "It's Japanese for 'three whites.' It refers to the whites of your eyes. Your iris should be touching the bottom lid of your eye, but instead the whites are showing at the bottom. They're also showing on the sides, which is normal. But since they're showing on the bottom, you are *sanpaku*—three whites."

"What?" Mona said.

"Look at our eyes," he said. "See how the iris touches both the top and bottom lids?"

"Oh yeah," Mona said, looking back and forth between them. "You both have really big eyes. They remind me a little of an infant's eyes." She poured herself more wine.

"Exactly," Nigel said. "It's interesting you mention that. When you're born, you're perfectly balanced. It's only after you've lived awhile that things begin to . . . deteriorate."

"Are you guys in a cult or something?" Mona asked.

To her surprise, Shiori giggled.

"Don't change the subject, Mona," Nigel said.

"Okay, Nigel, I'm willing to humor you, but first tell me what the hell you're talking about exactly. Sometimes I think you make this shit up on the fly."

"It's nothing fatal," he explained. "Being *sanpaku* is something you can repair. It just means you're imbalanced."

"Mentally?"

"Mentally, physically, sexually," Nigel said. "It also means you're prone to addiction and depression." He raised an eyebrow.

"One of your shoulders is a little higher than the other," Shiori said suddenly.

"It is?" Mona put a hand on each of her shoulders. "Which one?"

"The right one," Shiori said. "You should drink green tea. No coffee."

"No offense, Shiori, but how am I supposed to clean houses on green tea? Have you seen the houses around here? They're made of dirt."

"All you have to do is eat a macrobiotic diet for a few months," Nigel said. "Whole grains, leafy greens. No meat, no dairy. No fat or sugar."

"Which reminds me—I made dessert," Mona said. She got up and opened the fridge, where a plate of lemon bars was waiting. She placed the plate on the table. "I made these last night. They should be perfect. Please, help yourselves."

They paused, seeming to consider it. Nigel said, "Well, since you were gracious enough to make these from scratch—"

They came from a ready-mix box, Mona almost confessed.

"—Shiori and I will share one. Thank you, Mona."

Again, she wondered if she should really be associating with these people.

Nigel talked at length about his father. Apparently, he was the son of a semifamous inventor. He described the laundry detergent cap his father was famous for having developed, but all Mona heard was static. She watched Nigel's face while he talked, and, as she concentrated on his moving lips, she felt Shiori staring at her intently. She tried to ignore it but eventually felt compelled to meet Shiori's gaze, thinking perhaps she was trying to silently communicate something. Maybe she wanted another lemon bar or her own goddamn beer.

But as soon as Mona looked at Shiori, Shiori quickly looked at Nigel, and Nigel, still talking, glanced at Shiori before his eyes returned to Mona. Then it was back to the start, with Mona and Nigel looking at each other, until Mona was again compelled to meet Shiori's gaze, and Shiori looked at Nigel again, and he at her.

It felt, bizarrely, like a game of pinball. Nigel controlled the flippers, Mona was the main ball in play, and Shiori was the extra ball that came out of nowhere and threw everything into chaos before disappearing. She wondered who was putting the extra ball in play. Was she inadvertently hitting a button, or was it random?

After Nigel finished his story, they sat in a comfortable silence for several minutes.

"I've noticed something about you guys," Mona said after a while.

"Uh-oh," Nigel said.

"Now, don't be alarmed," Mona said slowly, "but . . . you both have killer cheekbones."

Nigel and Shiori looked at each other and smiled.

"Seriously," Mona said. "You could really hurt someone with those things."

"We enjoy your company," Nigel said, apropos of nothing. He held his hand out for Shiori, and Mona watched them clasp hands across the table. There was the three-way pinball of looks again.

"I like you guys, too," Mona said, and felt herself blush.

IN THE MORNING, SHE SAT INERTLY IN HER KITCHEN CHAIR. Her dining table had been pushed aside. Shiori entered the kitchen and weightlessly placed a heavy vat of chocolate pudding on the tiled floor, motioning for Mona to step in. Mona obliged. The pudding was still warm. She wiggled her toes and was overcome with euphoria. She noticed Shiori had pudding on her crazy spatula thumbs, and she wanted to put those thumbs in her mouth. She tried to move toward Shiori but the pudding had somehow dried like cement around her feet. The pudding thumbs became the dark nipples of Shiori's breasts. She heard Nigel moaning along to flute music and woke up.

Had they been hitting on her last night? She couldn't decide.

———

She'd always been terrible at reading sexual cues, or cues of any kind, and had a long and painful relationship with misinterpretation. In fact, now that she thought about it, misinterpretation was a constant theme in her life.

All Nigel's talk about his dad made her wonder about her own. Although, she'd stopped calling him Dad years ago. Mickey was his name. They'd been playing phone tag for two years and she hadn't laid eyes on him in twelve. He lived in Eureka—or maybe it was Seattle now. One of the last times she'd seen him had been in sixth grade. Her parents had been separated for a few months and she was splitting her time between the house she grew up in, where Mickey still lived, and her mother's new apartment. He'd picked her up from school that day. It was a surprise—she usually took the city bus home—and he'd been early; the bell had just rung and the school buses hadn't yet lined up in the parking lot. She and her classmates were just getting their backpacks on when he entered the classroom, and a few kids had approached him shyly, as if he were a local celebrity.

He'd been wearing his uniform: a yellow, mesh-backed cap with the words "Plumbers Have Bigger Tools" emblazoned across the top, a striped blue-and-white work shirt with his name stitched over the breast, and jeans with large holes in the knees. He smelled like a mixture of alcohol and cigarettes, with a low note of refried beans and the sweat of a hundred hangovers. A brown beard threatened to take over his whole face, and his skin was pebble textured on one cheek, as if he'd been sleeping on the ground. His eyes were what drew people in: clear, green, difficult to look away from. They were so animated they looked cartoonish—when he talked about money, his pupils seemed to turn into tiny dollar signs; when he talked about her mother, they were heart shaped.

His most distinguishing feature, though, was the hook. She always forgot about it until they were in public. The hook was made of steel, which he could open and close with his back muscles, and the prosthetic arm was made of fiberglass, onto which he had someone tattoo an American eagle, along with the words "We the People."

Her classmates had asked him the question every kid did: "How did you lose your arm?"

"I lost it by lying," he lied.

Usually he said it was because he didn't eat his vegetables or didn't go to church.

Her heart sank as he made his way over to her teacher, Miss O'Farrell. For some reason, Miss O'Farrell thought Mona was smart, even though she was an average student. She gave Mona books to read from her own library, books like *1984* and *The Stranger*. She carried the books in her briefcase and passed them to Mona when no one was looking, like contraband. Mona read them dutifully but never had the heart to tell her that she preferred her mother's taste in fiction—Lawrence Sanders, Sidney Sheldon, and . . . Jackie Collins, if nothing else was available.

"I'm Mick," he said, introducing himself. "Mona's dad."

"Hello," Miss O'Farrell said, and offered her right hand. He never shook hands with his hook, so he'd taken her extended right hand in his left one, which disoriented her. Then he held it for a beat too long so it looked as though they were holding hands. Mona blushed as if he'd just kissed her teacher on the mouth. Miss O'Farrell recovered quickly, giving his hand a squeeze before letting it go.

"Mona a good girl?" He spoke in the flirtatious voice he used on female cashiers.

"She's very bright," Miss O'Farrell answered, to which her father merely grunted. "She's also the fastest runner in the sixth grade," she added.

"Is that right?" He spun around and looked at Mona. He was beaming.

As they were leaving he shouted, "Race you to the parking lot!" and took off running across the playground. Mona hung back. He ran as though he were being chased by a demon. Then, to her horror, he stumbled at full speed and fell spectacularly onto his face.

The playground was laid out like a prison yard, a big concrete square surrounded by tall chain-link fencing. He was lying in the center of the square. He'd fallen as though he'd been shot in the back. One shoe had slipped off and was lying on its side, near his good arm. His hat rested upside down near his head. She and some of her classmates stood behind the fence, staring at him, their fingers and noses poking through the holes. A couple of stupid fourth graders climbed the fence to get a better view.

She remembered the noise he'd made. It sounded like bitter laughter, but she realized he might be crying. His expression never told her—he had a habit of smiling when he cried. He rolled over onto his back and called her name. She reluctantly shuffled over to him. When she got there she was careful to stand so that her shadow covered his face, which had been scraped on the pavement. He looked as though whatever he'd drunk that day had just now caught up with him. He was smiling and wiping tears away with his shirt sleeve, but she still couldn't tell which kind they were.

"I was just thinking about your teacher," he said. "She has the eyes of a hawkfish. I wouldn't mind taking her out. Is she married?"

He reached for the cigarettes in his shirt pocket and shook one out. It was flattened and on the verge of breaking. "My smokes are crushed," he muttered.

"You can't smoke here, Dad," she'd said.

When he finally got to his feet, he limped dramatically to the edge of the playground, dragging his leg behind him and moaning in continuation of his performance. He no longer had an audience— her schoolmates had scattered like cockroaches as soon as he'd sat up. She handed him his shoe and hat and he put them back on and then patted her cheek roughly, as if brushing imaginary crumbs off it, a gesture he often made in place of a hug or a pat on the back.

"Sorry I fell, pumpkin," he said, frowning. "My legs felt . . . wrong. I think my knee might be busted." He paused, waiting for a response. Getting none, he said, "I guess you think your old man is an ass."

"Why are you here?" she asked quietly. "I don't need a ride, I have bus money."

"I just bid a job down the street and uh, I dunno! I thought it'd be nice to pick you up for once. You shoulda seen this lady's house, Mona. You woulda been in *heaven*. She has a swimming pool the size of—"

"Why couldn't you wait in the parking lot like the other parents?" she'd asked.

"Hey," he said, looking hurt. "Don't be so sensitive. I said I was sorry, for chrissakes. I crawl under houses all day," he said, as if that explained everything.

As they walked to his truck in the parking lot, he put his arm around her and leaned heavily against her. He cleared his throat, and she could sense one of his talking jags coming on. As he fished out his keys, she twisted away from him and took off running down the street, toward the ocean and the apartment her mother shared with her new boyfriend. He didn't bother chasing her, but she could hear him yelling his head off. She was glad she couldn't hear the words. His mouth was a coffin she'd spent years wanting to nail shut.

He knew where she was headed and followed her in his truck, a

Frito-Lay truck in its previous life, tall, square, and snub-nosed with a large flat windshield. He'd had it repainted white with the words "Boyle's Plumbing" on each side in bright-blue letters. While she was catching her breath at an intersection, he pulled up alongside her. His face was alert with a mixture of hilarity and rage. The last time she'd seen that look on his face he'd just finished beating a possum to death with a tennis racket in the backyard.

"I'll drive you to your mother's," he said out the window.

"I'd rather walk."

"Suit yourself," he said, and pulled away.

The next time she saw him he pretended as if nothing had happened. He'd always been good at that.

BROODING. IT WAS LIKE BED SPINS; THE ONLY WAY TO STOP it was to put one or both of her feet on the ground. She slid her foot out from under the comforter and placed it on the floor. *Better.* She recited her new mantra: *Feelings are just stories: they have a beginning, middle—*

The phone rang, startling her.

A woman named Susan asked about housekeeping services. The woman apologized for the last-minute call, but she needed her house cleaned for a party that evening. Did Mona have time in her schedule?

She pretended to look at her calendar. "I think I can squeeze you in," she said. "What's your address?"

"11 De Vargas Lane."

Sounded familiar. "You don't live in the Angel House, by any chance, do you?"

"That's me," the woman said.

Now she didn't know what to say. "Yay," she said, idiotically.

THE CORNERS OF SUSAN'S MOUTH WERE JELLY FREE THIS time, her blonde hair clean and neatly combed. She wore the Taos uniform for Anglo women in their forties: denim jacket, strappy tee, hand-knit scarf, jeans, practical shoes with treaded soles. She greeted Mona at the door and then gave her the grand tour. She wasn't kidding about having a thing for angels. Mona had been expecting display cases overcrowded with hideous porcelain cherubs, but Susan had good taste in angels, if there was such a thing, which came as a relief, as there were fucking angels on every available surface, and she always did a better job if the client's taste matched her own to some degree.

In the living room, on a free-floating shelf that wrapped around the room, stood a series of foot-tall faceless angels made of hand-carved wood; in the dining room, a collection of hand-painted plates displayed in an antique hutch; in the hallway, angels made from coat hangers hung from hooks in the ceiling; on the walls, large and small canvases of angels painted in the style of Picasso, Clemente, Schiele. Mona was impressed in spite of herself.

The house had a turret, the winding staircase of which led to the master bedroom. Susan called it the Angel's Nest. Everything was white up there—walls, carpet, dressers, nightstands, the linens on the king-size bed. The bed faced a large picture window with a startling view of a mountain covered in aspen trees. Over the bed, the room's only decoration: an oversized canvas of two emaciated female angels. They were naked and appeared to be either wrestling or having sex. They looked like sisters—they both had messy dark hair, eraser-like bright-red nipples, and lots of pubic hair. Their wings were bloody, broken beyond repair.

"I didn't know angels . . . got naked together," Mona said.

Susan laughed. "Me neither, until I saw that painting."

"It's unsettling," Mona said. "Beautiful."

"Thanks," Susan said. "I bought it in Paris. It's one of my favorites. Anyway, you don't have to do much in here other than vacuum."

The entire house looked clean already, and she wondered why Susan called in the first place. They left the room and went back to the kitchen, where Mona had set down her cleaning supplies.

"Oh, and don't bother with the guest room. My dog's in there, sleeping."

"You don't have to keep your dog locked up," Mona said. "I love dogs."

"She's . . . not feeling well. If I let her out, she'll just get underfoot."

She picked up Susan's toaster, turned it upside down over the sink, and shook the crumbs out. There were dozens.

"Holy cow," Susan said.

She smiled. Clients always ate that up.

"Well, I'll get out of your hair. I have errands to run in town, but I should be back in a few hours. Think you'll still be here?"

"Hard to say," she said. "But if I leave before you get home, I can always bill you later."

"Perfect," Susan said. "Listen, I really appreciate your coming on such short notice. I had a good feeling about you."

"Me, too," Mona said.

"Help yourself to anything in the fridge."

She spent an hour in the kitchen, the dirtiest parts of which were the top of the refrigerator and the inside of the microwave, and another hour in both of the bathrooms. The bulk of her time would be spent dusting angels and vacuuming.

Food first. In the fridge, a pitcher of iced tea, feta cheese, plain yogurt, a bowl of tuna salad, and a bag of something in the meat drawer. She removed the bag and looked inside: brownies—bingo.

She wolfed down two. They were partly frozen and therefore some-what tasteless, but they had a slightly grainy texture she liked, and semisweet chips, and possibly some cayenne. She chased it with iced tea straight from the pitcher, wiped her mouth with her wrist.

As she dusted the angels in the living room, she imagined spending time with Shiori. Sans Nigel. What was her childhood like in Japan? Did she have crappy parents? Did she have to wear a uniform in school? Were the subways as crowded as they say? Was she ever molested by a businessman? Shiori didn't answer her questions. She just removed her pajama top, exposed her breasts, and offered them to Mona. Her nipples were large, brown, perfect. *"Here,"* Shiori said. "Suck *here.*"

"Boobs on the brain, Bob," Mona said.

He didn't answer at first. "Must you call them boobs?" he said finally.

"Boobs, Bob," she said. "Boobs!"

"I've never liked that word," he said. "Unless it's used to describe a person."

Her hands were clammy. So was her dusting rag. Dry mouth, racing heart. Must sit. Couch too soft. Must stand. Shaky legs. Must sit.

"Boob, I feel drooged," she said.

No answer.

She looked at her hands, which had always been her way of taking her drug temperature. They looked like two hard-ons, the erect veins of which resembled blue earthworms, each with its own tiny red heart. Angel dust. Wasn't that the shit that made you think you could fly? She imagined taking a slow swan dive off the top of the turret, flapping her arms on the way down. Her body impaled on a fence post, being devoured by turkey vultures.

She watched her hands with interest: the left one was picking up angels in slow motion; the right dusted the surface with a damp pink rag. The hands didn't feel attached to her body but they seemed to know what they were doing. "Dusting angels," she whimpered. "Angel dust."

Don't get all hysterical, she ordered herself. It's just hash. You love hash.

After vacuuming, which seemed to take hours, she gathered her supplies and put them in her truck. Then she went back into the house for a quick once-over. She walked from room to room. She heard the dog sniffing at the space under a door.

"I'm coming in," Mona said aloud.

She entered and quickly shut the door behind her. The light was dim, the curtains drawn, but she could make out the dog, a medium-size pit bull, wagging its skinny tail and staring at her expectantly. She bent down to pet the dog. The dog was wearing an enormous menstrual pad attached with a belt. She squinted at the collar; the word "Pretty" was stitched onto it in red cursive letters.

"Pretty," she said, and turned on the overhead light. She and Pretty locked eyes. Her eyes were almond shaped, the color of caramel, with blonde eyelashes.

"You're on the rag," she said. "How embarrassing, all out in the open and everything. Is that why she keeps you hidden in here?"

Pretty wagged her tail.

"Are you bored?"

Pretty licked her chops and swallowed.

"Do you have cramps?" she asked.

"I don't get cramps," Pretty said.

"Why aren't you fixed?"

"Trying to get pregnant."

"So you have a husband," Mona said.

Pretty shook her head. "I'm not tied down. I have sex with friends from the neighborhood. One of them has three legs." She sniffed her pad and then turned back to Mona. They stared at each other again.

"Well, I'm on my period, too, if that makes you feel any better."

"I know," Pretty said.

"Do you want to come home with me? I'll give you a good life."

"I have a good life," Pretty said.

"I need you."

Pretty yawned. "Go fetch your camera. Get some shots of you and me on the bed."

"Can't," Mona said. "I'm too fucked up."

Pretty sniffed the air. "Someone's coming," she said.

Mona bolted to the den and looked out the window at the driveway. No one yet.

Floor, feet, get moving. She found a notepad and pen in one of the kitchen drawers. DEAR SUSAN, she wrote in block letters. HAVE A GREAT PARTY. MONA. She fastened the note to the fridge with a magnet. Her handwriting looked more like foot writing. She laughed, removed the note, slipped it into her pocket.

AFTER MANAGING HER WAY HOME IN ONE PIECE, SHE MIS-takenly looked in the mirror. Her mascara had run, though not far, just around the crease delineating her cheekbones. Pupils, thumbtack-sized and depthless. Most of her hair had escaped its braid. She freed the rest and ran her fingers through it, and then bent down for a comb under the sink. When she looked in the mirror again, she saw her naked white skull for a single terrifying instant. She made a strange yelping noise and turned off the light.

In the living room she walked in circles and wondered why she didn't own a stereo. She heard knocking.

———

It was Shiori, wearing black cotton pajamas. "Come in," Mona said.

Shiori stepped into the kitchen. "I saw you pull into the driveway and drive over the bushes."

"Oh," Mona said.

"Are you all right?" Shiori asked. "Your eyes look really . . ."

"Fucked up?" She cleared her throat. "I cleaned this lady's house today and I got hungry so I ate some brownies. Turns out they had hash in them—or PCP? Either way, I'm definitely hallucinating. On the drive home I convinced myself that the highway was a church parking lot."

"You're here now," Shiori said. "You're right here."

"Right. Here I am." She laughed nervously and looked at her watch. It was only 5:00. It was going to be a long-ass night. What to do with herself? Writing in her diary was out of the question. She gazed at the television, at a loss.

"You should eat something," Shiori said. "Come over. We'll make dinner and keep you company." She took Mona's hand and held it loosely. "Don't worry. You don't have to be alone."

Keep her company—right. Shitty timing, though, since she was bleeding. Well, she didn't see it going that far anyway. They could do other things, perhaps. Shiori could simply sit on her lap, for example, maybe hump her leg. Mona would be fine with that.

"I'll come over after I change," she said. "But if you don't see me in ten minutes, would you mind coming back for me?"

"Of course," Shiori said, and squeezed Mona's hand.

She showered and changed into a pair of green silk pajamas—when in Rome—and then walked around to their half of the house. Her vision was fuzzy at the edges. You can totally do this, she told herself. Your parents were swingers, remember?

———

The door was open. "Come in," Nigel called. He was sitting in full lotus near the edge of the platform and patted the pillow across from him. "Welcome. Make yourself comfortable." She crawled onto the platform, settled into the pillow. Burning sage and sitar music wafted in from a back room. She wondered what it looked like back there. She expected to find out soon enough.

"Are you all right?" Nigel asked. "Shiori told me what happened."

"I'll be fine in an hour or two," she said, "but right now I'm in the pain cave."

Nigel paused. "'Pain cave.' What an expression."

She didn't have the heart or the energy to tell him that the expression wasn't hers. Her stomach was making strange music with what sounded like a Jew's harp.

"Can you hear this?" she asked Nigel, pointing to her stomach.

"No," he said.

Shiori came in carrying a sandwich plate and a glass of milk.

"Nothing fancy," she said, and sat beside Mona, a little closer than usual. Their knees touched. This feels intimate. She bit into the sandwich—almond butter with honey and sliced banana on toasted grainy bread.

"You guys eating?" she asked, her mouth full.

"We had a big lunch," Shiori said.

They seemed content to watch her eat. After two more bites and a wash of rice milk, she asked, "Why aren't you guys talking?"

"Embrace the silence for a few minutes," Nigel said. "Take a deep breath and go into yourself. Make conscious contact with the force that created you."

"Conscious contact," Mona repeated. "Okay."

"It can only be done in silence," Nigel said. "The French composer Claude Debussy said that music is 'the space between the notes'—"

He stopped talking suddenly. She heard the noise, too. Long, low, like someone shuffling a deck of cards. It took her a second to realize it was her, farting.

"Excuse me," Shiori murmured, smiling.

"Was that you or me?" Mona asked.

Shiori shrugged.

"I guess the force that created us has gas," Mona said.

Now her ears were burning and felt too large for her head. She clamped her hands over them. "Monkeys," she heard herself say. "Did you know that if you drop a cigarette in the couch cushions it can smolder there for hours before suddenly bursting into flame? Not that you have a couch."

Nigel didn't say anything, but he flicked his tongue at her. His red, pointy tongue. Shiori sat still, staring at her expectantly. Clock's ticking, she thought. Better choke the rest of this sandwich down. She stuffed the remaining crust in her mouth and emptied the milk glass. Nigel continued flicking his tongue intermittently.

"Did you know that male garter snakes have not one, but two penises?" she asked. "And they're both forked, just like their tongues. They keep the extra one hidden in their tail for emergencies."

Nigel nodded absently.

"Let me tell you about their mating habits," she continued. "Garter snakes hibernate in the winter, in a hole in the ground. In the spring they come out of the hole and wait at the entrance for the females, who take longer to wake up. Soon there are *hundreds* of them waiting and they form this vast writhing carpet outside the hole. It's, like, insane. Indescribable. Finally, the females slither out and onto the moving carpet. An orgy ensues. The females have sex with a shit ton of males, but—and here's the interesting part— afterward they're able to select which sperm they want to fertilize

PRETEND I'M DEAD

their eggs. It's called 'cryptic choice,' because it's not obvious from the outside."

Nigel responded by flicking his tongue at her yet again.

"Nigel, what's with that?"

"Pardon?"

"You keep doing that thing with your tongue. It's freaking me out."

"I'm not doing anything." He exchanged a baffled look with Shiori.

"Nice try," Mona said, and rolled her eyes. "Okay, look—I think I know what's going on here. I mean, you've made it pretty obvious. You guys want to have a three-way, right? Well, guess what? I think I'm up for it." She fumbled with the silk buttons of her pajama top. They were as slippery as wet lemon seeds, but she managed to unbutton each one. She peeked at her tits, which were partially exposed and looking pretty good. Nigel's eyes flickered over her chest before returning to her face. Shiori was staring straight ahead at Nigel.

Guess it was her move. She rested a tentative hand on Shiori's thigh, testing the waters, as it were. The water was warm and she could feel a current pass through her hand. Without thinking, she dove in slow motion toward Shiori's face, her lips brushing against her jaw before catching her small mouth. She waited a beat, treading water, but Shiori's mouth remained closed, impassive. She'd hit the shallow end, evidently, and felt a sharp pang in her chest. She pulled back and looked at Shiori's eyes, which were open wide, and then she quickly climbed out of the water and sat there, shivering, with her head in her hands.

"Mona," Nigel said gently. "I think you've misunderstood our . . . intentions toward you."

She moaned. "I should go," she mumbled. She got up to leave.

A misstep forced her backward, throwing her shirt wide open. She felt herself flush, and, mortified, she stumbled out of the house, the screen door snapping shut behind her.

"Why'd you let me do that, for fuck's sake?" she asked Bob, wiping her mouth with her sleeve. "Talk about humiliating."

"Nothing happened," Bob said. "Besides, did you really want to see Nigel's schlong?"

"No," she said morosely. She sat at her kitchen table and drank a beer. "I wanted to touch Shiori's boobs, though. I really did. I wanted to bury my face in them."

"You don't want to have sex with your neighbors, Mona," Bob said. "You're just lonely. Maybe it's time you got a dog. An older dog—"

Shiori's pale face peered through the window over her kitchen sink. Mona ducked but it was too late. Shiori let herself in and took a seat at the kitchen table.

"You again," Mona said. "I guess I should start locking my door."

"You ran away before we could explain," Shiori said. "We *do* want something from you, just not . . . *that*. Nigel and I have taken an interest in you and would very much like to be your mentors. We both feel we can teach you how to live well. How to be your best self. Nigel has been doing it for years. He had a small following in India—that's how we met, in fact. I was one of his students. I think he misses having that. He's a great mentor, if you give him a chance."

Join a healthy cult of some kind, Disgusting had advised. *Get a guru.* Is this what he'd had in mind?

"You guys should have had children," Mona said thoughtfully. "They're more . . . malleable. I'm too old for this crap. I also happen to think I could teach *you* a thing or two about living. For starters, you could read something published in this century. That would be your first assignment. You might want to watch a film every now and then—I could give you a list a mile long. And why not eat a little sugar once a week? I know you like it. Also, what man in his right mind turns down a threesome? Hey, don't get me wrong, I'm glad it didn't go down. It would have been a *huge mistake*. I can totally see that now."

Shiori blinked at her.

"Listen," Mona said. "Would you mind sitting on my lap for a couple of minutes? Or giving me your underwear?"

"My underwear?"

"I want to smell you," Mona said.

Shiori stood and smoothed the front of her pajamas. "You're not ready yet," she said. "But we'll be here when you are. We're going to watch the sunset now. You're welcome to join us."

"I think I'll pass," Mona said.

Shiori shrugged and walked out.

Mona snorted. "Can you believe these people, Bob? Talk about *gall*. Rich people are so, like, *out of touch*. You know what I'm saying?" She looked at the ceiling. "I need a favor. I need you to tell me if Mr. Disgusting's with you. I followed his directions. I moved all the way the fuck out here. Is he with you, or what? I bet he's sitting on your lap right now."

He didn't answer.

"I'm not expecting a long conversation—that's probably against the rules—but could you give me some kind of sign?"

The ceiling was vibrating, breathing.

"It's me, Mona," Bob said at last. "I'm right here."

She closed her eyes.

"Don't you recognize my voice?"

She opened her eyes. The ceiling looked shiny now, sweaty.

"It's been me all along. You can keep calling me Bob, though. I always wanted a three-letter name. Which reminds me, I think you should call your dad. You need to talk to someone other than me, and he's home right now, this very minute."

"So I guess you're really dead?"

"Call your father," he said. "He's waiting to hear from you. He's waiting for you to reach out to him."

"Jesus," she said. "Take it easy, Bob."

She checked her hands—the earthworms were still alive, their hearts beating visibly under her skin. Her thoughts, however, seemed lucid enough. She stood before her bookshelf, felt the familiar urge to reshuffle. She wanted to break up the blocks of red, pink, and green with some negative space. Perhaps it was time the white-spined books came out of hiding. She opened the closet—they were right where she'd left them, lined up on the top shelf. She began adding them to her bookcase, but it was all wrong. Wrong, wrong!

They needed their own shelf. She cleared a space for them on the shelf she reserved for bird figurines. This time she arranged them so that their titles formed sentences: "Man walks into a room with the pharmacist's mate as I lay dying of accidental blindness and assorted fire events, of white noise and housekeeping and the secret lives of people in love. The elephant vanishes to the lighthouse east of Eden. You remind me of me, Natasha. The mysteries of Pittsburgh and Ulysses are an invitation to a beheading, stories in the worst way about grace in the age of wire and string, the ambassadors and anagrams of a farewell to arms, already dead." This chewed up what would have been the dinner hour.

"Pick up the phone, Mona," Bob said.

"All right, all right."

She brought the phone to the closet and sat on her hamper, figuring she'd be able to concentrate better in an enclosed space. Mickey answered on the sixth ring.

"Well, hello," he said warmly. "Hello, hello. Been a while since I heard your voice."

"Two years," Mona said.

He grunted and then there was a silence. She asked him how the plumbing business was.

"I'm not a plumber anymore. I don't fix toilets anymore, I sell them. I work for a manufacturer now. Clients are a whole different breed. Tell you what, the lady I pitched to this morning? She really chapped my ass. One of these days, I tell ya, Bang, zoom, to the moon, Alice!"

"I ate some hash by mistake today," she said. "At a client's house."

He didn't respond, but she could hear him breathing.

"A client's hash," she repeated. "I ate it. By mistake."

"Wait, what're you doing with clients?"

"Cleaning. I told you that in the letter. Did you get my letter?"

"Ah, Christ. Don't work for yourself, girlie. Go work for the federal government. Benefits, pension, 401(k). You gotta thinka your retirement. Don't make the same mistake as me."

Did he just call her girlie? Yes, he did. "What color are my eyes?"

"What?"

"My eyes. What color are they?"

"I don't know," he said. "Brown."

"I'm regretting the brownies, Mickey. I really am."

"Don't call me Mickey. I hate that. Call me Dad," he shouted. "Dad!"

She held the phone away from her ear. He was in worse shape than she was. Much worse.

"Two words," she said. "Alcoholics Anonymous."

He laughed. "I'm done with the double A. Besides, I'm not an alcoholic, I'm just bored."

"Right," she said. "Makes perfect sense."

"I'm serious. I only drink when I'm bored or in pain. Strictly, uh—how do you say it—*medicinal.*"

He stumbled over the word, as he did all multisyllabic words, drunk or sober. He had trouble getting his mouth around "Massachusetts," for example, along with "unfortunately," "sophisticated," "vocabulary," "educational," and "apologetic."

"You have no idea what it's like to wear a hook for thirty years. It really fucks up your neck and back. I've had three surgeries and now they got me hooked on oxy. I'm almost dead."

The pity card. Used to work like a charm. At eighteen he apprenticed at an auto body shop that serviced race cars. One day he was carrying a tire across the parking lot. Not sure how—she'd never asked. Sometimes she pictured him rolling the tire across the lot; other times she saw him hugging it to his chest. The explosion had been massive—a tire bomb, the paper called it—and he'd been thrown fifty feet, through the plate-glass window of a dentist's office next door.

The paramedics hadn't been able to get his gurney in and out of the elevator because his arms couldn't be strapped down—they'd swelled to over twice their size—and he screamed whenever they were touched. They were filled with pus and debris from the tire, which had confused her at first—how did little bits of rubber get inside his arms? The surgeons tried to remove the debris, but they didn't get it all, and his left arm was broken in eight places, and the bones of his right arm had been pulverized, so they kept it in traction for several months. She wasn't sure when the gangrene set in, but because his arm was in traction right there in front of him, he'd been forced to watch it eat its way to his elbow.

"It was like watching a plant die," her mother used to stage-whisper to friends and relatives. "You could smell it all the way down the hall. By the time they amputated, his hand looked like an old glove. A crushed, black leather glove."

The glove imagery occupied her imagination for weeks afterward—she'd been six or seven when she first heard it—but it came in handy later. She kept the image in the back of her mind and could bring it forward at will. It was money in the bank, a kind of emergency fund; when her father did something mortifying, the image of the empty glove helped her forgive him. Unfortunately, by the time she reached junior high, she'd unwittingly drained the potency out of it.

"I'm forty-seven," he said now. "Forty-seven years old. You know how I stayed alive this long? All these years?"

"Booze?"

"Fear," he said.

Interesting. Maybe he had some actual wisdom to impart. Wouldn't that be nice? Some fatherly advice? In her time of need?

"Fear keeps you alive?"

"A spectacle of fearsome acts."

Oh. Well, he just gave himself away with "spectacle." And "fearsome." Definitely not in his lexicon. Must be a line from a movie. He was a poor enunciator, yes, but not when he was reciting something. Then the words tumbled out perfectly, like a stutterer who doesn't stutter when he sings. Whose line was it? She was good at this game. She'd probably be able to recognize it if he kept going.

"Fearsome acts, huh? Like what?"

"If somebody steals from me, I cut off his hands. If he offends me, I cut off his thumb. If he rises against me, I cut off his head and stick it on a pike. Raise it high up so all in the streets can see." He paused. "That's what preserves the order of things. *Fear.*"

Dammit. It was on the tip of her tongue but she couldn't place it, which was a shame, because he'd never tell her.

"I never had a son," he said. "Civilization is crumbling."

Wait a minute now. She could see the actor's face. He had a mustache. A black mustache. Lunatic eyes, like Mickey's.

"Daniel Day Lewis!" she said. "Hah!"

"What?"

"Uh, the movie you're quoting," she said. "*Gangs of New York.*"

"I'm not quoting anything."

"Oh, *Dad.*"

He giggled. "How's your mother? Still beautiful?"

"Probably."

"Still married?"

"I believe so."

"She wanna see me?"

Mona laughed.

"I don't understand why we can't be friends. I mean, we were married fifteen years!"

"Yeah, well, she's kind of brain damaged from the concussions you gave her."

"What're you talkin' about, concussions."

"I guess you don't remember kicking her in the head? With your boots?"

"Whoa! Wait a minute. I never hit your mother. Never once. Did she tell you I hit her? Let me tell you a secret about your mother: all those bruises were self-inflicted. She beat *herself* up. Don't you—"

She hung up, crawled out of the closet, checked her hands again. Little less wormy. It was going to be all right. She'd pass out soon enough.

———

"Hey, thanks, by the way, for your brilliant suggestion, Bob. Nice one. Real nice. I feel way better now."

She took herself to bed. Alone again, she realized the depth of her need. It yawned widely, expanding inside her, a sizable black hole. Exhausted, she resigned herself to being sucked under and dragged through its muck for several hours. She closed her eyes and turned to face the wall, her head full of pins and needles. The dogs were howling outside. Think pleasant thoughts, she ordered herself. She imagined following the dogs into the woods. They led her to a log cabin where a man stood in a clearing, chopping wood in the failing light. It was him, Mr. Disgusting. He'd been waiting for her all along. He dropped the ax, picked her up, and carried her toward the cabin—

But then the dogs surrounded them and started chasing them through the trees. Disgusting dropped her and took off running. She tried to follow but stumbled, fell. Her legs were cement. She was too tired to lift her head.

Why not offer herself to the dogs? Let them have their way with her. They could chew her face off and she'd die the way she'd always suspected, a friendless, fuckless wonder.

A friendless, fuckless wonder, she repeated. You are a wonder. Friendless. Fuckless.

Tears stung her eyes. Feelings are just stories, she reminded herself. They have a beginning and an end.

"The End," she'd like to say.

HENRY AND ZOE

SHE COULD HEAR YOKO AND YOKO'S PHONE RINGING through the wall. She looked at her own. Three weeks, and not a single service call. Not one!

She turned on the television and settled into a Merchant-Ivory production on PBS, breaking her rule of never watching a period piece unless she was on her period. Helena Bonham Carter and Beefeater were a hellish combination, no question. She considered wandering out to the highway, hurling herself against a speeding windshield.

She missed Yoko and Yoko. Not their sanctimoniousness, but their physical presence on the other side of the house. They were attending a series of workshops in Italy, and they'd taken their cellos with them and wouldn't be back for over a month, and now the house felt more lopsided than usual, like the unweighted end of a giant seesaw. She was up in the air, her feet dangling, and she needed Yoko and Yoko's dreadful music to bring her back to earth.

Maybe the Merchant-Ivory soundtrack was to blame—Puccini would turn anyone to mush. She muted the volume on the portable rescued from a Dumpster. Better. Then the phone rang. Her phone!

A man named Henry Moss introduced himself and asked for Bee's Knees Housekeeping. He sounded embarrassed, as if her business had an unsavory name, like Busy Beavers in the Buff. Which wasn't such a bad idea—if she cleaned houses naked, she'd probably have a lot more going on than *A Room with a View*.

After introductions he explained that he'd received a flyer and asked, "So how does this work?"

"Well, my rate is twenty dollars per hour, but I can drop by and give you an estimate, and we can take it from there."

"Very good," he said. "What about references?"

She said yeah, sure, she could give him some of those, and she gave him Sheila's number in Florida, along with three names of former clients in Lowell. If everything checked out, she told him, they could meet the morning after next.

Time to put the gin away and turn off the television. Now that her plans for the next forty-eight hours involved leaving her house, she could do something more productive, like allow herself positive thoughts of the future. Maybe moving to New Mexico wasn't Big Stupid Mistake No. 502, after all. Henry Moss would become her first steady client, he'd tell all his friends how great she was, and before long her phone would start ringing off the hook.

HIS HOUSE, A TIDY RED ADOBE CASITA WITH MILKY TUR-quoise trim, sat on a narrow lane extending off the town plaza. She parked behind a vintage orange-and-cream Range Rover in the driveway. Two burgundy-colored chili ristras hung on either side of the mahogany front door. There wasn't a doorbell, so she knocked. She didn't remember posting a flyer on this door.

The man who answered was well over six feet and had messy hair the color of an Irish setter. His lips were chapped. His eyes were a shade of blue she associated with Ukrainians and hummingbirds. A pair of dirty reading glasses sat on the tip of his nose, and she wanted to remove them and clean them with her apron.

She shook his hand, which was warm and dry and much bigger than hers. She placed him in his midforties. He seemed pleasantly surprised by the looks of her, and she was glad she had put some effort into her appearance. Her hair wasn't exactly clean, but she'd made an attractive pile of it on top of her head and she was wearing red lipstick, a navy-blue blouse, jeans, and an apron from the forties. Clients relished seeing her in an apron—a source of comfort, she imagined, the idea that someone was taking care of them.

She sensed he was a private person, unused to having strangers in his house. A short hallway opened onto a pueblo-style living room with low ceilings supported by hand-plastered walls decorated with sun-bleached cow skulls.

"So this is the living room," he mumbled. "It's pretty basic, I guess."

The floors would be difficult—neither the woven kilim rugs nor the uneven Saltillo-tiled floor would tolerate an upright vacuum. She'd have to sweep the floors and lug the rugs outside. They were too large to shake, however, so she'd have to beat them with a broom. She pictured herself on the back patio, beating the crap out of the rugs.

The kiva fireplace was overflowing with ash. She wondered what he'd been burning, as it wasn't quite cold enough for a fire. Perhaps the ashes were left over from last winter. In any case it would need emptying and cleaning, so she added an extra half hour to her estimate. Judging from his taste in furniture, he was single. No woman would tolerate so much leather. A clove-colored leather couch with matching love seat, and a hunter-green leather armchair and matching ottoman—these she would clean with Murphy Oil Soap, one of her tricks. A large white animal pelt—not a polar bear, but something big—lay on the floor in front of the enormous television. The lamps, she noticed, were all the same: banker's lamps with green glass shades.

Next, the kitchen, which was full of restaurant-quality stainless steel appliances, all smudged and covered in fingerprints.

"The people at Home Depot said to use a special cleaner on the stainless steel," he said. He opened a cabinet and handed her a bottle. It had never been opened.

"They're just trying to make money. This stuff is way overpriced, not to mention toxic," she said, setting the bottle on the counter without looking at it. "Olive oil works best. Trick of the trade."

He looked down at her over his glasses. "I'll take your word for it," he said, and smiled.

She followed him past a small office and bathroom, down a long, dimly lit hallway lined with a mosaic of framed photographs, all featuring the same dark-haired girl. The closely grouped photos reminded her of a shrine, minus the candles, and were dwarfed by a large, life-size oil painting of the same girl, aged eight or so, sitting on a park bench, wearing a pink gerbera daisy behind her ear and a white cotton dress, her bare feet dangling. The heavy-framed painting was the focal point of what she imagined must be an altar to his daughter. His dead daughter? The one he killed while driving drunk?

He opened a door at the end of the hallway. "This is my daughter Zoe's room. She stays with me on weekends."

Okay, not dead, just idolized and worshipped to make up for

the messy, drawn-out divorce. She poked her head into the room. Unmade bed, scattered clothes. On the walls, a poster of Kurt Cobain, another of Orlando Bloom, and framed abstract drawings of horses.

"How old?" Mona asked.

"Twelve," he said. He seemed uncomfortable suddenly, as if she were prying. "Would you mind changing her sheets each time? She likes to eat cookies in bed."

"No problem." Mona liked to eat cookies in bed, too, but only changed her sheets once a month.

He opened another door. "I sleep in here." Another unmade bed. His white sheets were printed with orange morning glories. His nightstands looked antique and had splotched mirrored panels on them. The closet doors were mirrored. Another mirror in a gilt frame hung above the headboard. She could see herself and Henry in one of the mirrors. He was looking sideways at her.

"Do you do laundry by any chance?" he asked.

"I do it all," she said. "I'll even iron your sheets if you're into that."

"Uh, that won't be necessary," he said, as if she'd suggested something crazy.

She inspected the master bath: green slate floors, a large, doorless, two-headed shower, and two sinks, each with its own framed mirror. The sinks were made to look like large oval bowls resting on a wooden vanity. He'd spent some money in there.

As they walked toward the front of the house, she asked what he did for a living.

"I own the Blue Mango Cantina, but I have another . . . project in . . . Santa Fe, so . . . I'm only around on weekends." She got the feeling he was making it up as he went along. "It's a little complicated. I just stay down there during the week," he added.

———

"Are you a chef?" she asked.

"No, but I love to cook." He tilted his head at her. "Do you do something other than . . . ?" He made a vague gesture at her apron.

Because she was white and well spoken, people assumed she must do something "other than." Clearly, cleaning houses wasn't good enough. Or it shouldn't be, anyway. She must be in some kind of rut. Would he have asked if she were Hispanic? Of course not. She watched him squirm a little—she was probably glaring at him without realizing it—and decided to let him off the hook. "I take photographs." Not a total lie.

Visible relief on his face. Usually they preferred that she be in college, taking classes toward something practical, like a business or nursing degree. But this was Taos, after all, which was overrun with people calling themselves artists. "Well, you're in the perfect place," he said. "You can't beat the light around here. What sort of photographs—landscapes?"

"No," she said. "I take pictures of myself, mostly." Naked, she wanted to add. On your sofa. With a broomstick up my ass.

"Interesting," he said, nodding. "Where you from again?"

"Massachusetts by way of California."

"Oh right. I know that from your references. They spoke very highly of you, by the way. And that's where I'm from originally," he said. "Boston, I mean."

"What pahht?" she asked, exaggerating the accent he was conspicuously lacking.

"Beacon Hill," he said.

Rich prick. "Aw, that's nice."

"So where do we go from here?"

"I suggest weekly visits to start. I'll probably spend about five hours the first time and four hours the second time. After that, I'll charge you my minimum, which is three hours. My schedule is open right now so you have your pick of days. Most people prefer Fridays."

"Actually, I prefer Mondays," he said.

THE FIRST TIME IN A CLIENT'S HOUSE WAS A SORT OF SEDUC-tion: she would do something beyond the call of duty to make them feel special, and by the third week they'd wonder how they ever lived without her. For Henry, she cleaned the filthy coffeemaker inside and out. She did the same with the cappuccino machine, removing the stubborn milk stain from the steaming rod with a piece of steel wool. She cleaned out his silverware drawer and refrigerator. She washed the walls, scrubbed the floor by hand.

Now the bathrooms. She started with the basics: mirrors, sinks, shower, and then cleaned the toothbrush holder, the toothbrushes themselves, and the toothpaste tube. She removed the hair from his hairbrush and soaked the brush in soap and alcohol. She eliminated the mineral deposits in the toilet bowls with a pumice stone. She folded the toilet paper into a point, like they do in hotels.

In the hallway, she dusted the Zoe shrine, which she suspected wouldn't go unnoticed, examining each picture as she cleaned it: Zoe eating spaghetti with her hands, blowing out candles, jumping on a trampoline, playing piano, holding a green balloon, licking an ice cream cone, sitting on a horse, hanging upside down from monkey bars, blowing a kiss to someone outside the frame. Her favorite was a close-up of Zoe at age seven or eight, wearing eye makeup and a platinum wig with mascara running down her face.

Zoe was alone in every photograph. As she got older, her facial expressions became more inscrutable. There was a guarded blankness about her, and she seemed to have stopped smiling at around age nine. In the most recent photographs she'd acquired a uniform: heavy black eyeliner, black T-shirt, denim miniskirt, black Converse high-tops.

She obviously had a secret or two. Mona wondered if many of them revolved around Henry. Mona had spent years keeping Mickey's horror-show high jinks from her mother. Not telling her mother was essentially like tossing the secret into an abandoned well—without nourishment and in spite of its hoarse screaming, it would eventually die. Later, in junior high, she wondered if the secrets were feeding on each other, perhaps gaining strength and intelligence in their numbers, scheming to balance on top of one another, so that eventually one or all of them would climb out of the well and wander into town for everyone to see.

She thought of the secret vacation her father had taken her on when she was eleven. A weekend at the Tropicana in Vegas. They'd driven there in his plumbing truck. Instead of heading for the casino straightaway, he surprised her by asking, "If it was just you and Mom here, what would you do?"

"Well, first we'd go shopping," she said. "Then we'd get our hair done and Mom might get a manicure. Then we'd walk around and eat donuts."

"That's it?" He looked disappointed.

She shrugged. "Yeah. Then we'd go to the movies when it got dark."

"Okay," he confirmed. "That's exactly what we'll do."

But her father took her "shopping" in a pawnshop. Instantly bored, she kept her eyes on the owner, a nerdy man with glasses, and his ten-year-old son, who kept staring at her father's hook. Lost in his own world, her father wandered around the shop for what seemed like forever, carefully picking up guitars and then putting them down again. He handled each one warily, like a specimen in a jar. Mona gave him a few minutes, then walked over and stood right next to him, hoping to remind him that she was there and that they were in a pawnshop and not in a regular store, buying new jeans as she had hoped.

He picked up another guitar and said, "I probably never told you this, but I used to play guitar before I lost my arm. I wrote songs and was in a band and everything." She watched his eyes fill up with tears. It gave her a panicky feeling and she tried to think of something to prevent any further spillage. He never talked about what he was like before the accident.

"You had more hair back then, too," she said, and smiled.

He put the guitar down and looked at her appreciatively, as if she'd just said something profound. "Did you know me and your mom saw the Doors on our first date? They were at the Whiskey."

"What's the Whiskey?" she asked.

"The best nightclub around," he said. "Your mother got completely hammered and puked all over my Mustang. I still liked her, though. She was wearing white patent leather go-go boots that night. Man, oh man."

In his stories about her mother—to Mona or to anyone else—her mother was always the drunk and out-of-control one. But also the beautiful one.

Before leaving, he bought himself an old Nikon, and then told her to pick out ruby rings for both of them. "Rubies are lucky," he said. She thought pointing out favorites would be the extent of it, but then they actually tried them on and everything. She chose a small ruby surrounded by diamond chips, her father a pinkie ring with a thick gold band. "We'll take 'em," he told the owner, to her astonishment.

"Semper fi," the owner said as they were leaving.

Her father merely nodded. He liked men to think he'd been in Vietnam.

At the hotel hair salon she managed to talk him into getting her a perm, something her mother would never allow. Her father wanted one as well, which made the hairdressers laugh. Bald on top, his red hair was long on the sides and back, so they said they could do it, if that's what he really wanted. "Curly hair is in," he said, flicking his hair back with his hand. He flirted with the hairdressers the entire time, but Mona didn't mind because they were laughing as if he were the funniest man they'd ever met. When they put the solution in, he screamed, "It burns!" and did his imitation of the possessed girl in *The Exorcist*.

They emerged three hours later looking like Little Orphan Annie and Bozo the Clown. He bought her an ice cream cone and they headed for the movies. Mona was relieved to see no children's movies playing; she had an aversion to Disney films. She had a choice between *Ordinary People* and *Raging Bull*.

"I heard *Ordinary People* is a total downer," he said.

They bought tickets for *Raging Bull* and sat near the front, like she wanted. She watched the kissing scenes carefully, trying to figure out the transition between regular kissing and tongue kissing. She glanced at her father from time to time and noticed that he cried during most of the boxing scenes. When the movie ended, he declared, "That's the best movie I've ever seen."

The rest of the weekend she spent mostly alone, lounging by the pool and drinking virgin daiquiris while her father played blackjack. On their last night she ordered room service and lounged in the Jacuzzi tub. The towels were bigger and thicker than the ones at home and she made sure to use all of them, drying off with one, wrapping one around her body and another around her head. When she came out her father was back from the casino and sitting at the desk with a drink, trying to load film into his camera.

"Give me a hand with this," he said.

She helped him feed the film into the spool. He took the first picture while she was brushing her teeth. She spat out toothpaste and told him to cut it out. He ignored her and snapped a few more, and she gave him the finger.

"Wait." He smiled. "Do that again."

She crooked her middle finger and smiled widely for the camera.

"You look like a model with your tan," he said. "Come sit on the bed." She gave him a dirty look and took the towel off her head. "No, leave the towel on. You look like Natalie Wood." She didn't know who that was, but assumed she was someone glamorous. "Come on, Mona. You know you love having your picture taken."

True—if she saw a stranger taking a photograph on the street, she tried like hell to get into the frame somehow.

"We've had such a good time," he said, still trying to convince her. "I just want something to remember this trip by."

"You have the camera," she said. "And your ruby. And you won't forget that perm." She laughed.

"I think the rest of my hair's falling out," he said, looking worried.

"All right," she relented, wrapping the towel back around her head. "I'll pose for your stupid pictures."

Delighted, he refreshed his drink and directed her to sit on the edge of the bed and cross her legs like a lady. "Put one hand on your hip and the other on the back of your head."

"Take it from above," she said.

He stood on a chair.

"Make sure you get my profile," she said, turning.

"Don't worry, you look wonderful," he said with a fake accent.

She can't remember how he enticed her to remove the towels, but it seemed natural at the time. She liked the pictures, despite the drastic tan lines. They were back home by then and the school year had just started. When he showed her, he said, "See what a beauty you are? You look just like your mother." She was thrilled by this prospect.

A few months later she caught him showing them to his fat friend, Fat Jim, in the living room. She watched Fat Jim run a finger over her black-and-white figure and heard him comment on her flat chest and lack of hair *down there*. Her father said nothing, just nodded in agreement. She felt dizzy and quietly backed out of the room, thankful she hadn't been seen, and then spent an hour in the bathroom, watching herself cry in the mirror.

Later, in high school, her therapist anticipated—and seemed to crave—a different ending, but her father never laid a finger on her. He moved away to Sacramento when she was thirteen. Still, she doubted he would have tried anything. He seemed a little frightened of her by the end.

HENRY DIDN'T STRIKE HER AS BEING A PERV. ON THE OTHER hand, maybe her perv radar was on the blink and a little reconnaissance was in order. She walked into his office and eyed his desk drawers, then stopped herself. Nothing going on here, she told herself. She looked at her watch—already 3:00. She swept the floors quickly and then mopped her way out of the house.

On the way home she stopped at the Agave, a dive bar and taco stand on the edge of town, and treated herself to a taco plate and a glass of crappy chardonnay. The bar was empty except for the bartender and another loner like herself, a bone-thin Native American woman with open sores on her face, sitting at the end of the bar.

The only Native Americans she ever saw were at the gas station, filling their tanks, or at 7-Eleven, buying six-packs and cigarettes. The woman at the bar was drinking something with cranberry juice. If Mickey were here, he'd whisper, "Looks like she chased a fart through a keg of nails," his favorite expression for homely women. Then he'd try to get into the woman's pants. She imagined the various ways he'd go about doing that—he'd buy her a few drinks, offer her a bump of coke, openly gape at her chest. When that didn't work, he'd make up stories about how he'd lost his arm—sniper fire, a land mine, a prison camp in Laos—or tell her about the time he'd met Christopher Walken, who'd bought him a drink and told him he should go into acting.

Stop thinking about him, she chided herself. She'd thought about Mickey more in the past two days than she had in years. Maybe it was a sign—maybe he was utterly alone and dying of cancer, and he desperately wanted to make amends but was too—

"Why are you staring at me?" the woman at the end of the bar called out.

Mona looked over her shoulder—no one there.

"I'm talking to you," the woman said. "You keep staring at me."

"Sorry," Mona mumbled.

"Maybe she likes your face," the bartender said to the woman. "Maybe you remind her of her sister." The woman rolled her eyes and they smiled at each other. The bartender turned to Mona and asked, "Another?"

"No," Mona said. "I'm finished."

AT HENRY'S THE FOLLOWING WEEK SHE FOCUSED ON THE living room, dusting the vigas with a damp mop, and reconstructing what he and Zoe might have done the past weekend. There were Dylan CDs in the stereo, a stack of movies on the coffee table—*The Crow, Groundhog Day, The Nightmare Before Christmas*—an empty pizza box, six empty beer bottles, and two cans of Coke on the kitchen counter. In Zoe's room an empty pint of Chunky Monkey on the nightstand next to a dog-eared copy of *Interview with the Vampire*.

When she stripped Zoe's bed she found a bloodstain the size and color of a plum on the mattress. It reminded her of a birthmark, and something about it brought tears to her eyes. She scratched the stain with her fingernail and felt the urge to gouge it out of the mattress with a pair of scissors. Instead, she sat on the bed and stared at Zoe's nightstand drawer, willing herself not to open it.

Protect your karma, she ordered herself. It's forever.

Inside the drawer, a set of colored pens, a handful of rubber bands, a necklace with a butterfly pendant, and a small red journal. A master snoop, she took a mental picture of the drawer before removing the journal, noting its exact position.

Unfortunately, there was only a single, undated entry:

> Dear Diary,
>
>   Yesterday was San Geronimo Day and me and Dad went to the Pueblo. A big crowd was standing around the village square. It was very hot and the wind kept blowing the dust around. Indian clowns ran through the crowd, shouting and acting crazy. They were naked except for homemade hula skirts and their bodies were painted with black and white stripes. A few of them were fat. They snatched little kids from their parents and carried them on their shoulders to the river. The river is sacred.

The clowns dunked the kids in the river. I wished I was one of them. It's supposed to be a blessing.

She appreciated Zoe's style. She replaced the journal carefully—facedown, its spine flush with the back of the drawer—then wandered into Henry's room. On his nightstand, two Sue Grafton novels, *J Is for Judgment* and *K Is for Killer*. He was certainly better read than her father; the only book she'd ever seen Mickey read was *E.T. the Extra-Terrestrial*, a novel based on the film rather than the other way around, and he never even finished it.

She opened Henry's nightstand drawer. No journal, just maximum reserve tip condoms, a bag of shake, a one hitter, and, hidden at the back of the drawer, a large prescription bottle. She looked at the label—Dilaudid. The stuff they salivated over in *Drugstore Cowboy*. Well, this was a first. She'd seen plenty of habit-forming narcotics in people's houses—Xanax, Valium, Demerol, Percocet—but *Dilaudid*? She counted the pills—only nine left—and wondered if she could get away with stealing a couple. Or just one. They were 10-milligram pills—one was plenty. She asked herself if she really wanted one. The answer was yes. She could go home and wash it down with a beer and then spend the evening contemplating the calluses on her feet. But maybe she should wait and see—he might be the pill-counting type.

She opened the other nightstand drawer. A case of Rolaids, a bottle of Pepto-Bismol, a pair of scissors. She slid her hand between his mattress and box spring. Her fingers brushed paper. Lifting the mattress slightly, she saw four little chapbooks with plain covers. She pulled one out and leafed through it: no pictures, just old typewriter text on newsprint. Poetry?

She zeroed in on the words: "The horse came in buckets all over her back. She was covered in cum. She moaned and continued fingering herself." Whoa! Bestiality! Another first. She turned the pages— the woman in the story went on to fuck all of the barn animals, including pigs. She just couldn't get enough of corkscrew cocks. At one point a farmer spied on her. After the woman finished with a pig, Mr. Green Jeans took her from behind. *The End.*

She shuffled through the remaining three. Each one was dedicated to a specific fetish: golden showers, foot fucking . . . and then this: "We took turns spying on our teenage kids through the keyhole. After Becky sucked Robbie's cock, he fucked her tits. I noticed my husband had a hard-on. 'We know you're watching, Mom and Dad,' Becky called out. 'You should join us.'"

A family orgy ensued, mother with son, father with daughter. Incest erotica, she thought. Fucking gross. She was unable to stop reading, however, and gradually became aware of two rumble fish swimming around inside of her. One fish was Repulsion, the other Arousal. They swam in circles for several minutes, sizing each other up. Then the fighting began. She continued reading and the fighting intensified. She climbed onto the bed, the book in her left hand, her right hand down her pants. It didn't take long, only a minute or two. Afterward, she replaced the books. You are a slimy little creature. Wretched, vile, despicable. You should seriously consider seeking—wait, is that a hidden camera? There was a hole in the wall she'd never noticed before. It was the size of a quarter and too high to peer into, so she inserted a finger into it. No camera. She opened the armoire. No camera there, either. It was just her and her filthiness.

In an effort to cleanse herself, she spent an hour on hands and knees, vigorously scrubbing the floors with vinegar and water. She cleaned all the baseboards, too. Incest pornography = child molester? Probably not. If all three booklets were devoted to incest, then maybe. He clearly just had a taste for the taboo. So did she, apparently. And so what if he thought of his daughter when he jerked off? It was none of her business. She was a fucking cleaning lady, not the Incest Police.

By the time she left, her knees were red and swollen and her back was killing her. On her way home she stopped at the grocery store, bought some leafy greens and a bottle of salad dressing for dinner. After the stunt she pulled at Henry's, she felt undeserving of a proper meal.

At home, she broke another of her rules by dragging out a box of old journals from the closet. She'd been saving the journals for her future biographer, but never allowed herself to look at them—too depressing. Most of them were from high school, but she had one from around the time her parents split up, the year she'd been Zoe's age. She rifled through the box, searching for it. She remembered it being purple and having a lock.

It was at the very bottom of the box, of course, and the key was missing. She brought it to the kitchen, popped the lock with a sturdy butter knife, and then sat at the table. When she opened the journal a photograph fell out. A picture of her childhood home in Torrance. The house was even smaller than she remembered. She grew up on Newton Avenue—a street of modest one-story homes built close together and in the Mission style, with smooth stucco siding and red-tiled roofs. In the seventies, shortly after Mickey and her mother bought the house, Newton Avenue became popular among Asian families who'd been buying up a lot of the businesses in the area. Korean families had lived on either side of Mona's house, and a family of Samoans lived across the street. The neighborhood was nestled up against the hills of Palos Verdes, where wealthy people continued to buy property even though their houses kept falling into the ocean. These same wealthy people used Newton as a shortcut home, and their BMWs and Benzes often careened at high speeds past the house. Her father was fond of throwing things—small rocks, garbage, dirty looks—at speeders while he watered the lawn.

On the very first page of the journal was a drawing of Tom, her father's best friend and former business partner. She'd been secretly in love with Tom for two years. She remembered having done the math at one point: by the time she was eighteen, Tom would only be thirty-nine, which meant they could still get married. She was twenty-four now, which made Tom—wherever he was—forty-five. Around Henry's age.

She was impressed by the level of detail in the drawing. He was smiling, and she'd captured the gap between his two front teeth, a gap that had made her want to writhe around on the carpet. His resemblance to Mr. Disgusting was startling, embarrassing. It made her feel like a robot, and not a smart one. A robot from the fifties, perhaps. Was she really so transparent?

> Dear Diary,
> Tom's been sleeping on the couch. He sleeps naked. When I come into the living room he doesn't put clothes on. His body is very long with lots of little muscles. He has a hairy behind. His thingee is regular-looking with black hairs around it. His balls are shiny. Mom says Tom is a scumbag.

> Dear Diary,
> Tom's mouth is shaped like a piece of toast when he yawns. He has a tattoo on his arm that says "Rat Patrol." He

said he used to run with a gang. I told him I didn't know he liked to run! He thought that was funny. Then Dad came in and he stopped talking. I wish we could be alone.

Dear Diary,

Dad's friends are here. Tom, Fat Jim, Ed the Electrician, and another guy. They're watching the fight on TV. Dad made me take his boots off in front of everyone. Except he tricked me this time and they all laughed. But not Tom. I think it's because he's in love with me. I'm in my room now. I hope he comes to see me.

The boot trick. He'd asked her to remove his cowboy boots, which wasn't in itself out of the ordinary. She'd approached his outstretched leg and straddled his calf as usual, while his friends looked on, bemused. She faced away from him, the boot between her legs like a horse's head. Grabbing the heel, she gave it a good pull, but he flexed his toes so the boot wouldn't come off. She had a vague notion of the subtext, but continued the performance like a good sport. Everyone (except her and Tom) seemed really entertained by the whole thing.

Dear Diary,

Tom gave me a ride on his motorcycle tonight. He told me to hold on tight and we went really fast up and down the street. I didn't want it to be over. My hands were cold so I put them under his shirt. Dad was really mad when we got back. He was making hamburgers and he threw mine against the wall. It left a red mark. I wasn't hungry anyways. He always makes mine bloody in the middle.

———

Dear Diary,

Dad had his friends over to watch the fight on TV.
Then Tom and Dad got in a fight and we had to go to the
hospital. Tom held my hand in the waiting room and told
me he was adopted.

A night to remember: Sugar Ray Leonard knocked out Thomas
"The Hitman" Hearns in the fourteenth round, after which Mickey
insisted on giving her a boxing lesson. "Punch me in the stomach as
hard as you can," he'd said.

Everyone stopped talking suddenly and stared at them.

"Leave her alone, Mick," Tom said from the couch. "The poor
kid's tired."

"Hey," her father said. "*You* leave her alone. I'm trying to *teach* her
something, Fucknuts."

She hesitated at first, but ended up punching him in the solar
plexus. His face turned bright red and the room went quiet and still. "I
told you to punch me in the stomach," he said, after catching his breath.

Before she could fake an apology, he slapped her. He missed her
face and hit the top of her head, messing up her hair, which made her
feel stupid, and also ugly. Tom quickly got to his feet and gave him
a good shove. Mickey lost his footing and fell onto the coffee table,
landing on the plant aquarium her mother had left behind. The glass
shattered and he made a strange yelping noise before rolling off the
table and onto the maroon carpeting.

There was a lot of blood. It was coming out of an artery in his
wrist. Thin, fake-looking spurts. It hit the wall, the ceiling, a nearby
lampshade. "Whoops," he said. He clamped his wrist to his chest and
held it there with his stump. Fat Jim wrapped a T-shirt around it, but
it was obvious he needed stitches.

The emergency room was crowded, and they would be waiting awhile. Mickey told them to head in while he finished his cigarette outside. She and Tom found a seat in the waiting room and Mickey staggered in a few minutes later.

"Help! Help me!" he screamed.

The makeshift T-shirt bandage was gone and he had his good hand cupped over his stump, which was covered in blood and looked recently severed. The two front desk nurses stopped what they were doing and gaped, along with everyone else in the waiting room.

"My arm, oh, God help me, my arm," he whimpered.

"Gurney!" one of the nurses yelled, and rushed over to him.

"I can wait," she heard him say. "It doesn't hurt that bad."

SHE PAGED THROUGH THE REST OF THE JOURNAL. TOM, TOM, and more Tom. Funny, she hadn't recorded his rejection of her, but she remembered every detail. It had been late in the evening, after ten, and they were in the living room of the old house on Newton, sitting side by side on the leather love seat. Her father was passed out on the other couch, mouth open, snoring softly. Tom was shirtless and had his bare feet up on the coffee table and a beer bottle between his legs. This was her last chance to declare her love; in a few days, Tom and Mickey would be moving to Sacramento to start another plumbing business.

They were watching *Cat People* on cable and Tom kept making fun of it, but he didn't turn the channel. During one of the racier scenes, she placed a tentative hand on his thigh. He didn't seem to mind so she moved it closer to his crotch. She could feel his leg stiffen suddenly—a good sign, she thought.

She was mistaken. He picked up her hand like it was some dead thing and dropped it back in her lap. "You're eleven—"

"Twelve," she said.

"You're just a kid," he said, and took a swig of his beer. "You don't know what you're doing."

"You can put your hand in my underwear," she whispered. "I don't mind."

He gave her a startled look and glanced at her father, still out cold. She watched him drink most of his beer in one swallow and set the bottle on the coffee table. He turned to face her and leaned back against the armrest, placing both of his hands behind his head, like the police tell you to do. He looked at her as if she were a bunch of numbers he was trying to multiply.

"I'm not a virgin," she said, trying not to stare at his armpits.

He took a deep breath and seemed about to say something, but then changed his mind.

"I've been to third base," she said. "With someone your age."

She watched his neck redden. He didn't look impressed. He asked who it was and she just shrugged. He glanced at her father again and cleared his throat. "What's his name?" he asked.

She shook her head. She felt stupid, stupid for not knowing, stupid for bringing it up. He removed his hands from the back of his head and crossed his arms. She stared at the tattoo on his bicep: no picture; just "Rat Patrol" in old-fashioned letters. He was frowning at her. She could tell he thought she was being cagey, but she was telling the truth.

"Where was this—school? Was it a teacher?"

"Here," she said. "After a party. He came into my room."

Now something was happening to his mouth. His lips curled and bunched up.

"It was dark," she explained. "I couldn't see him."

He winced and put his head in his hands. She thought he might be jealous.

"But it wasn't like that," she said quickly. "It's . . ." She shook her head. *It's you I love,* she wanted to say. *I want us to get married.* She touched his shin with her fingers. *I even love your shins.*

"When was this?"

"A while ago, when Mom still lived here."

He took his hands away from his face. "Where was I? Was I here?"

She nodded. "We danced that night."

He blinked at her.

"Three whole songs," she added.

Fleetwood Mac, the *Tusk* album. She could tell he didn't remember, or didn't care, that his mind was somewhere else, and she wanted to remind him that it had been the weekend she'd lost Spoon and Fork, they were gone, gone, disappeared to fucking Idaho, and she'd been crying for something like twelve hours, and her eyes were all puffy and her parents were drunk, really drunk—her father passed out on the patio, her mother on the couch, and it was over between them—and she remembered seeing Tom carry her mother to bed, which had made her wild with grief, like those angels in Gothic paintings, and she'd wanted to scream and beat her fists on the closed door and maybe even tear out some of her hair, but she'd poured herself a drink in the kitchen instead, her first ever, and choked it down like medicine, and then she'd gone around and drunk from half-empty cups in the living room, and after a while she noticed that she'd stopped shaking and felt pretty good, so she offered to massage Ed the Electrician's shoulders, thinking it would make Tom jealous when he was done with her mother, but when he finally came back he simply ordered her to bed. She remembered asking, "Will you carry me? Like you did with Mom?" And his face had softened a little and he picked her up like she weighed nothing. She circled his shoulders with her arms and he spun her around a couple of times and said, "Where to?"

"My room," she said.

It was only fourteen steps away, but he'd taken them slowly, carefully, pausing between each one, long enough for her to feel little again, and safe, and unsinkable.

In her room he flipped on the light and laid her down on the bed and then stood there for a minute, swaying slightly. She was hoping he'd lie down next to her, and then maybe on top of her, that he would kiss her and grind against her like she sometimes did to her favorite blanket. Instead, he told her that a million anchovies had turned up dead in the marina that morning. "They swam into the marina in the middle of the night and got lost," he said. "A million of them. They couldn't find their way out. Eventually they ran out of oxygen, and now there's this huge floating mass of dead anchovies in the marina." He kept raising his eyebrows at her, as if to say, "Are you getting this?" He seemed to be trying to warn her of something. And she'd smiled and thought, I'm getting that you're drunk!

She'd never seen him like this before, wasn't sure how she felt about it, and before she could say anything he clumsily draped a blanket over her and then shut off the light and stumbled out of the room, pulling the door closed behind him.

She woke to someone tapping on her window. The house was otherwise silent, asleep. She figured it must be him, but why was he outside? Did he sleepwalk out of the house and get lost in the marina? Was he running out of oxygen? The tapping was confident, insistent. And then suddenly he was there in the room with her and she realized he'd been tapping on the door, not the window, and the way he was tiptoeing around made her think that he wanted her to be asleep, was counting on it. He sat on the edge of the bed and put his head in his hands, and when she asked him what the matter was he stuck his hand under the covers and immediately started searching for something in her underwear. Something he'd misplaced. That's what it felt like: hunting for keys in a drawer in the dark.

Except his fingers felt like keys—the wrong keys. They were thick and rough and had teeth. When she tried to move away, the pressure changed. Now he was reclaiming something she'd stolen from him—something vital—and she felt a little guilty, because he seemed to be having an attack of some kind, what with all that ragged breathing. She'd said his name and told him to slow down, and that's when she realized it wasn't Tom at all.

"Why didn't you tell me?" Tom asked. "Or your dad?"

"Well, because I thought it was you at first," she said. "I wanted it to be you."

"Fuck," he muttered. "What did you do—did you . . . scream?"

"No," she said slowly. Screaming had never occurred to her. "I pretended I was dead."

He didn't say anything.

"Are you mad at me?" she asked.

"For what?"

"For not screaming," she said.

He shook his head. "Of course not, Mona. It wasn't your fault. You know that, right?"

"I like you," she said. "I love you."

She hoped he would pull her toward him and kiss her, but she knew the mood was ruined.

"I wish I was going to Eureka with you. I'm going to miss you so—"

"Listen, Mona. I like you, too, but I'm way too old for you—don't you get that? If you were my age, you'd realize that you don't really know me. I'm actually not as nice as you think. I've been to prison—a few times."

"What for?"

"All kinds of things. I was in a gang with a bunch of . . . awful people."

"Bank robbers?"

He smiled. "Not quite. I wasn't very nice to my wife, either, and I ended up in jail. It took a few years, but I realized that all of my bad qualities were just, uh, I don't know. They were like fat and gristle clinging to a bone, but the bone was the real me, and the real me was strong and perfectly good. I just needed to have that rotten meat cut off me, burned away."

If she were a bone, she thought then, her father would be the fat and gristle.

"It was him," she murmured. She made no move to indicate who she was talking about; she didn't glance in his direction or nod her head or point a finger, but he seemed to know who and what she meant.

"Jesus, Mona," he said sadly. "That might be worse than the thing itself. Your dad is a pain in the ass but he loves you, and he's been good to me. He gave me a job when no one else would and made me his partner. I owe him a lot."

SHE FELT HER FACE FLUSH. PERHAPS SHE DIDN'T HAVE DADDY issues, as Sheila always claimed, but rather Tommy issues. She wished he were here right now so that he could devour her, chew off her awful fat and gristle, and she closed her eyes and became aware of a low hum, felt it vibrating inside her, the memory of his voice.

For the next several hours Mickey chased her around the living room in the old house. He was naked and angry, but she couldn't tell if he was after her, or the slice of pizza she happened to be holding in her hand. His stump looked pink and warm and it wiggled as if it had a mind of its own, a large, recently severed earthworm squirming around in the dirt, searching in vain for its other half. She took a bite of the pizza and discovered it wasn't pizza at all, but rather a piece of the carpet in Henry's office.

She woke up hungry and confused. The dream seemed Significant. Henry, Henry, her only source of income. She got out of bed, ate a peanut butter and jelly sandwich, and made a vow to stop snooping in his house. No digging, she told herself. No scouting for imaginary evidence.

YOKO AND YOKO WERE IN AGREEMENT. THEY WERE BACK from their workshop in Italy and full of fresh pearls. She'd spent an evening with them presenting her case against Henry. They'd been alarmed by her snooping, but she said it was warranted by reasonable suspicion, i.e. the shrine. They said that wasn't reasonable at all. She pointed to exhibits A (the drugs) and B (the incest porn). The burden of proof—wasn't that what it was called? Besides, she knew a thing or two about perverts, she'd said, and she told them a few stories about Mickey. "He used to let his junk hang out of his shorts," she said. "On purpose. In the supermarket."

"Embrace your personal history," Nigel advised patiently. "Then put it behind you, where it belongs. Your past does not drive the train. Aren't you tired of carrying it around? It's old, it's rotten, and believe me, it reeks. I can smell it from where I'm sitting—"

"Okay, okay, Nigel," she said. "I get it."

HER GOOD BEHAVIOR WAS REWARDED: OVER THE NEXT COUple of months she received a dozen service calls, all of whom became steady clients. Six of them were referrals from Henry. She showed her appreciation by buying him an African violet for his kitchen window, along with a rubber plant for his entryway, and by continuing to keep her nose out of his drawers and closets.

But not her camera. She didn't photograph the contents of his drawers and closets—nothing like that—but she'd recently resumed her life's work, which was to take pictures of herself cleaning and/or pretending to be dead, occasionally while wearing an item or two of his clothing. No big deal, she told herself, because she'd stopped snooping, stopped hunting for additional proof. This was called putting her past behind her. Moving on. And his house was hard to resist. Roomy, well lit, filled with objects that photographed well in black and white—all that wood and leather and animal fur, all those mottled vases and large, abstract prints; that tiled floor, that fireplace.

In fact, she was setting up her camera and tripod right now because she'd just purchased a new leopard-print apron and wanted a few shots in the living room. Her photo shoots generally took under eight minutes. In and out, no nonsense. She had the steps down to a science: extend tripod legs, adjust tilt handle, mount camera, turn it on, check framing in viewfinder. Set timer to five seconds. Get into position. Three, two, one: leap off the couch with enormous Clyfford Still print in background.

Repeat. Move your arms this time. Really kick your legs out.

Action shots were a new thing.

She checked the results. Nice blurring effect on her hands and feet. Perfect lighting, as usual. Her teeth—she was always smiling in the action shots—actually looked kind of white.

Reset timer. In position. Three self-portraits with face buried in feather duster.

Again reset, in position. Sitting on the couch—

Henry's head in the doorway—fuck!

She ducked as though he'd thrown something at her and then scrambled behind the couch on all fours.

"Hello?" he said.

She heard his leather slippers shuffle in her direction. They stopped near the coffee table. He was looking at her camera, no doubt. She remembered rehearsing this moment in the past—way back when, in Lowell—but she couldn't remember any of her lines. Hiding behind the couch obviously wasn't the way to go. What the hell was he doing home?

"I see your foot," he said.

She moved her foot and groaned.

"Mona," he said.

She waited a few seconds and then peeked at him over the back of the couch. He had bed head and was wearing a pair of reading glasses and a cashmere bathrobe she knew very well, having posed in it while holding a butcher knife in the kitchen once, a month ago.

"What are you doing?" he asked, peering at her over his glasses. She got to her feet and stood there, blinking, trying to think of something to say. It's over, she thought miserably. Over!

"What is this?" he asked, looking back and forth between her and the camera.

She felt her mouth hanging open. "Well, this is gonna sound a little strange," she said, her voice quivering. "But I love your living room. The lighting, I mean."

"You take pictures," he declared.

She looked at the floor.

"And then?" he asked.

"What do you mean?"

"What do you do with the pictures?"

143

"Nothing," she said quickly. "They're just for me, for my records."

He removed his glasses and slipped them into the pocket of his bathrobe, then looked around the room. She watched his eyes land on her cleaning bucket.

"Records?"

"You know, like a diary," she said.

He seemed to perk up slightly at the word "diary."

"A housekeeping diary," she said.

"Mind if I look?" he suddenly asked, pointing at her camera.

Well, yes, she minded. It had been well over a month since she'd emptied it, so there were perhaps two hundred photographs on there. Before she could respond, he expertly removed the camera from the tripod and started fiddling with the buttons. She flashed to that series of her lying on his bare mattress, naked except for her silly French hostess apron, her long hair fanned over the pink ticking. And those ones of her scrubbing his shower walls, wearing one of Zoe's blue wigs. She hoped those shots of her pretending to fall down the stairs weren't on there, but the bathrobe–butcher knife shots definitely were, not to mention all the pictures she'd taken at other people's houses over the past few weeks. People he knew, no less. His friends.

She watched his mouth tighten as he scrolled through. This was really, actually happening. She closed her eyes and willed herself not to cry. He would probably erase everything. All that work, down the drain. And then what?

Without a word he handed the camera back to her, and she noticed her hands were shaking. She mumbled an apology, but he was already walking away. He paused in the doorway and motioned for her to follow him.

"Should I bring my things?" she asked.

"No," he said.

She put her camera down and followed him toward the front door, panic scratching the back of her throat. Fired, she thought. Fired and . . . sued, possibly. Or just blackballed. She'd have to close up shop and search for other work. What else was she qualified to do? Nothing.

He led her past the front door and down the hallway. Where was he taking her? What the fuck did he want?

To humiliate her, maybe. She kept her head down and stared at his hairy calves as she followed him into the office.

"Have a seat," he said.

She sat in the comfortable chair by the window, he in the chair behind his desk. Here we are in the principal's office, she thought. He pulled a checkbook out of a drawer. His bathrobe fell open and she could see one of his pink nipples. She'd never pictured him naked before. Why was that? More important, why was she here? She imagined him removing his bathrobe and touching himself.

Dear God, I'm sorry for calling you Bob. Please don't—

"Well, you said you were an artist," he said, and chuckled.

She shrugged.

"Are you a painter as well?"

She considered saying yes—he seemed to want to hear that—but he might know she was lying. The only painting she'd ever made was of Spoon, and she'd never finished it.

"I sculpt occasionally," she said, then instantly regretted it.

"I know a lot of sculptors," he said. "What's your medium?"

Fuck. What's my medium, what's my medium? "Clay," she said. "And . . . marble."

"Marble and clay," he repeated, and smiled.

"Actually, just clay," she said, and shook her head. "No marble."

"Well, you're a talented photographer," he said. "Seriously."

"Thanks." She tapped her crooked tooth with her finger and wondered if he was mocking her. Several minutes seemed to tick by. He bit his lip and began writing her a check. He was going to fire her, after all. She imagined herself cleaning the whirlpool jets in the guest bath with a toothbrush and then she saw herself putting her cleaning bucket in the bed of the truck while trying not to cry.

"Am I fired?" she asked.

"No, no," he said, and shook his head. "I just haven't paid you in a while. What you're doing is okay with me. I totally get it."

"You do?"

He nodded. "We're all dying, aren't we? We all want to stop time. To make a mark. And also to make meaning out of the work we do. I imagine your job feels trivial a lot of the time."

"I'm twenty-four," she said, for no reason.

He nodded thoughtfully and handed her a check. The numbers were legible—he'd overpaid her by forty dollars—but his handwriting was straight-up chicken scratch. She folded the check and placed it in her apron pocket. He's loaded, she thought. High on Dilaudid.

"I'm sorry I barged in on you like that," he said. "I didn't mean to scare you. I'd just woken up and I was . . . confused. I forgot you were coming today." He coughed into his fist and then stared at his hand for several seconds. "I'm, uh, sick! I mean, that's why I'm home." He looked at her face and took a deep breath. "The truth is, I'm a very sick man. I think you know that already. I mean, you've probably seen . . . signs." He waved his hand, as if the signs were everywhere.

She nodded. A very sick man indeed. No question about that.

"But, I want to ask a favor of you, Mona." He placed his hands on the desk. "I realize it's hard to keep this kind of thing to yourself, but please don't tell anyone. Especially my friends. Or anyone at all—it's a small town." He shook his head. "Anyway, believe me, it'll all come out soon enough. I'm about to undergo more aggressive . . . treatment. But for now I want to protect Zoe."

Oh man, she thought. Oh man.

"What do you say?" he said. "Can we keep each other's secrets for a while?"

She gazed at her hands folded in her lap. She had no real proof that he'd ever touched Zoe. If she went to the police it would be his word against hers, and her word meant nothing. He was a successful restaurateur and she was a cleaning lady, a nobody, a ghost. She didn't even have a real business license. She wasn't bonded or insured. And then there were the pictures. Jesus. People would be upset about that. She could be convicted of fraud, sent to jail—

Assuming they were talking about the same thing. Could he be referring to his addiction? Could she come out and ask? *Excuse me, but are you talking about drugs or incest—*

"Are you okay?" he asked, raising his eyebrows.

"Sure, yeah," she heard herself say. "I'm fine. I guess I'm just wondering—" She shook her head. "Never mind."

"Go ahead, Mona," he said. "Please. Don't be shy."

She was about to ask, *Which secret am I keeping?* But then he said, "Are you wondering what kind of cancer I have?"

"Wait—what?"

"Oh," he said. "Shit."

Her clothes felt strangely heavy and she realized she was sweating. She touched the back of her neck—cold, damp—and then wiped her hand on her apron.

"I assumed you knew. I mean—I thought—because you're so thorough—" He shrugged. "I don't know what I'm saying."

Cancer. Of course. It explained pretty much everything: the Dilaudid, the weed, the vomit she sometimes found near the toilet, the bloody

Kleenex she often saw in the trash. Maybe even the weird-ass erotica. If you're dying, you may as well jerk off to whatever the hell you want.

I thought you were a pervert, she wanted to confide. A pill-popping pervert. Isn't that funny? Ha ha.

"Anyway, it's stomach cancer," he said. "In case you're wondering. They caught it early, so I actually have a pretty good chance. Of beating it, I mean."

"Okay," she said. "That's good."

"So do we have a deal? Can we be quiet about this for a little while?"

She nodded and tried to smile, and then they actually shook hands across the desk and she felt like she might throw up. He looked pretty nauseated, too.

SHE HAD YET TO LAY EYES ON ZOE IN PERSON, BUT SHE WAS able to piece together her weekends with Henry. She knew what movies they watched, what they read, what they ate. In Zoe's wastebasket she found drafts of a book report on *Of Mice and Men*, a geography report on the state of Louisiana, and a history report on the Pueblo Indians. In Henry's trash, empty bottles of Maalox and cigarette butts. She hadn't seen Henry since that day, six weeks ago now, but judging from the amount of hair loss—she found loose strands on his pillow, in the shower, all over the sinks—he'd started chemotherapy.

He also seemed to be engaging in retail therapy. Like most rich people she'd worked for, he was careless with receipts. He left them in shopping bags strewn all over the house. She collected the receipts each week and placed them in a neat pile on his office desk. A week later she'd find them in the garbage.

One day she saw a few shopping bags she didn't recognize. After examining the receipts, she discovered they'd spent the weekend in San Francisco. He'd bought himself and Zoe leather jackets, an assortment of hats, and designer jeans. Then she found a receipt from a lingerie store totaling $352. So he had a girlfriend, she thought. A girlfriend he showered with expensive lingerie. And here she thought she'd been overcharging him.

She wondered what Zoe's leather jacket looked like. It was black, no doubt. She wandered into Zoe's room and took a look in her closet. Typical train wreck, but nothing new. She must have carted all the booty to her mother's. In fact, she was probably at school right now, showing it off to her friends. Well, good for her.

On her way out of the room she noticed a pair of panties—midnight-blue silk with black lace trim—crumpled up on top of the bureau, and the scales fell from her eyes. This guy didn't have a girlfriend. Zoe was his fucking girlfriend. She opened the top drawer of the bureau. There, on top of Zoe's cotton briefs and socks, lay a neat pile of undergarments with the tags still on: several pairs of black French knickers, $50 each; three baby doll nightgowns, $75 each; two $60 black lace bras; several pairs of crepe briefs, $30 each.

She stared at the tags, dumbfounded. The poor girl's boobs were still growing, for chrissakes. She'd probably just sprouted pubic hair two weeks ago. Picking up the underwear on top of the bureau, she took a tentative sniff, then chastised herself: you've masturbated in a client's house—on his bed, no less, to his incest erotica—and now you're sniffing his daughter's panties. You got problems.

But this was worth investigating, she reminded herself. Perhaps he was in the process of seducing her and hadn't touched her yet. I'll save you years of self-mutilation, Zoe, and psychotherapy, and antidepressants, and bad sex with strangers.

Starting in Henry's closet, she frisked his coat pockets. Nothing but Blistex, a bottle of Visine, a few nickels. She picked up each of his shoes and shook them. Nothing there, either. She was surprised and disappointed—as a kid she'd ransacked her parents' closet on a regular basis, hunting for quarters to buy candy with, and had found all manner of disturbing items. She remembered the photograph she'd come across in one of Mickey's jackets, a blurry close-up of two people fucking. Her parents, presumably, but who could tell. Well, they could, obviously, but she wasn't about to ask them. On second thought, it may have been her father and Heather, their cleaning lady. She didn't remember much about Heather, only that she was thin and blonde and nervous looking, but her father's alleged affair with her had been one of the final straws for her mother. That and the broken nose he'd given her when she confronted him about it. In any case, the irony wasn't lost on Mona. Her father boned the cleaning lady and now, thirteen years later, she was cleaning houses and sticking her nose where it didn't belong. She had yet to have sex with a client, but at the rate she was going—ah, what was this, hidden behind a sleeping bag on the top shelf? A small leather toiletry bag. She wrestled it out and placed it on the bed. Inside were ten or so empty prescription bottles. She examined the labels. More Dilaudid, more Percs, all prescribed to Henry.

She replaced the toiletry bag and moved to his office—nothing incriminating in his desk drawers, just a bunch of papers and office supplies along with a big bag of weed and a hand-blown pipe. Then, hidden under a stack of phone bills in his filing cabinet, she found a handwritten letter on bone-colored paper.

Dear Zoe,

By the time you read this you'll understand why I cherished our time together so much. You'll also understand how special our bond is. What we have is very unique—I think you know that. It's so hard to be away from you, especially with the likelihood that in a few years we won't have this time together. I love you so much. You are, and always will be, the greatest thing that ever happened to me. It's been difficult for me to see you only on weekends and holidays. I hope I'm well enough to take you to Wyoming again this summer. The time we spent there last year was the happiest of my life. I taught you how to ride a horse, shoot a rifle, and make pie crust. You became a woman on that trip and although I was unprepared, I like to think I rose to the occasion. I know you're probably still embarrassed about the whole thing, but I think it was very special and I'm glad I was there. When I'm gone you might miss what we

THE LETTER ENDED THERE. SHE PICTURED HERSELF CON-fronting him at his restaurant, in front of his employees. "I found your little love letter, kid fucker!"

If only she had the balls. If anything, she'd consider leaving it in plain view on the kitchen counter—no, on his pillow.

Maybe she'd simply write a letter of her own: *Dear Henry, I regret to inform you that I can no longer clean your house. I think you know why. Good luck with your cancer.*

In the end, however, she did none of these things. She replaced the letter and finished cleaning the house as if nothing had happened.

At home that night she watched television for a solid three hours. At ten o'clock, flipping through the free-movie channels, she came across the opening credits of *Raging Bull*. She watched

De Niro, alone in the ring and wearing a hooded leopard-print robe, box in slow motion to weepy Italian opera music. Mickey would have been in tears already. Maybe he wasn't such a bad guy. So he was a drunk—so what. So he'd spent most of her childhood in a blackout—well, who could blame him, really, after losing an arm. So he'd taken a few pictures of her naked and showed them to his friends—big whup. It wasn't like they were beaver shots, for chrissakes. They were black and white and, as far as she remembered, fairly tasteful.

At any rate, she'd certainly had it better than Zoe, hadn't she? He'd done the best he could, given the circumstances. She pictured him trying to play tennis—there had been a brief phase where he'd tried to become a jock—and felt a sudden wave of affection for him. She picked up the phone.

"I was just thinking about you," he said, as if they'd just spoken yesterday.

"Really?"

"Yeah," he said.

There was a long silence.

"Well? What were you thinking?"

"Two things I remember about you as a baby," he said. "You hated to walk on grass, and you always had to be sucking on something—you used to suck on my stump."

"Gross," she said.

"Oh stop," he said, and laughed. "It was adorable. Remember that game we used to play in the pool?"

"No," she lied.

He seemed excited that she didn't remember. "Your grandparents' pool."

"Okay."

"You were such a funny kid," he said, clearing his throat. "You made up this game where you'd pretend to be drowning. Remember?"

"Vaguely," she said. Part of her was curious to hear what new details he'd make up and which ones he'd leave out. But the other, larger part of her wanted to hear the story because she liked hearing about herself in the past. It was like hearing about some other person.

"You'd splash around and make a big scene, then you'd float facedown and wait for me to jump in and save you. So I would, of course. But you were so dramatic! And you could hold your breath forever." He paused and she waited for him to continue. "I think you liked all that attention," he said finally.

She bristled at the word "attention." She remembered the game, but she'd never thought of it that way before. She'd called it Pretend I'm Dead, and had always played it more for his benefit than her own, as it had given him a chance to outdo himself. He'd only agreed to play when they had an audience. She'd float facedown, he'd dive into the pool, swim noisily over to her, then drag her by the arm to the pool's stairs. Sometimes he lifted her out of the pool altogether and carried her to the lawn. She thought they were both exceptional—he at pretending to be frantic, she at pretending to be dead.

But she was surprised he remembered it at all. His memory had always been faulty, to say the least. One of her duties as a child, in addition to cutting his steak, ironing his shirts, and tying his shoes, was to fetch his nose spray, which he always seemed to misplace. The nose spray he used in conjunction with the "Chinese brain powder" he snorted on a regular basis, which he claimed "helped with his memory." After he was sufficiently coked up, he'd regale her with stories from his childhood for several hours. As she got older, the stories turned into painfully long lectures on the dangers of drug and alcohol abuse.

Maybe he was back on the blow. In any case, it was infuriating that he'd been misremembering the game all these years.

"Well, just for the record, that's not why I played that game with you," she said. "I did it so you'd feel like a good dad for a few minutes. And it's you who likes attention, not me."

"You should have been an actress," he said, ignoring her.

"What—you think that's going to work on me? I'm not a kid anymore."

He sniffed. "How old are you?"

"Twenty-four."

"Still a baby," he said, and sniffed again. He was either wired, or else on the verge of tears. She decided on the former.

"You're the baby," she said.

"Hang on a sec." He put down the phone and blew his nose. "God, you have a mean bone," he said afterward. "That's why I never call, you know. You seem to think I was a lousy father or something. Your mother put all these crazy ideas in your head, and you've been carrying them around for years. You should see a therapist or something."

She laughed. "This is me *after* therapy. Five years. It's you who needs therapy."

"Well, five years wasn't enough," he said. She could tell by his voice that he really believed what he was saying.

"You're in *denial*," she said. "It's really common among *addicts*. I learned that in *therapy*."

"Turn down your TV. You're shouting."

"Listen, this isn't why I called," she said. Why *did* she call?

"I need a wife," he said. "Not therapy."

"Where's Tom?"

"Tommy's living like a king in Mexico."

"New Mexico?"

"Old Mexico," he said. "He moved down there a few years ago. Has a maid, a cook, lots of girlfriends. But I haven't heard from him in over a year. I think he might be dead."

"Maybe he's just avoiding you," she said.

"Nah," he said. "We're like brothers. We share everything, even women. You know, he and your mother had a—"

"Wait!" Mona shouted.

"What?"

"I don't want to hear about it," she said quietly. "I just wanted to tell you that your favorite movie's on ENCORE right now." She hung up, resolved to never call him again, and returned to *Raging Bull*. She stared at the screen and let her eyes go out of focus. Cry, she ordered herself. Let it out.

She remained dry-eyed instead, even after several swigs of Beefeater.

A FEW WEEKS LATER SHE LET HERSELF INTO HENRY'S HOUSE and set her cleaning bucket on the floor of the entryway. She removed her shoes, put on an apron, and was about to head to the kitchen when she heard a noise, a groaning noise in the walls followed by the sound of water running. The sound was coming from the back of the house. "Hello?" she called out, startled. No response.

She tiptoed down the hallway, her heart thumping. Strangely, Henry's bedroom door was closed. Was he sick again? Did he stay home from work? She put her ear to the door. Someone was sobbing in there—a girl. She knocked twice, loudly. "Hello?" No response. The sobbing suddenly stopped. She counted to three and threw open the door. Henry was lying on the bed next to Zoe. They were both naked from the waist down, and Henry was stroking Zoe with a wet washcloth while she cried silently.

Mona leaped onto the bed, straddled Henry, and began pummeling him with her fists. Then she put her hands around his throat and squeezed—

No. She entered the room with a baseball bat. Henry leaped off the bed and she swung the bat at his junk—

No. She entered the room holding one of Henry's Japanese cooking knives. He jumped off the bed and tried to attack her. She held the knife out in front of her, sliced the air a few times. He lost his footing and fell to his knees. She plunged the knife into his chest. He gasped. Zoe screamed. Blood bubbled out of his mouth.

"Get dressed," Mona said. "Hurry! I'm getting you the fuck out of here!"

The fantasies varied from week to week, depending on her mood. Sometimes they completely revolved around the savage beating she administered to Henry. The beatings were bloody and intimate. They rolled on the floor, grappling and biting, tearing at each other's clothes and hair. She pressed her thumbs into his eye sockets. She kneed him in the face. There were broken bones and teeth. Other times Henry was just an extra and it was all about her and Zoe—their special bond, their new life together in some faraway place. Sometimes she fantasized beyond the initial rescue and she and Zoe were in Mexico, where they'd hunted down Tom, who'd instantly fallen in love with Mona and married her, and now Zoe was their adopted daughter. In either case, the naïveté behind the fantasies embarrassed her, as did the pleasure she derived from them. She caught a glimpse of herself after a particularly vivid one—she and Zoe were on a road trip, headed to Philadelphia to be interviewed by Terry Gross, who'd somehow heard about their incredible story—and saw that her cheeks and chest were flushed, as if she'd just had an intense orgasm.

Maybe she needed to get laid. But that would involve small talk, the thought of which exhausted her. She was exhausted in general lately and had been sleeping in her work clothes for several nights in a row. Last night she'd passed out with her shoes on.

A few months after finding Henry's letter, she spent part of a Saturday afternoon at the local bookstore, browsing the fiction section. In one of the aisles, a young girl sat cross-legged on the floor, reading Salinger's *Franny and Zooey*. Mona recognized her outfit—a black button-down blouse and a purple denim miniskirt. She'd spent ten minutes removing a chocolate stain from that skirt a few weeks back.

"Zoe," she blurted before she could stop herself.

Zoe looked up at her and smiled slowly. She had the guilty look of someone who was bad with names.

"You don't know me," Mona assured her. "But I know you . . . sort of."

Zoe narrowed her eyes and looked her up and down. You sound like a freak. You're scaring her. "I'm your cleaning lady," Mona said quickly. "I clean your house."

Zoe blinked several times.

"Your father's house?"

"Oh!" Zoe said. "Right. You're . . . *Mary*."

"Mona," she corrected.

"Oh yeah." She snapped the book shut and stood up. Mona had been carrying Zoe in her fantasies for weeks—she liked to carry Zoe out of Henry's room and then out of the house and even down the street—but Zoe was way too big for that, she saw now. She was just an inch or two shorter than Mona. She glanced at Zoe's chest—little boobies!—then back at her face. Her eyelids were smeared with shiny purple shadow and she had several piercings in her ears. She immediately felt the now familiar urge to kidnap Zoe and take her out for ice cream, but Zoe seemed . . . *beyond* ice cream.

"My dad totally loves you," Zoe said. "He practically creams his jeans when you wash out the garbage cans." She laughed and then covered her mouth with her hand. She had braces. When did she get braces?

"Sorry," Zoe said, and rolled her eyes. "That was gross. I don't know why I said that."

Well, you are your conversation, she heard Nigel's voice say.

Zoe scratched her head. Her fingernail polish matched her eye shadow. Mona wanted to kiss those fingers.

"I'm glad he notices things like that," Mona said. "It, uh, adds to my job satisfaction." She paused. "Or whatever. You have good taste in books, by the way."

"Oh, well, I have to read this other one—*Catcher in the Rye?*— for school, but they're out of it, so I figured I'd read a few pages of this one, but I dunno. It's a little . . . weird, I guess." She bit her lip and stared at the cover, tracing the title with her finger. She was suspiciously self-possessed. Mona still remembered a line or two from *Franny and Zooey* and considered reciting them, but that would be lame, number one, and would probably scare the piss out of Zoe. She realized now that she didn't know how to talk to kids. Were you supposed to ask them about school?

"Is your dad here?"

"Yeah, he's right over there." Zoe pointed toward the magazine section, but the only man Mona saw was emaciated and completely bald.

"Where?" Mona asked.

"Right there," Zoe said, pointing. "Dad!" she called out.

Mona wanted to shush her, but it was too late. Henry looked at them and smiled weakly, then put down his magazine and walked toward them. She looked over her shoulder toward the exit, thought about making a run for it.

"Hi, Mona," he said. "Long time no see." He smiled at her. His lips were a red, worn-out rubber band, and his eyebrows had fallen off. He was extremely pale and gaunt, and looked much too vulnerable to be out in public. A large, walking eye white. He continued smiling at her. He likes me, she thought. "It's so good to see you," he said. It's good to see me.

"Likewise," Mona said.

"You'll have to pardon my appearance. I know I look like death warmed over."

Well, yes, that was exactly what he looked like. Was she supposed to acknowledge the missing hair and eyebrows, or pretend everything was normal? She had no idea.

"Dad!" Zoe said, punching him softly on the arm. "You look like a skinhead. A *healthy* skinhead. Or no, wait—a monk. A Buddhist monk."

He laughed and put his arm around her. "Thanks, pumpkin. You always know just what to say."

"I'm gonna shave my head," Zoe said. "Out of solidarity."

Henry laughed. "No, you're not."

"I should, right?" Zoe asked Mona.

"Don't answer that, Mona," Henry said.

He pulled Zoe closer and kissed the top of her head. Of course he worshiped her—he was dying, and she was his only daughter. Writing her love letters and showering her with gifts was the fucking least he could do. He was innocent. He was Michael fucking Landon. Mona, on the other hand, was just a large, dumb animal.

"How you doing, Mona?" he asked.

"Good, good!" she croaked. "Good," she said again.

"Has my buddy Adam called you? I gave him your number last week. You may end up hating me for it—he's a real slob."

"Nope," Mona said. "Nope. Not yet. Not yet. But I've heard from all the others. Thanks for that. You practically built my business, like, single-handedly."

"Aw," he said. "I doubt that."

"Thank you," she said again. Stop repeating yourself, dummy.

He winked at her and she noticed that his eyelashes were missing, too. It didn't do much for a person's eyes. "Still taking pictures?"

"Oh yeah," she said, and tried to smile. "Still, uh, doing that. Yeah."

He looked at Zoe. "Mona's a very talented photographer, Zo," he told her. "Might be famous someday. She's got a really good eye."

"Ha ha," Mona said nervously.

"Dad!" Zoe said. "You're embarrassing her."

"Okay, okay," he said. "But we just love having you, Mona—can I say that? You've made things *so* much easier. Right, Zo?"

"Yep," Zoe said. "She even folds my underwear, Dad."

"I know. She folds mine, too."

They both looked at her appreciatively.

Mona shrugged. "Just doing my job!"

They stood there for several seconds, smiling and nodding at one another.

"Well, we're gonna scoot. Ready, sweetie?"

"I gotta put this book back," Zoe said. "I don't want it."

"I'll take it for you," Mona said.

Zoe handed her the book and said thanks.

"Good to see you again, Mona," Henry said. "And thanks so much for your hard work."

"No problem," Mona mumbled. "My pleasure."

She watched them walk arm in arm toward the exit. Henry

looked back at her as they walked out the door. She dropped her head and opened the book, her hands shaking. "Maybe there's a trapdoor under my chair," she read. She closed the book and set it on the nearest shelf.

Walking home, she tried to imagine shaving her head for Mickey. She doubted it ever would have occurred to her to make such a noble gesture, especially at Zoe's age, but then she remembered a game she'd sometimes played with herself as a kid, wherein she'd tuck her right arm inside her shirt and pretend to be Mickey. She couldn't believe how impossible and time-consuming it had been to simply write her name, button her blouse, brush her teeth. Even something as routine as using the toilet had felt alien and disorienting with one hand, and she remembered feeling less like Mickey and more like a clumsy, useless baby. Still, it had been important to her to walk in his shoes for a few minutes, even if it meant falling on her face.

THE RESCUE FANTASIES HAD VANISHED NOW, OF COURSE. Each time she cleaned Henry's house she saw new evidence of his illness: blood splattered on the rim of the toilet, bloodstains on his sheets and pillows, vomit on the floor next to his bed. On one occasion she found shit in the shower. Just a nugget, what would have been a floater if it had landed in the proper place. It looked sad, lying there next to the drain. She picked it up with a paper towel and flushed it down the toilet.

Maybe it was the poop that triggered the new batch of fantasies, because they started again that same day. The daydreams were still heroic and absurd, and were sometimes accompanied by the heavy strings of the *Raging Bull* theme song, but this time it was Henry she saved, and sometimes Henry looked like Tom.

BETTY

FROM A DISTANCE SHE COULD PASS FOR SPANISH BUT UP close she was just ridiculously tan with dyed black hair. This may explain why the woman trailing behind her across the store parking lot kept yelling *hola* in her direction. She pretended not to hear and continued wheeling the cart toward her truck.

"Por favor, please," the woman called out in a tired voice.

Por favor, please, Mona repeated to herself, and smiled. She stopped walking and turned around. It was the petite redhead she'd noticed earlier, squeezing peaches in the produce section. She'd liked the expression on the woman's face because it had seemed to say "Wow, these peaches are superripe" and "Sadly, I don't especially like peaches" simultaneously.

Somehow she'd failed to notice the woman's outfit before: low-cut green angora sweater, leopard-print velour leggings, white leather high-tops. The woman's cleavage was sun damaged and livid red. Her hair was a similar red, but brighter, obviously enhanced

---

with a rinse. Like most redheads, she probably thought she looked best in green.

"Gracias," the woman said as she caught up. She was older than Mona initially thought: late forties, early fifties.

"I speak English." First words of the day.

The woman removed her enormous sunglasses and looked Mona in the eye. "Oh, right," she said.

There was something unnatural about the woman's eyes that Mona couldn't put her finger on.

"You do cleaning, right?" the woman asked. "I noticed your, uh, apron."

She nodded, offered her hand. "Mona," she said.

"Betty McKenzie," the woman said, grasping Mona's fingers rather than her whole hand. She suspected Betty was one of those people who always introduced themselves with their full name, even when meeting three-year-olds.

She realized what was strange about the woman's eyes: she was wearing blue contacts on what were already very blue eyes, which made them inescapably, unyieldingly blue, a color that made Mona think of fate or acts of God.

"Wait a minute. I've heard of you," Betty said. "I mean, you were recommended to me once."

"By whom?" Mona asked. "If you don't mind my asking."

"Adrienne Payne," Betty said.

Ah, Adrienne, the pain-in-the-ass vegan and a referral from Henry. She'd made an unusual request: she asked Mona to refrain from bringing animal products of any kind onto her property, as it "disturbed the energy" in her house. This included the obvious—meat and dairy—but also the leather shoes Mona preferred to work in, along with her leather belt. Adrienne was otherwise fairly low maintenance, so this

didn't seem like such a big deal. Mona figured she would just eat car-
rots if she got hungry. But there was something about Adrienne's
house—the "energy," perhaps—that made Mona ravenous, and she
often found herself craving fried chicken, Frito pie, hamburgers, and
milk shakes. Still, she managed to respect Adrienne's wishes and ate
neither meat nor dairy in the house or even in the yard.

Things ended badly, however. Mona had been scheduled to clean
while Adrienne was out of town, mushroom hunting in some for-
est in the Pacific Northwest, which was Adrienne's idea of a good
time. Lunchtime had rolled around and Mona grabbed a burrito at a
nearby taco stand and brought it back to the house. What the hell, she
thought. It was a thousand degrees outside and the AC was busted in
her truck.

Adrienne came home early, of course, and let herself in unan-
nounced. She caught Mona sitting at her kitchen table, thoughtfully
chewing a piece of roasted pork that she'd picked out of her mostly devoured pork burrito, all of which Mona later suspected she may have
been forgiven if she hadn't also been feeding small pieces to Adrienne's miserable cat, Pookie-Ooh, also a vegan, though not by choice,
obviously. Pookie-Ooh was clearly very happy, probably for the first
time in his life, because he didn't even acknowledge Adrienne when
she walked in, even though she'd been gone for more than a week.
Mona could still see the outraged expression on Adrienne's face—it
was as if she'd caught Mona having loud sex with a real live pig right
there on her kitchen floor, or as if Mona had been doing something
truly despicable to Pookie-Ooh, such as holding him down and sticking a pencil up his ass. It was by far the dirtiest look Mona had ever
gotten and she'd felt perfectly justified in gathering her things, leaving the house without a word, and never returning. Adrienne left nu-
merous messages, but Mona never returned her calls—a ballsy move,

really, considering that her business relied almost exclusively on word of mouth.

Evidently Adrienne had recommended Mona's services before the Pork Burrito Disaster.

"How do you know Adrienne?" Mona asked casually.

"She used to be a client of mine," Betty said.

"What do you do?"

"Oh, lots of things." A common answer on the part of the middle class in Taos, an endangered species rapidly nearing extinction. "Hang on a sec and I'll give you one of my cards." She trotted over to the only classic American car Mona could identify by sight—a 1960 convertible Cadillac. The car was sandwiched between two mud-splattered pickup trucks and painted the most beautiful shade of midnight blue Mona had ever seen.

Mona imagined Betty was in the Witness Protection Program. Her real name was Denise and she'd been married to the Mob for twenty years. To avoid doing time, she'd turned state's witness and the feds relocated her to New Mexico from Queens or Jersey. This would explain her accent and taste in cars. And clothes, too, now that she thought about it. Then she noticed the license plate:

PSYCHIC, in all caps.

Betty handed her not one but a handful of business cards. Mona glanced at one out of politeness. Betty's name was printed in a font two sizes too big, with a list of services underneath: psychic readings, channeling, astrology charts, energy work, aura cleansing—blah, blah. She smiled and slipped the cards into her back pocket.

"Nice wheels, by the way," Mona said.

"Oh, thanks," Betty said. "It's called divorce."

"Wow." A few seconds ticked by in silence. "Well, I should go," she said. "My ice cream's melting."

_____

"Could I get one of your cards?" Betty asked.

"Sure," Mona said. "Of course." She rummaged through her bag, pretending to search for one. She'd run out of cards months ago. "Guess I'm out," she said sheepishly. "Could I just give you my number?"

BETTY CALLED TWO HOURS LATER AND MONA GAVE HER THE usual spiel: twenty dollars an hour, cash only, with a four-hour minimum the first day, and a two-hour minimum moving forward.

"That's it?" asked Betty. "You should charge more. You'll never make it in this town on that."

"Are you flirting with me?" Mona joked.

Betty laughed. "I'm serious."

"Well, this is a first," Mona said. "Make it twenty-five an hour, then."

"Done," Betty said.

"But if you're trying to get me to up my rate, your place is either really clean or really scary. I bet you're ankle deep in cat hair."

"No, but I do have several cats," Betty said, sounding worried. Mona wondered if "several cats" was code for "dozens of strays."

"I love cats," Mona lied. She was fond of cats, but love had never entered into it. Still, Betty could live in a litter box, for all Mona cared.

She asked for Betty's address, but Betty said she didn't have one. "I live way out on the mesa. There aren't any street names out here. You take 73 south over the Gorge Bridge. After 8.7 miles, you'll see a dirt road on the right. Follow that road for exactly 1.4 miles. My place is on the left."

Mona had trouble understanding why anyone would willingly live on the mesa, but then she'd never been a fan of wide-open spaces.

Betty's double-wide trailer looked like it rolled off the back of a truck and down a ravine, but it was painted casino pink and stuffed with oversized antiques, as if it were a palace, and had an attached make-shift carport on one side, where Betty kept her Caddy. She didn't have any close neighbors, but a cluster of newly built, wheat-colored houses stood up the road a ways, huddled together with their backs turned, as if conspiring against her.

The inside of the trailer reminded Mona of a flea market after a dust storm. Betty collected walnut furniture, jewelry boxes, antique keys, vintage perfume bottles, printed matchboxes, old photographs of strangers, and snow globes, all of which were coated with brittle red dust. The dust likely blew in through the window screens and the cracks in the walls. It had even made its way into Betty's kitchen cup-boards, leaving a grainy residue on all her dishware. As Mona emptied the cupboards—she planned to wash all the dishes—she wondered if Betty had a healthy collecting impulse or an overactive hoarding in-stinct. She decided on the latter, especially after finding hidden boxes of menus, stamps, calendars, key chains, bottle caps, dice, playing cards, marbles, and postcards. In the freezer she found not food but a stockpile of angora sweaters neatly stacked in separate ziplock bags. Betty also appeared to collect deaf Persian cats. The cats bellowed ev-ery thirty seconds as if being tortured.

While Mona cleaned, Betty stayed in the living room, giving readings to clients over the phone. From what Mona could gather, she required a handwriting sample including their name, date and time of birth, and a couple of questions they wanted answered. Mona didn't bother trying to eavesdrop; Betty was clearly performing—Mona could hear it in her voice—and live performance made Mona's skin crawl. She had always preferred a screen between herself and actors.

When Mona was done, Betty followed her outside and thanked her for a job well done. To Mona's surprise, she asked if Mona could come not once but twice a week. Mona wavered, said she'd have to see what her schedule looked like. Since Betty "worked from home," she was inclined to say no. She didn't want to be trapped in a trailer, especially with a so-called psychic (and possible lunatic), twice a week every week. But then she did the math: twice a week equaled $150, which equaled $600 a month, which covered most of her rent. And, if she cleaned the place twice a week, chances were she'd be in and out in no time, possibly in under an hour.

"Actually, I think I can swing it," Mona said. "I mean, now that I think about it. Monday and Thursday afternoons would work."

"Are you in a cult, by any chance?" Betty asked then.

"Not that I'm aware of," Mona said. "Why?"

"You're giving off cult energy."

"Really? That's weird," Mona said, and shrugged.

"Your aura has lost its pulse."

"Well, I'm *very tired*," Mona said.

Betty shook her head. "It's beyond that." She leaned toward Mona, took a dainty sniff, and then wrinkled her nose. "Smells like leather and burned coffee."

"Auras have an odor?"

Betty nodded. "Sometimes, yes."

"Well, I drink half a pot of coffee a day," Mona said. "It's probably coming out of my pores."

Betty looked genuinely dubious, and Mona felt a wave of affection for her.

"Another thing I noticed is that you don't talk much," Betty said. "I think your throat chakra is blocked. Are you a passive person?"

"Probably," she said.

"I have some exercises you can do," Betty said. "Some of them involve screaming. Have you ever just screamed your head off?"

"No," Mona declared.

"Do you have trouble saying no to people?"

"No," Mona said. "I mean yes."

"Then these exercises will be perfect for you."

"Super," she said, trying to sound energetic. "Well, it was great talking to you, Betty. See you next week."

SEVEN WEEKS LATER, SHE STIFLED A FROWN AS SHE REMOVED Betty's hair from the bathtub drain—red pubic hair made her queasy. Betty stood in the doorway, absentmindedly watching her work. That first day was a fluke; Betty turned out to be one of the rare clients who followed her from room to room, ostensibly to "keep her company."

She finished cleaning the tub and then started in on the hardwater stains in the toilet bowl. Most of her clients would be embarrassed to watch her clean their toilet with a pumice stone, but not Betty.

"Look at you, scrubbing away with that thing!" Betty said, in the voice she used with her cats.

I am not an animal, she wanted to say. She put the pumice stone away and cleaned the toilet rim using the ridiculous potpourri-scented Windex Betty insisted upon, which was hot pink instead of blue.

"I just got a flash of you in a past life." After a dramatic pause, Betty said, "You were an African woman living in a hut in the middle of the bush."

She looked over her shoulder. Betty was wearing the solemn expression she reserved for channeling Mona's past lives, which apparently numbered in the hundreds. In each of these past lives Mona was overweight and destitute, relegated to a life of domestic servitude. She also had a habit of contracting a venereal disease and dying young. Betty appeared to be staring at Mona's ass crack, her eyes out of focus. She wasn't wearing her psycho contacts today. Without them, her natural eye color was a lighter shade of blue—less flinty, more forgiving.

"You were walking down this long dusty road with an enormous jug balanced on top of your head," Betty went on. "A beautiful jug. And you had this big poufy skirt on . . . and your hips were swaying from side to side." She put her hands on her hips and made a disturbing swaying motion. Mona was still fascinated by Betty's ability to deliver utter tripe with a straight face.

"So I was poor and fat," Mona said. "Again."

"Maura," Betty said. "I didn't say you were fat, for God's sake. And I've told you a thousand times: I can't help what I see."

Mona flushed the toilet.

"I didn't ask for this gift, Maura," she said, and sniffed.

Betty had a habit of punctuating her sentences with people's names. Too bad she was using the wrong one—she'd been calling Mona "Maura" since the day they'd met. For whatever reason, Mona neglected to correct her and now, almost two months later, felt it was too late. She suspected that only a deeply fucked-up person would allow her client to call her by the wrong name, week in and week out. But she was also delighted by the irony of it, considering Betty's profession. Betty was apparently gifted enough as a psychic to get away with charging a hundred dollars an hour, and her calendar was fully booked. She also hosted a call-in show on KTAO, where she gave readings on the radio. The show aired at midnight.

Betty was able to detect Mona's outright lies, however. A few weeks into their arrangement, Mona called at the last minute and said she was having a particularly bad menstrual period. She went on to explain that she'd been to the gynecologist and they'd found polyps on her uterus. But not to worry, she'd said—the polyps were asymptomatic and could be treated with medication. Still, she had unusually heavy bleeding and would have to cancel for the week. This was an excuse she'd perfected in high school and had been using to great effect ever since. Bulletproof, as they say.

"Why are you lying?" Betty had asked, in a small voice.

"Pardon?" Mona said.

"Why. Are. You. Lying."

Her instinct was to hang up and never answer the phone again. Instead she said, "Uh, I don't know, Betty." As soon as people heard the word "polyps," they usually accepted it, no questions asked.

"Well, what's really wrong with you?"

"I'm just so . . . tired lately. I haven't been sleeping well and I have this sort of low-grade depression thing going on."

"That's all you had to say," Betty said. "Polyps! Honest to God, Maura. Does that excuse ever really work?"

"Yes, actually," Mona said. "I've been using it for years and it hasn't failed me once."

"Well, I'm not your average customer," Betty said. "So you should know better than to try that stuff with me."

"Yeah, I'm starting to realize that," Mona said.

NOW SHE WAS ON ALL FOURS, CLEANING THE BATHROOM floor with Windex and a damp rag. Betty, still in the doorway, watched her work. Because Betty seemed to think she lived in an Italian villa rather than a trailer, the tiles were porcelain and imported from Rome. As per Betty's request, Mona cleaned the floor by hand. You couldn't simply use a mop, no sir.

"Can I make a quick confession?" Betty asked.

Betty's confessions were precisely the reason she felt so tired lately. She didn't bother answering; she kept her back turned like a priest, and cleaned around the toilet.

"As a teenager I wanted to poison my mother," Betty said. "I'd finally worked up the courage to tell her my brother was molesting me. First she didn't believe me, then she said it was my fault, that I had somehow seduced him—me, an eight-year-old, seducing a thirteen-year-old—can you imagine? So I almost put rat poison in her wine that night. I always regretted not doing it."

"Is she still alive?"

"Unfortunately." Betty sighed.

"Say three Hail Marys and ten Our Fathers," Mona said, and made the sign of the cross.

"I'm not Catholic," Betty said.

"I know. It was a joke."

What deserved punishment, in her opinion, was treating your cleaning lady like a garbage disposal, as if the poor chick didn't have enough of your dirt under her fingernails already. Last week Betty confessed to an intense hatred of both old people and children. She said that sometimes, when she saw a child laugh, she wanted to slap the smile right off its face. The week before, she confessed to a fear of dying alone and to fantasies of being sexually humiliated in public. With each new confession, Mona felt increasingly drained and bloodless.

The bathroom finished, Mona progressed to the bedroom. Betty followed and stretched out on the bed. Mona always had trouble deciding where to start, as the room was crammed with collectibles.

In the corner stood a small bookcase filled not with books—Betty read only palms and trashy magazines—but with twelve prominently displayed porcelain dolls. Mona had trouble touching them with her bare hands, so she dusted the doll case only when absolutely necessary and then only while wearing rubber gloves. Betty never seemed to notice. The dolls reminded her of the ones she'd had as a kid; Mickey had bought three for her eighth birthday. Fixed to wooden stands, they had real hair, hand-set glass eyes with long eyelashes, porcelain faces and limbs, embroidered dresses trimmed in lace, and moles painted on their cheeks. Spanish ladies. He'd even gone so far as to buy a display case for them, which he placed near the foot of her bed.

She remembered thinking of the dolls as house guests who had outstayed their welcome. At night her irritation turned to dread because she discovered that the dolls could see her. In fact they were staring at her. They kept a lidless vigil over her, biding their time until she fell asleep, whereupon they would somehow bludgeon her, or strangle her, or smother her with a pillow.

"Why are you sleeping in the closet, honey?" her mother asked one morning. Mona explained her predicament. "They're not staring at you," her mother said. "They're staring into space. They can't see you."

"Yeah they can."

"Can they see you right now?"

"Yeah."

"But they're faced the other way. They don't have eyes in the back of their heads, silly. They're blind."

But they were far from blind, and she didn't have to be in their direct line of vision to be seen. The activities she usually did in her bedroom—dressing and undressing, reading, writing in her diary, sleeping—were no longer private, and the dolls were a hostile audience. She tried putting the damned things in the closet, but she still felt their presence from behind the closet door, even when she buried them under clothes. She remembered waking in the middle of the night and feeling pinned to her mattress, fully conscious yet unable to move, her arms and legs buzzing, her breath shallow, and imagined one of the dolls astride her chest, looking her dead in the face. She wanted to bring the dolls to the garage and smash their faces with a hammer, but she never worked up the nerve.

Unlike the dolls Mona had as a child, Betty's were all dressed as brides. The bridal theme made sense, given Betty's obsession with marriage. According to Betty, Mona would one day be married to a man with a goatee and squinty eyes. This man also had a bad knee and sometimes walked with a cane. The cane belonged to his grandfather and happened to pull out into a knife, if needed. "I can see him standing next to you," Betty sometimes said, when Mona was doing the dishes or dusting. "Every time I see him lately, he has bags under his eyes. I think he has insomnia."

"He sounds really appealing," Mona said. "I'm super excited to meet him. He'll probably stab me to death with his cane."

"He's the love of your life," Betty said.

Mona was supposed to have two children with this mysterious man, one of whom would eventually struggle with addiction. The marriage was supposed to last twenty-three years, which seemed like an awfully long time, after which Mona would meet husband number two. Unfortunately, Betty couldn't get a good look at her second husband, but knew that he was tall, often wore a hat, and didn't have facial hair.

Betty herself had been a bride once, fifteen years ago. His name was Johnny, and they'd met in Vegas, where they'd both been living for a number of years, Betty as a professional psychic, Johnny as a professional gambler and alcoholic. Johnny approached Betty at a gas station while she was filling her tank and asked her to dinner. They married two weeks later. The marriage lasted all of three months, which seemed about right to Mona. She could imagine how a person could be initially bewitched by Betty—she had undeniable charisma and a number of physical charms, including a sizable rack and shapely calves—but after a few months, Mona imagined, those bewitching qualities would start to seem . . . just plain witchy.

Mona could only guess as to why it hadn't worked out. Betty claimed that Johnny left her suddenly, in the middle of the night. He was from New Mexico originally and they'd lived here for the last three weeks of their marriage. Betty stayed, even though she had no friends or family in the area. Mona could plainly see that Betty was still desperately in love with Johnny and wanted to keep an eye on him, make sure he didn't marry someone else.

She still wore an engagement ring. Not the one Johnny gave her, but a ring she'd purchased herself. It was a vintage ring with a platinum setting and a huge, impossible-to-ignore diamond. "So you're engaged to yourself," Mona said when Betty first explained the ring. Betty frowned and said she didn't like to think of it that way.

Mona cleaned the mirror above Betty's bureau. She dampened the rag with more Potpourri Windex and started in on Betty's vintage perfume bottles, which required special attention. They were delicate things and had a way of making Mona feel apish, slow-witted, and, now that she thought about it, a little like Lenny in *Of Mice and Men*. She'd already broken one by accident. She'd had it in her palm and was sort of petting it with the rag—gently, she thought—and it had somehow shattered. Luckily, Betty hadn't been home at the time. Normally Mona would have left a note about it, but it happened on the same day she found the poem under the nightstand, and she'd been too distracted. The poem was handwritten, untitled, and addressed to no one:

> Betty has a machete.
> She keeps it in her closet.
> Don't ever scorn her
> Or she'll hunt you down
> And hack you
> To pieces.

A silly poem, probably a joke, but disturbing nonetheless, particularly the last two lines. She'd actually rooted around in Betty's closet looking for the damned thing, but found only a disturbing collection of rabbit fur coats from the eighties. She looked under the bed just for the hell of it, and, lo and behold, there it was: the machete, an antique, it looked like, its handle bound in crisscross leather. Mona had finished cleaning and hightailed it out of there. She put the broken perfume bottle in a paper bag and threw it in the trash.

"Maura," Betty suddenly said from the bed, "let's call it quits. You've done enough for today and everything looks great."

"Really?" Mona said. "Cool." She dusted the last perfume bottle and began to gather her things.

"Wait, don't leave just yet. I want to try something with you," Betty said. "In the living room."

Crap, Mona thought. She's going to read my palm and tell me I'll always live hand to mouth. Again.

"Don't give me that look," Betty said. "I'll still pay you the full amount." Betty thought everything was about money.

They went into the living room, a tiny space made even tinier by an enormous red velvet couch, a marble-topped coffee table, and Betty's psychic throne, an ornate walnut chair upholstered in pinkish-gold brocade with a high, straight back. Betty took the throne, Mona the couch.

"Okay," Betty said. "I want to do a little experiment with you. I'm going to think of a number between one and twenty. You're going to first see it, then read it to me. You're going to have to look me right in the eye and really concentrate."

"Oh God," Mona said.

"Just try it," Betty said. "It won't kill you."

She would rather have a rock thrown at her head.

"I'm thinking of a number," Betty said. "I'm projecting it nice and large."

Mona stared at Betty's perfectly shaped left eyebrow, but could only concentrate on the strange guttural noise one of her cats was making outside. The cat sounded as if it were repeating the word "ouch." *Owww-chh*, it kept saying, over and over.

"Betty," Mona said, "is that your cat? It sounds like it's in pain. I'd feel really bad if it got eaten by a coyote while I was reading your mind."

"She's fine," Betty said. "She's just in heat. Now stop stalling and look at me." She pointed to her eyes. "*Here*."

Mona locked eyes with Betty. A whole minute seemed to go by. This was, by far, the most eye contact she'd maintained in months. Perhaps ever. Betty's blue eyes, she noticed now, were flecked with some other color—gold? No, copper. Jesus, they were stunning. No wonder she covered them with contacts—they were too beautiful to be seen naked. They needed protection. The contacts were like gloves, then. She realized it was probably time to say a number. "Eleven," she said.

Betty shook her head. "You have to really concentrate."

She counted to twelve and wondered if blue-eyed psychics were more successful than brown-eyed ones. Probably. "Eighteen," she said.

"You're guessing," Betty said. "Don't guess. Just wait until you see it."

"Fourteen."

"Very good!" Betty said, clapping her hands. "Now it's my turn. Think of a number and project it nice and big so I can see it."

"Project it where—on my forehead?" Mona said.

"Just hold it in your mind."

"Maybe we should be wearing aluminum feelers on our heads," Mona said. "Might make things easier."

"Do you have a number?" Betty asked impatiently.

"Yes." Two-oh, two-oh, two-oh, two-oh, she repeated to herself, visualizing the number.

"Twenty," Betty said, after five seconds.

"Good guess," Mona said. "I must be inadvertently cuing you somehow."

"Oh, please," Betty said. "I'm psychic, silly! When are you going to stop mocking me?"

Probably never, Mona thought.

"Okay, Maura," Betty said. "You're up." Mona stared hard into Betty's eyes again, waiting for a number to come into her head. She was about to say "nine" before Betty stopped her and said, "Try again."

"Five," Mona said.

"Yes!" Betty said. "I knew you'd be good at this. Okay, my turn."

Mona thought of the number three. She repeated it to herself, but was careful not to move her lips or blink. She projected it onto a drive-in movie screen in her mind.

"Very good, Maura. I can see your number more clearly now." Betty paused. "The number three, that is!"

"Whoa," Mona said. "You're freaking me out."

They went back and forth several times. It didn't get any easier for Mona, but after staring into Betty's eyes for a minute or two, she could suddenly see the numbers, large silver numbers on a blue background. When she read the number out loud, a kind of euphoria washed over her. She felt drunk and in love.

As she was leaving, she asked, "Why do you think I can see the numbers? I'm not psychic."

"Everyone has some psychic ability," Betty said. "It's just a matter of being open. You have to learn how to see first and then you simply read what you see. Sometimes it's very clear-cut; other times it takes some interpretation on your part. Then there are certain other kinds of knowledge that are already there, inside you, and the process of seeing and reading is a process of recovery, of recovering knowledge you already know."

Mona tilted her head as if she were hanging on Betty's every word, but she was actually in screen-saver mode—physically present, yes, but the rest of her was miles away, in her apartment, disrobing and climbing into bed.

When she did finally go to bed that night, she slept a miraculous twelve hours straight, without once getting up to do the usual things: guzzle water, despond, pee, eat peanut butter from the jar with her fingers, despond again.

ON THURSDAY BETTY DIDN'T FOLLOW MONA AROUND, BUT stayed on her throne in the living room, reading her favorite magazine, *National Enquirer*.

———

"You see the irony in the fact that you live in a trailer and subscribe to the *Enquirer*, right?" Mona said at one point.

"Pffh! This is hardly what you'd call a trailer," Betty answered.

When Mona was finished cleaning, Betty invited her to sit down. "I can't read your mind today," Mona said. "Took too much out of me. I was so tired I almost died in my sleep that night."

"You're a crack-up," Betty said with a straight face. "What I want to do today is actually very different. It requires the opposite of concentration."

Mona sat down heavily and removed her sneakers, suspecting she'd be there awhile. She wished she had something better to do, but the sad fact was she didn't. Her only plans that evening were to bathe and watch television, and Betty was better than television. Or network television, at least.

She stiffened when she saw the large box of loose photographs at Betty's feet. She'd always equated the viewing of other people's personal snapshots with hearing about the dream they'd had the previous night.

Betty rummaged through the box and pulled out a small handful. She shuffled the photographs like a deck of cards, then dealt one to Mona, placing it facedown on the table in front of her. "Okay, here's how this goes: I want you to turn the picture over, look at it, then say the first words that come into your mind. No thinking and no editing. Just say whatever pops into your head. Okay?"

Mona recalled the last time she saw a photograph lying facedown in a client's house. She'd been at the Baxters', a sweet but oddly formal couple in their late forties, dusting Mr. Baxter's office, when she saw the photograph lying on top of his filing cabinet. She absentmindedly flipped it over, expecting a picture of one of their dogs, but was confronted instead with a close-up of someone's dark, hairy asshole. Mrs. Baxter's, she'd imagined.

"Ready?" Betty asked from her throne.

"I guess so," Mona said.

She flipped the photograph over. No asshole this time, just a man on a horse. This must be Johnny. The man had long black hair, dark skin, and was wearing head-to-toe denim. He was sitting bareback on a white Appaloosa with gray spots and a blue eye. In the background stood a snowcapped Taos mountain under a pink sky.

"Feel free to really handle the picture," Betty instructed. "You know, with your hands."

Mona held the photograph closer and peered at the man's unsmiling, handsome face. "He looks like the stoic type," she said.

"See, now you're thinking. No thinking allowed. Just spontaneous words and phrases. Whatever pops into your head."

"My thought bubble is pretty empty, Betty, to be honest. It always is at the end of the day. You have no idea how many chemicals I inhale on a daily basis. I'll probably die of brain cancer in five years."

"I just said I'm not interested in your thoughts," Betty said. "Just look at the picture and tell me if any images or words come to mind."

You forgot to say please, Mona thought irritably. Words were in fact coming to mind. Not just words, but snatches of poetry—very specific snatches from a very famous Plath poem. Fuck it. She wants to know what's on my mind, I'll tell her.

"Daddy," Mona began. "I have had to kill you." She paused and looked at Betty, who was literally on the edge of her seat.

"Don't stop!" Betty commanded.

"Bean green . . . language obscene . . . I could never talk to you. Clear beer, neat mustache. Love of the rack and the screw. There's a stake in your fat black heart. Daddy, Daddy—" She stopped there.

She'd almost recited the rest of the last line—"you bastard, I'm through," but thought it might be too recognizable, not to mention dramatic and over-the-top.

"Wow," Betty said, pleased. "You gave me goose bumps, Maura. That's called 'channeling,' and you are gifted."

It's called "plagiarism," Mona thought. But thanks.

"'Fat black heart'—I wonder if Johnny has heart disease," Betty said anxiously. Mona shrugged.

Betty shuffled the deck again and placed another photo face-down. This time Johnny was in a hotel swimming pool with his back to the camera, treading water in the deep end, his long hair in a bun. He was looking over his shoulder, squinting toward the camera, but his expression was unreadable. The phrase KING OF KINGS was tattooed across his shoulders in big black letters.

"Nice tattoo," she said. "That's a Jesus reference, I take it."

"No thinking!" Betty said. "First words that come into your mind."

She closed her eyes and improvised. "Sweet children, bitter children, bright red teeth within a womb. A fist pounds on a steel door. Freezer burn, bloody gloves, blue feet—the clock is ticking." Jesus, she thought. I'm giving *myself* goose bumps. Maybe I *am* good at this.

"Oh my God, he's going to have a heart attack!" Betty said, her eyes filling up. "He's going to die for two minutes and then be brought back to life, and then he's going to need surgery."

Mona was genuinely taken aback. "Are you kidding? I didn't say that."

"Trust me, I know what I'm talking about," Betty said, wiping her eyes.

"You never told me you were married to a hot Mexican dude," she said, trying to change the subject.

"Be careful who you call Mexican around here," Betty said. "Johnny and his family, along with everyone in their neighborhood, trace their lineage back to the Spaniards who conquered New Mexico in the 1500s. They identify as Spanish, not Mexican."

"You're definitely still hung up on the guy, that much is clear," she said.

"Can we do one more?"

"Sure." She made a mental note not to mention hearts or blood.

The last photo was a close-up of Johnny's face, a face Mona suddenly recognized. "Wait a minute, I know this guy," she blurted. She detected an instant change in the atmosphere of the trailer—subtle, but palpable—and thought of leaves on a tree turning over, baring their spines in anticipation of a downpour.

"What do you mean, you know him?"

She backpedaled. "I don't *know* him. I met him once, when I first moved to town. He bought me a drink."

"Where?"

"At that bar where he works—the Tom-Tom Room."

"TT's," Betty said, nodding. "Go on. Tell me everything."

"Not much to tell. I happened to sit next to him at the bar and he bought me a drink before his shift started. He works the door, he said."

"He bought you a drink?" she asked, incredulous. "Really?"

Mona gulped. "Not like that—I told him I was new in town. He was just being friendly."

Betty looked away and took a breath through her nose. She's letting it go, Mona thought. She's putting it aside to process later. Impressive.

"So how did he seem to you?" Betty asked languidly. "Happy, sad, angry, what?"

"I don't know." She shrugged. "It was months ago. He seemed fine. He was wearing orange."

She remembered their brief exchange well. He'd introduced himself as John, not Johnny. When he went to order their drinks, he asked, "What's your poison?"

"Oven cleaner," she'd said with a straight face.

Her sense of humor sometimes made people—herself, included—uncomfortable, but he'd laughed easily. She remembered liking his mouth and the way he tipped his head back to laugh, exposing his throat. Good-looking, for an older guy. He'd bought her a beer and introduced her to the bartender. When she left, a little over an hour later, he'd offered his hand for a shake, and then faked a buckling of his knees when she grasped his palm. "Jesus," he'd said. "Talk about an iron grip."

"Thanks," she'd said, and blushed.

But she couldn't tell Betty any of that. Everything between her and Betty was different now.

"Are you any good with a camera?" Betty asked suddenly.

"Really good, actually," Mona said, then kicked herself. She could see where Betty was headed.

"How would you feel about taking some pictures for me? I'd pay you, of course."

"You mean, how would I feel about spying for you," she corrected.

"All I need are a couple of decent pictures. The ones I have are over a decade old."

"And why do you need them?"

"Because then I'd know for sure when Johnny's going to die."

"This is going to sound crazy, but why don't you just call him and ask how he's doing?"

"Believe me, I've tried. He wants nothing to do with me. Whenever I see him around town, he runs the other way. It's like he thinks I'm a vampire or Satan or something. Do you know what it's like to be in love with someone who hates your guts? Hell is what it is. Hell on earth."

"Have you tried therapy?" she asked.

"He's my soul mate."

"If he was your soul mate, don't you think he'd know that? I mean, wouldn't it be mutual?"

"He knows, he knows. I mean, deep down. He's just scared. He had a terrible childhood. He was sodomized—"

"Betty, listen—that Daddy stuff? It's called poetry. Poetry by a famous person. Have you heard of Sylvia Plath? There's nothing the matter with his heart."

"Maura, you don't know how this works, okay? It came into your mind when you looked at the picture. It could be poetry or a brand of toilet paper. Either way, it counts."

"Well, what am I supposed to do, follow him around with my camera? I don't think he'll appreciate that."

"All you'd have to do is go to TT's with your friends, hang around, have a drink or two, and take some pictures."

"I don't have any friends," Mona said. But the idea of spying on him actually appealed to her, more than a little. She'd always wanted to be a private eye.

"You'll figure it out, Maura," Betty said. "And I'll pay you fifty bucks per picture."

"Fifty?"

"Five-oh," Betty said. "That's how much I want them."

"So if I come back with ten good pictures, you're going to fork over five hundred dollars?"

"You won't get ten pictures," Betty said. "But yes. So let's see . . . if you take pictures this weekend, then have them developed, then bring them with—"

"Ever hear of digital cameras?"

"I don't have one of those."

"Yeah, but I do," Mona said, hating herself. "I can print the pictures at home and bring them with me next week."

Betty beamed at her. "You're an angel, Maura."

EVERY WEEKDAY AT DUSK, JUST AFTER SHE GOT HOME FROM work, she heard the near-distant sound of drumming and chanting. She'd always assumed it was coming from the Pueblo, which was a mile or two from the house, and imagined fifty or so Tewa Indians, some wearing elaborate headdresses and body paint, dancing around a bonfire, chanting for salvation. Or money. Or happiness. Or rain. Or whatever it was people chanted for.

And now, at last, she was seeing it live. She felt like a dolt—the music hadn't been coming from the Pueblo at all but from loudspeakers inside the Tom-Tom Room, which was attached to a small hotel just down the road from her house. The drummers and chanters were in fact genuine Tewa natives, hired to put on a show for the tourists, but there were only five or six of them and they weren't dressed in traditional garb. Instead they were wearing T-shirts, jeans, and running shoes and kept glancing at their watches. When they finished their set they took their beer to go and were replaced by a blues band whose entire repertoire consisted of songs about jail.

She sat at the horseshoe-shaped bar, drinking a vodka tonic and waiting for Johnny. In an effort at disguise she wore a straw cowboy hat, except it wasn't very low profile as it was pink and mangled on one side. She doubted Johnny would recognize her anyway—she'd met him only that one time, nine months ago now.

The problem with spying in a bar, she soon realized, was that you got tanked while you were waiting for something to happen, and she'd never been one to nurse a drink. By the time he showed up she was half in the bag. He looked exhausted. In fact his weariness seemed stitched into his skin. He'd also gained a few pounds. His cheekbones had been as sharply prominent as coastal cliffs but now looked buried in sand, and his gut peeked over the waistband of his Wranglers. Despite the fat and fatigue, he was still easy on the eyes.

He stayed at the door for the most part, checking people's IDs. She didn't feel like whipping out her camera, but she reminded herself that she could use the extra money, having knocked over a Tiffany floor lamp at the Baxters' the previous afternoon. Naturally, she didn't have insurance, so she offered eight free visits as a gesture of goodwill. Except the fuckers took her up on it, which she hadn't anticipated. Their asshole fetish was fitting. So, rather than work off the damage, she'd just pay them in cash. Perhaps then she'd feel less indentured, and would stop calling them names like Mrs. Balloon Knot, Ass Hat, and Pucker Poo under her breath.

After procrastinating for most of the evening, she managed to get two pictures of Johnny, one while he leaned over the bar to whisper something to the bartender, and another returning from the bathroom. He looked right at her after the flash went off both times, and she made sure to look the other way.

She showed up again the following night. This time her disguise consisted of a pair of weak, red-framed reading glasses she'd purchased at the drugstore. The place was mostly empty except for a handful of single men at the bar and a few couples in the dining area. She was early again and strategically chose a bar stool that would give her a decent view of Johnny later on.

He turned up early, too. Halfway into her second vodka tonic, he waltzed in and sat directly across from her at the bar. He still looked tired, but more alert this time, and wore a pressed cowboy shirt. His hair was wet and pulled into a ponytail and he was chewing gum. He gave her the once-over but didn't seem to recognize her. Then he ordered dinner from the bartender and proceeded to ramble about some motorcycle he was planning on buying.

His dinner arrived and she watched him work on a plate of ribs. He briefly examined each rib before chewing the meat off quickly and unself-consciously, sucking on the bone a little before tossing it in the bread basket. He licked each of his fingers before wiping them on his napkin. She wondered if he ever even thought of Betty. Her instinct said no. Something—the finger licking, perhaps—told her he was a present person, untormented by the past.

It was strange knowing so many random facts about him. She knew his middle name (Michael), his sun sign (Cancer), his moon sign (Gemini), his brother's name (Daniel), his favorite dessert (Ding Dongs), where he was ticklish (just above the knee). She also knew about his fetish for underarm hair on women, a fetish Betty had indulged while they were together.

She'd never seen someone so engrossed in their meal. This is your chance, she told herself. Don't be a pussy. She removed her camera from her purse, turned it on, and made sure the flash was off before setting the camera on the bar. She took several pictures while pretending to fiddle with the settings. Then she felt Johnny glaring at her. He's onto you, dumbass. She put the camera away and invented a story for herself: You're a healthy, well-adjusted twenty-five-year-old who enjoys socializing and interacting with others. It's Friday night, so naturally you're waiting for your date. Your date is . . . late, unfortunately, goddamn him. She looked at her watch and pretended to be irritated. Johnny finished his meal and took his seat at the door, but he kept squinting in her direction. Look busy, she told herself. She rummaged through her purse for a pen and wrote a list on a cocktail napkin:

> Deposit cash
> Buy string mop, vacuum bags, ice cube trays, mustard
> Dye hair, pluck eyebrows, moisturize
> Buy new bra
> Paint some pictures
> Join healthy cult

"May I?" A stranger sat next to her before she could answer. Your date has finally arrived. Act happy. Get rid of the dorky glasses. She crumpled up the list and deposited it in her purse, along with the glasses, which were giving her a headache.

The man had a handsome face and very hairy hands and forearms. He was probably hairy all over. You're okay with hairy dudes, she told herself.

"Looks like you're ready for another," he said, nodding toward her almost-full glass.

"Yep."

He ordered her another vodka tonic and a Chimay for himself. Damn, a yuppie, she thought. His name was Anthony, he said, and he was from New York City. He'd come to Taos for two reasons: to attend a wedding and to hike some famous trail.

She hated serious hikers. For starters, they had terrible taste in footwear. She glanced at his shoes: brown leather slip-ons with perforated sides—tolerable. Then she noticed his beige nylon cargo pants—unacceptable.

"How long you in town for?" she asked.

"I leave tomorrow morning."

Clothing aside, his attractiveness immediately increased by 40 percent.

"What do you do?" he asked.

"I'm a cleaning lady," she said.

He smiled and blinked a couple of times, apparently waiting for the punch line.

"I'm kidding," she said. "I'm a designer."

"Me, too," he said. "What do you design?"

She took a long sip of her drink. Interiors, she almost said. "Hats," she said instead. "And luggage occasionally."

"Wow."

"It's not as glamorous as it sounds. It's a very tricky market." She was suddenly envious of her imaginary occupation. "What about you?"

"I'm trained as an architect, but I design fire escapes and elevator shafts for office buildings."

"Interesting," she said.

"Not really," he said, and laughed. "What do you do for fun?"

"I drum," she said. "I'm a drummer."

He nodded. "I can totally see that."

If only it were true. She felt tears well in her eyes and quickly looked away, waiting for them to recede, and noticed Johnny standing at the door, talking and laughing with some locals. Poor Betty was more than likely in her living room watching *Judge Judy* reruns, surrounded by her deaf cats and thinking of Johnny every ten seconds.

"You have beautiful hair," Anthony said, apropos of nothing. "Are you Spanish?"

She turned and looked at him. "Mick and spic," she said, and smiled. "But mostly mick."

———

He looked at her squarely. "You realize that's racist, right?"

"Of course," she said.

"Just checking," he said.

She drained the rest of her drink. "Are you a spic?"

"Wop," he said.

Which explained the gold horn and serpent chain under all that chest hair.

"You look a little like Frank Zappa," she said.

He was visibly offended, as if she'd told him he resembled a tree shrew.

"I meant that as a compliment," she said.

He shrugged. "You don't look like anyone."

"No?"

"Also a compliment," he said.

Two hours later he invited her back to his hotel room. She was drunk by then and having difficulty seeing out of her left eye, so she said yes. On the way out, she photographed Johnny openly. He covered his face with his hand like a celebrity. "I like your face!" she yelled.

WHEN SHE ARRIVED AT BETTY'S THE FOLLOWING MONDAY, Betty was sunbathing on the hood of the Caddy in a green paisley bikini two sizes too small. She was slick with oil and looked like one giant freckle. Mona noticed red hair curling out from her bikini bottom and averted her eyes. Betty hopped off the hood and gave her a greasy hug.

"You're awfully chipper," Mona said.

"I took the day off." She blotted her face with a towel. "Let's go inside and see how you did!"

Betty covered her throne with the towel before sitting down. Mona dropped her cleaning bucket in the kitchen and joined Betty in the living room. She handed Betty an envelope containing her work. Betty flipped through the photographs, staring hard at each one. "Oh, Maura. These aren't very good," she said. "Three of them are blurry and the rest are too far away."

"Well, what were you expecting—Sears portraits? He works in a bar. It's dark."

"I thought you said you were a professional."

"I said I majored in photography. I never said I graduated."

"Well, these aren't worth fifty apiece."

"Fine," Mona said. "But you should at least give me some money for all the alcohol I had to consume."

"That's not what we agreed on." Betty thought everyone was a closet alcoholic, and she refused to be an enabler.

"I would have died of boredom otherwise. I spent, like, fourteen hours in that bar."

"I'll give you a hundred dollars."

"Fair enough, I guess," Mona said. "Listen, I'm sorry the pictures aren't what you wanted, but the good news is I got laid on Friday night."

Betty looked surprised, but that was because Betty wondered how brunettes with B cups ever got anywhere with men.

"The bad news is he had the smallest dick I've ever seen. It was like, this big," Mona said, holding up a thumb. "In fact, I felt like a child molester when I, uh, touched it. But it's weird, because he had very large hands—"

"Ooh! I just got chills when you said 'child molester.'" Betty shivered. "Something in your voice."

"Was I a pedophile in a past life?" Mona asked. "That might explain a few things. Anyway, lucky for me, he made up for it in other areas, if you know what I mean."

Really, it was Mona who'd made an ass of herself that night. In his hotel room Anthony had undressed her carefully, tenderly, and then asked if he could put his face down there. "If you insist," she'd said.

"Thank you," he'd said soberly, still fully dressed.

"Don't thank me yet," she said. "I don't know how, uh, fresh—"

But he already had his mouth on her. Not just his mouth, but his whole face. What was he doing with his nose? Something incredible. Or wait—was that his chin? She sat up and looked down at him.

"What are you doing?" she asked, genuinely curious.

He opened his eyes and stopped moving. "Please just let me do this."

She lay down again and studied the drapes. He was handling her cunt deftly, as if he'd designed it himself, and she thought back to their conversation in the bar. An architect, he'd said. Fire escapes and elevator shafts. What do you design, she imagined asking him now. "Vaginas," he would say this time. "For office buildings."

In fact, for many months now, her body had felt like an office building—neutered, utilitarian, without ornament—but he seemed to be remodeling it. His left hand cradled her fire escape, and the fingers of his right hand were inside her elevator shaft. His tongue—or was it his thumb?—kept grazing the elevator button, over and over and over. She tried to move away at one point, but he had her pinned. He seemed to be using his upper jaw to hold her in place. She couldn't remember when exactly the inappropriate laughter started, but she could feel it bubble inside her for a while. Then it began to leak out steadily, filling the room. It felt as natural as the sweat from her pores, and stopping it was beyond her capacity. It reminded her of the time she'd put Palmolive in someone's washing machine. Thankfully, he seemed amused and carried on with the business at hand.

This was before he'd revealed his tiny member. She'd managed not to laugh then, thank Bob. In any event, it was the first time she'd been in the sack with someone since Mr. Disgusting. At least it had been uncontrollable laughter rather than tears. At least she hadn't clung to him and talked about her feelings.

"Anyway, small package aside, he didn't have squinty eyes or walk with a cane, so we're probably not getting married," Mona said.

Betty didn't answer. She was staring at one of the photographs. "He needs a haircut," she said. "And a shave. But God, I miss those hands. And those eyes!" She looked ready to cry.

"I had a feeling this wasn't a good idea."

"I'm fine," Betty said, composing herself. "Just do what you need to do in here. I'm not going to keep you company today. I'm too upset."

Mona went into the kitchen. Thirty minutes and you're out of here, she told herself. She washed the eight cat food dishes and wiped down the counters, then headed for the bathroom, where she spent an additional fifteen minutes. Without Betty looking over her shoulder, cleaning the trailer was almost pleasurable.

As she was vacuuming Betty's bedroom she saw something sticking out from under the bed. It looked like a bone. She crouched down and lifted the bed skirt. It wasn't a bone, but a porcelain limb—an arm. The arm was attached to one of Betty's creepy porcelain dolls, except this one didn't fit in with the others—she had brown hair instead of blonde, and brown eyes instead of blue or green, and she wasn't dressed as a bride. Instead, she wore a Mexican-style red dress and had a mole painted on her cheek. Evidently, she wasn't Betty's type, so she'd been banished, separated from the rest. Mona dusted her off with a clean rag and wondered how long she'd been living under the bed—years, probably. Her dress was tattered and smelled vaguely of cat piss. "I'm getting you out of here," she whispered, and placed the doll in the bottom of her cleaning bucket. She covered her with rags, and then finished vacuuming.

"Leaving already?" Betty asked, as she was gathering her things. She was still sitting on her throne. Her mascara had run and her hair was a mess. She looked like she'd just lost an important oil-wrestling match. One of her cats sat at her feet, licking her ankles.

Mona shrugged. "Cleaning this place twice a week is overkill. Not that I'm complaining."

"I've been thinking about whether or not to tell you something, Maura."

Uh-oh, she thought, another goddamn confession. She probably hacked a baby to pieces with that machete of hers. Her own baby.

"Can I see your palm?"

"My hands are dirty," Mona said.

Betty made an impatient gimme gesture. The poor woman's wrecked, Mona thought. Show some mercy. She sat down on the couch and offered Betty her palm. Betty put on her glasses and traced one of the lines in Mona's palm with a red fingernail.

"This is difficult for me," she said. She petted Mona's palm a few times with her oily hand. "Even though I've been doing this for thirty years." She removed her glasses and looked Mona in the eye. "It's your life line, Maura. It breaks at around age twenty-seven."

"Okay," Mona said slowly.

"Now, sometimes a break can signify a divorce or some other crisis—the death of a parent or child—but yours is permanently broken. It doesn't pick up again. See?" She pointed to the line in question. Mona peered at it. It did indeed appear to have a permanent break.

"Oh yeah," Mona said. "I can totally explain that. When I was little I placed my palm on a very hot iron. The line probably burned right off."

Betty looked at her like she was deranged. "Doesn't work that way, Maura. Look, ordinarily I wouldn't tell someone their life line ended before age thirty. It's just too terrible to hear. But I feel close to you. I consider you a good friend. And if it were me, I'd want to know."

Unbelievable, Mona thought. "So you're saying I have roughly a year to live? What about my two husbands and two children?"

"I've thought about that," Betty said with her chin in her hand. "Maybe I was seeing one of your past lives. I'm guessing it was the one immediately before this one."

Mona felt a laughing fit coming on. You can't laugh right now, she told herself. Do. Not. Laugh. She put a hand over her mouth and breathed deeply through her nose.

"You're in shock," Betty said. "Which is understandable. You have a lot of thinking to do. I just hope you don't hate me, Maura. I'm doing this out of love."

Mona stood up. "I don't know what to say, Betty. I'm going home."

"Let me pay you, at least." She reached for her pocketbook and handed Mona a hundred and fifty dollars in cash. "Listen, you don't have to come on Thursday if you don't want to, but would you mind taking a couple more pictures of Johnny? You can say no, of course. And I'll pay you fifty per picture no matter what. It'll be good for you to get out there and have some fun. Maybe you'll get lucky again."

"I'll have to think about it," Mona said, avoiding Betty's eyes.

LITTLE DID BETTY KNOW THAT MONA WELCOMED AN EARLY death. The thought of checking out early had been her pacifier for many years, something she'd always sucked on in the middle of the night when she couldn't sleep. If Betty had said her life line ended at age ninety-eight, or eighty-eight, or seventy-eight—that would be cause for alarm. Granted, twenty-seven was a little young to die. Perhaps that's why her hands were trembling. Then again, a lot of great people die at that age. Not that there was anything to worry about, as Betty was a total charlatan. And a sadist, now that she thought about it. She obviously just ended their relationship. Did she really expect a dying woman to clean her toilet? She wondered if Betty engineered the whole thing on purpose. If so, she'd just taken passive-aggressive to a new level.

At home she showered and then wandered around her apartment in her bathrobe. She entertained the thought of death in a year, which made her pleasantly drowsy. She'd sleep well tonight. She stared at the various things she'd collected in the nine months she'd lived in Taos. If Betty was somehow right, Mona had far too many possessions and, with no husband or children, they would all end up in the trash. The idea disheartened her. Perhaps she could arrange for an Egyptian burial. Or perhaps it was time she started paring down and purging. Although, without all her stuff, what the hell would she do with herself? She spent huge amounts of time simply admiring her knick-knacks. It occurred to her that she wasn't so different from Betty. They both lived alone and were companionless, and they both found solace in surrounding themselves with useless objects. The difference was that Betty collected things that were ostensibly worth money, while Mona collected things of value only to herself, like empty frames, broken watches, vintage handkerchiefs, bird figurines, and throw pillows.

Which reminded her: she had one of Betty's precious dolls. She retrieved the doll from her cleaning bucket. For some reason this doll didn't repulse her as much as Betty's brides. "You look Spanish," she said. "I bet your name is Carmen or Maria or Sofia." Avoiding the doll's eyes, she carefully cleaned its face and limbs with Windex and spot-cleaned its dress with Resolve. In the bathroom she shampooed and conditioned the doll's hair in the sink. Carmen-Maria-Sofia was creepy—there was no denying that—and Mona imagined waking to find the doll standing over her with a miniature butcher knife in her porcelain hand. Stop with the drama, she told herself. This doll's your friend. You need a friend. Why don't you get out of the house for once and take your little friend out for ice cream?

They headed to the Tom-Tom Room instead. Mona decided she would indeed take more pictures of Johnny. Why not? She'd get right in his face this time. What was he going to do—beat her up? Her new tactic would be to photograph the entrance from outside and make sure he was in the frame. She didn't know why she hadn't thought of it before. This business of going inside and getting shit-faced was counterproductive. If she simply photographed him at his post, he would be stationary and likely in focus—not that it mattered. Betty had said fifty no matter what.

Johnny wasn't there yet, so she sat in her car and waited with her camera in her lap. The native drummers had just finished their set and were making a beeline for their rusty van in the parking lot. The sun was five minutes from the horizon and looked like an oblong glob of Murphy Oil Soap. The rest of the sky was on fire. If Yoko and Yoko were around, they'd be drooling all over the place.

She turned to Carmen-Maria-Sofia in the passenger seat. "You forgot to put your seat belt on," she said. "And I can see your underwear." As she reached over to adjust the doll's dress someone tapped on the window, startling her.

It was Johnny. He was dressed in head-to-toe black, and the front of his T-shirt was covered with what looked like tiny metal shavings. She pictured him filing the bars of a cage and then quickly realized it was scratch-ticket dust. He must have scratched twenty tickets on his way to work.

"Hey, Oven Cleaner," he said.

She rolled down her window and smiled. "Oh, hey. I remember you. Sort of."

"Why you spying on me?"

She snorted. "I'm not spying."

"Yes, you are, and you're taking pictures," he said, pointing to the camera in her lap.

"You know, there's a support group for people like you," she said. "It's called Paranoia Anonymous. Ever hear of it?"

"How do you know Betty?"

"Betty who?"

"That Betty," he said, and pointed to the doll.

Mona massaged the back of her neck. "I'm her cleaning lady," she confessed, and looked down at her camera.

"Betty has a maid?"

Mona winced at the word "maid."

"I'm surprised she gave you that doll. If I remember right, she's pretty attached to those things."

"She didn't exactly hand it over," she said. "I, uh, kidnapped her. I'm going to use her as a bargaining chip in case something goes wrong."

He laughed. "Like what?"

"Well, in case she doesn't pay me."

"What are you going to do—break the doll's kneecaps?"

"I was thinking of smashing her face with a hammer."

"How much she paying you?"

"Enough," she said. "Hey, if you wouldn't mind posing for some head shots, I'll totally split the money with you."

———

200

He laughed. "Think I'll pass." He looked wistful all of a sudden. "I suppose she wants pictures to channel her bullshit."

"Yeah," Mona said, nodding. "She's convinced you're about to die of a massive heart attack, but I think that's my fault—I sort of put the idea in her head."

He put his hand on his chest and frowned.

"Don't feel bad," Mona said. "I only have a year to live."

"Listen, my shift starts in an hour. Why don't you come in and have a drink? I want to talk to you about something."

"You're not going to kidnap me and then torture me, are you?"

He shook his head and gave her a quizzical look. "I'm not mad. Tell me your name again, though."

"Mona," she said.

He opened the car door for her. "Should I bring my camera?" she asked.

He laughed. "No."

She brought the camera anyway. Inside, he directed her to sit at one of the tables and then brought her a draft from the bar. "On the house," he said, placing it on a coaster in front of her. He sat down heavily. He had what looked like sheet creases on the side of his face. She brushed imaginary crumbs off the tabletop and then sipped her beer. He smiled tightly at her.

"How long you been working for Betty?" he asked.

"Couple months."

"So you've figured out she's not right in the head."

"She's pretty weird," Mona admitted. "But I wouldn't say she's barking mad or anything. Although, I found this crazy poem once about a machete—"

"I wrote that," he said quickly, and laughed. "Holy crackers. I can't believe she still has it."

"Still has the machete, too."

"Well, that was my inspiration. That and her off-the-wall temper." He added a stick of gum to the wad in his mouth and chewed solemnly. "I'll tell you a story about Betty, just to give you an idea of who you're dealing with. You see these scars?" He pointed to three white marks, one on his left eyelid and the others under his right eye. They looked like miniature quarter moons. "Betty and I went out to dinner one night and I told her I was leaving her. This was ages ago. She freaked out and got really drunk. Only, she doesn't drink, so I had to carry her to the car. I put her in the backseat and she passed out. I was going to drive her home and then go sleep at my brother's.

"So I'm driving down 74, which is two lanes, heading to her trailer, and it's pitch-dark, no moon or nothing. I'm doing about eighty. Then all of a sudden she's awake. Wide awake and screaming. So what does she do? She sits up and puts her hands over my eyes—while I'm driving. And not just peekaboo style—she's trying to claw my eyes out with those fucking talons of hers.

"There's traffic coming in the other direction. I can see the headlights through her fingers. I take my foot off the gas and one of my hands off the wheel and try to snap her wrist. Meanwhile, we sail off the highway and the car rolls into an arroyo." In a gesture she recognized from hours of staring at him, he ran a finger over the scars beneath his eye. "We should be dead. Actually, I shouldn't say 'we'—she didn't have a scratch on her."

"Was this in her Cadillac?"

"No, thank God. And it's mine, by the way, not hers."

"She told me she won it in the divorce."

He shook his head. "Not part of the deal. I never signed it over to her. She forged my signature." His jaw tightened.

"You don't have a heart condition by any chance, do you?" she asked, trying to change the subject. "Betty's pretty convinced you're going to keel over any second."

"Listen," he said. "You and I have met for a reason." He parked his gum in the side of his mouth. "We were supposed to meet, I mean."

She rolled her eyes. "You sound just like her."

"Well, that's one thing we both believed in: there are no coincidences."

"Terrific."

"This is going to sound crazy, but you're supposed to get my car back for me, and I'm supposed to introduce you to my nephew." He started chewing again. "I just figured it out right this second."

"By 'get my car back' you mean steal it, right?"

"It'd be the opposite of stealing, since it's my car."

"Well, if you're the rightful owner, why don't you go and get it yourself?"

"Because it's complicated."

"It sounds pretty straightforward to me."

His face reddened and he looked at his hands. "Betty has some dirt on me," he said. "That's all I can say about it."

"How am I supposed to get your car back? Just out of curiosity."

He leaned toward her and lowered his voice. "You go to the radio station, right? At around midnight, when she's on the air, and you just take it. I have a set of keys, okay? Then you drive it to my brother's place in Arroyo Seco. Ten miles. That's it. You put it in his garage, he drives you home, and it's all over in an hour." He smiled at her. "Or maybe my nephew gives you a ride." He winked. "Anyway, I'll be here, see, so she won't suspect nothing."

"Uh, won't she suspect something when she sees you tooling around town in it?"

"I'm moving to California next month. And anyway, she won't report it stolen because it's not really hers. You see? It's all a game."

"So she will know you're in on it."

"Yeah, but she can't prove it," he said. "It's complicated, like I said. You just have to trust me."

She imagined herself behind the wheel of the Caddy and smiled. Then she imagined Betty chasing after her with a machete.

"I don't know," she said. "What's in it for me?"

"My nephew."

"Is he, like, a male prostitute or something?"

"No! He might be your new boyfriend. He's weird, like you. Artsy-fartsy or whatever. You're perfect for each other."

"Maybe I don't want a boyfriend."

"Yeah, you do. I can see it in your face. Listen, I'd give you money if I could, but I'm broke. You can ask anyone. So meet my nephew and just think about it. You don't have to worry—I'm not holding you to anything."

"You should probably let me photograph you now. As a gesture of goodwill."

He hesitated. "Fine," he said. "What should I do?" He brushed hair out of his face with a thick hand. "Should I smile?"

"No, look natural. Look in my direction but not right at me." She took a few pictures. "Now look off to the side. You should look like you're talking to someone. Tell me your nephew's name." She continued snapping away.

"Jesus."

"What?"

"That's his name—Jesus."

"You mean Jesús? I can manage the Spanish pronunciation."

"No, it's Jesus. He was born on Christmas. His mother's white."

And out of her mind, obviously. "How old is he?"

"Twenty-seven. Trust me, you'll like him." He smiled. "Come by tomorrow night around ten and I'll make sure he's here."

They'd probably be mutually horrified by each other and the meeting would be over in five minutes. He'd excuse himself and go to the restroom, then climb out a window. Or vice versa.

But maybe not. Johnny seemed utterly confident of their destiny together. She was touched by his conviction and enthusiasm. Could she really date someone named Jesus? Well, it wouldn't last long— after all, she might be dead in a year. Perhaps dating Jesus would somehow get her into heaven, if it existed.

HE LOOKED NOTHING LIKE HIS NAMESAKE. IN FACT HE looked like a Spanish greaser. He wore pomade in his black hair and was dressed in a plain white T-shirt, a belt with a Western star and wings on the buckle, dark jeans, and gray suede shoes. His eyes definitely qualified as squinty, but he may have just needed glasses.

"Nice to meet you . . . Jesus," she said.

"Likewise," he said. "But listen, you can call me Jesse if you're more comfortable with that."

"How many people call you Jesse?"

"Lots," he said. To her surprise, he did some silent counting on his fingers. "Ten or twelve, at least."

"Lame," she said. "I'll stick with Jesus."

He shrugged. "Makes no difference to me."

They were sitting at a small circular table Johnny had reserved for them. It was one of a handful on a platform overlooking the stage and dance floor. The VIP section, as it were. Johnny had a perfect view of them from the door, which was roughly fifty feet away, and his eyes swept over their table every fifteen seconds, like a spotlight. It was country night, unfortunately. Live music and line dancing. The crowd, which was sizable, especially for a Tuesday night, could be summed up by the phrase "big hats, no cattle." Luckily the crappy band was between sets, so they didn't have to shout to be heard.

Not that they were talking much. They'd covered the basics in ten minutes: he was a college dropout; he lived alone; he had two jobs; he worked in a plant nursery during the day and waited tables at night; he painted pictures in his spare time—religious figures were his subject, though he wasn't religious; he grew up in Cordova.

"Near that church with the miracle dirt?" she asked.

"Not far from there."

She explained how she'd stopped at that church when she first came to Taos and stocked up on holy dirt. "I used to bathe in it, practically."

He tipped his head back to laugh, just like his uncle. "Did it work?" he asked. "Are you cured?"

"Still need crutches occasionally," she said.

Now there was a lull. Jesus seemed slightly uneasy. They ordered a third round of margaritas. He slurped them down like water, just like her, so they had that in common, but he was too pretty for her. His teeth were too white and straight and she could tell he had a washboard stomach—on purpose. No bueno. Still, there was something about his skin that made her want to bite him.

"So your uncle seems to think we're destined to be together."

He shrugged. "He thinks everything's a sign. It gives his life meaning."

"Has he done this to you before?"

He took a long sip of his drink and held up two fingers.

"Get out of here," she said.

———

"But it's been a while. He's seeing fewer 'signs' now that he's clean. Thank God."

"AA?"

"GA," he said. "He hasn't set foot in a casino in two years. A miracle."

Should she mention that he was covered in scratch-ticket dust yesterday? No, she decided. Leave it alone. Maybe scratch tickets didn't count.

"What were the other girls like?"

"The first one sold him a winning lottery ticket. Her name was . . . Debbie, I think. This was, like, six years ago or something. She worked at 7-Eleven. He was positive we were going to live happily ever after, which ended up being, like, ten minutes. The second one was a blackjack dealer at the casino here in town. He won some money at her table and gave her my phone number along with a tip. Or instead of a tip, knowing him. Her name was Magdalena, which he thought was extremely significant. Turns out she had four kids. I was like, what the fuck."

"And here you are again. You must be an optimist," she said. "Or a masochist."

"Actually, I just want to make John happy. He's had a hard life. Plus, he lives for this shit. And he's moving to California in a month, so I figured what the hell." They were silent for a minute and she watched him fidget with his cocktail napkin. "Are you an optimist?" he asked. "Is that why you're here?"

"No, I'm just desperate and hard up," she said, and laughed. "Seriously."

"Where do you hang out usually?"

"In my living room."

"Do you have roommates?"

"Just me, myself, and I," she said. "We bicker constantly."

"Do you have friends?"

"I haven't gotten around to making any, but it's on my list."

"I'll be your friend," he said, and smiled.

She was startled by the lack of irony in his voice and thought of Mr. Disgusting. He'd said the same thing on their first date, and look what happened there.

"You look confused," he said, "but I'm serious. We should be friends."

"What happens when you fall in love with me? Or vice versa?"

"I won't."

"Why not? Am I hideous? You can tell me."

He motioned for her to come closer. She leaned toward him and got a whiff of his musky cologne.

"Gay," he whispered.

"Oh," she said. And here she thought she had gaydar. Well, it explained why he noticed that her shoes matched the stripe in her shirt earlier. So the pressure was off. She felt her neck and shoulders relax.

"I have a feeling I'm not your type anyway," he said.

"You would be if you were wearing ten extra pounds and a mustache," she said. "And a hairnet, maybe."

He laughed.

"Your uncle doesn't know, obviously."

"No one in my family does. I'm very discreet. I've never dated anyone from around here. I'll have to tell them eventually, but it's . . . hard. I'm an only child and my parents want grandchildren—bad. It's, like, all they talk about."

"Here's what I think we should do: let's put on a show for your uncle. Let's pretend it's love at first sight. It'll be fun."

"But we've been sitting here for twenty minutes."

"So we've had a couple of drinks and we just realized we're made for each other," she said. "Happens all the time."

"What are we supposed to do—make out?"

"No, no," she said. "We gaze into each other's eyes, like this. Then eventually we hold hands across the table. Then you touch my leg or something. Then we leave in a hurry."

They leaned toward each other until their faces were a foot apart. "Boy, this is really intimate," she said. "Do I have bad breath?"

"You're fine. You have nice eyes."

"No, you do."

"Listen, there's another reason I wanted to meet you—John asked you to get his car back, right?"

"Yeah."

"He's been trying to get me to do it for years. Just say no."

"Just say no," Mona repeated. "That never occurred to me. I was going to tell him I have polyps on my uterus."

He laughed. She reached over and touched his earlobe, then watched his face redden. "You're really good at this," he said.

"This is the best date I've been on in a while, believe it or not."

He awkwardly brushed a strand of hair out of her face. "I think we might be overdoing it."

"Nonsense." She glanced at Johnny. He was sitting on a stool at the door, beaming at them. She took Jesus's hand and kissed it, then held it to her cheek and closed her eyes. "I really, really like you." She sighed.

"You're going to give John a fucking heart attack. He's totally staring at us. He's probably making wedding plans already."

She lowered his hand away from her face and held it across the table. "I suppose we should get out of here before the band starts up again."

They finished their drinks and walked toward the door, holding hands. Johnny was still sitting on a stool, talking on a cell phone. He winked at them as they passed. "You kids be careful," he called out.

"Where you parked?" she asked.

He pointed to a bicycle.

"Do you want a ride?" she asked.

"It's only a couple miles." He walked her to her truck and opened the door for her. "Listen, I'm sorry this didn't work out, but call me if you want. I work a lot but we can hang out now and then."

"Sure," she said. "Thanks."

While they were exchanging numbers he noticed Carmen-Maria-Sofia lying on the passenger seat. "Is that yours?" he asked.

"No," she said. "I found it under Betty's bed yesterday."

He scowled.

"You know her?"

"Oh yeah. We had a really fucked-up relationship. I was staying with John in Vegas the summer he met her, and since he worked nights, she looked after me during the day. It was only a week, but it was the longest year of my life."

"Did she give you a death sentence?"

"She told me I was gay. This was before I knew what that meant. I was only ten. She was very graphic about it—told me about anal sex and all kinds of stuff. Scared the shit out of me.'"

"She can be kind of insufferable."

"Are you going to keep that doll?"

"Why—you want it?" she asked.

"God, no," he said. "I hate dolls."

She told him about the Spanish ladies she'd had as a kid, along with their side effects: paranoia, paralysis, anxiety, insomnia. "I wanted to take them to the garage and smash their faces."

"Why didn't you?"

"I just couldn't summon the energy. I was too passive and non-confrontational. And I was afraid they'd somehow reassemble themselves and gang up on me."

He nodded as if that made perfect sense and then startled her by wrapping his arms around her and squeezing.

"You poor thing," he murmured, directly into her ear.

She felt herself bristle. Don't pity me, Jesus, she thought.

A WEEK LATER SHE ARRIVED AT BETTY'S AS SCHEDULED. Betty met her in the driveway. Despite the insane heat, she wore a white cap-sleeved angora sweater, matching white leggings, and white patent leather high-heeled sandals. Her eyes were glowing.

"I've missed you, Maura! I almost called you a couple of times, but I stopped myself. I wanted to respect your boundaries."

"I have a present for you."

Betty clapped her hands. "You didn't!"

"I certainly did," she said. "I think you're going to like them."

They went inside and sat in the living room. "Your aura is pink and lavender, Maura. You've met someone, haven't you."

"I found Jesus."

"Oh my God," Betty said. "What happened? Tell me everything."

"I don't want to talk about it."

"Well, you look fantastic."

"I have a confession to make."

Betty looked frightened. "You've fallen for Johnny."

She laughed. "No, nothing like that." She opened her mouth and then closed it. Just say it, she ordered herself. Say the words. Spit them out. "Here's the thing," she said, and then paused again. "My name," she said too loudly. "My name is . . . Mona. Not Maura. Mona."

Jesus, that was easy, she thought. Betty sat there, blinking.

"M-O-N-A," she said, for good measure.

Betty regarded her with swimming-pool eyes. "Why didn't you say so before?"

"I wish I knew," she said. "Whenever I thought about telling you, my throat would close up and I felt like someone was suffocating me with a pillow."

"It's your chakra. I told you it's blocked."

She put a hand on her throat. "Well, I feel better now. Much better." She took a deep breath and let it out. "Anyway, I know you're dying to open your present, so here."

She handed Betty the photographs and watched her flip through them, oohing and aahing every few seconds. "How'd you get so close this time?"

"Zoom lens," Mona lied.

"He looks so tired," she said. "He's not taking care of himself." She selected one from the pile and touched Johnny's face with her fingers. Then she pressed the photograph to her chest and closed her eyes. She looked like she was swooning. Mona could see her eyes moving beneath her eyelids. When she started speaking her voice was thick and throaty.

"A kitchen. Open cabinets. Messy counters. Dog food on the floor. Newspapers. Empty boxes. There he is. He's fixing something with a screwdriver. It's . . . a broken toaster oven. A pot is boiling over on the stove. A woman. Black hair. Red blouse. Her name begins with an *L*. She's crying, mumbling, something about the post office. He's ignoring her." She opened her eyes and placed the photograph on the coffee table. "I'm not sure what I was seeing there, but I think he's moving out. Or she's moving in."

"Hey, what happened to your voice? It sounded really . . . different."

"I was in alpha," she explained.

Whatever that meant. Christ, she wasn't far off—he was in fact moving. But maybe she knew that because she staked out his house in her spare time? Spied on him from the sagebrush? In any case, it was a very convincing performance. She could see why Betty made so much money. Speaking of which.

"So you're pleased? I really stuck my neck out this time."

"I can tell," Betty said. "I didn't think you'd get quite so many, but I was going to give you five hundred dollars anyway—just to show my appreciation." She handed Mona a bank envelope from her purse.

"Thanks." She resisted the urge to count it.

"You should go shopping," Betty said. "Buy yourself some shoes. Or get a massage. Or a facial."

"Why bother, when I'm dying?" She cleared her throat. "Look, you don't tell someone they have a year to live. You said you did it out of love, but that's, uh—not love. That's just cruel and hateful. You're pushing sixty. You should know the difference by now."

Betty winced. She hated to be reminded of her age. "Mona," she said slowly, trying it out. "Mona. Mohhhh-na. Listen, Mona." She smiled. "Let me tell you something. I said you would die at twenty-seven, but you didn't even ask how I came up with that number. Do you see the number twenty-seven written next to your life line? No, you do not. The fact is your life line ends abruptly, but you could live to be thirty-two or thirty-eight or even forty-five, okay? It's impossible to get an exact number. Also, your palms change over the course of your life. They're not like fingerprints. I only said twenty-seven because you were dead already. You weren't really living. You were just coasting along like a zombie. And look at all you've done in the time I've told you. It's only been a week and you're already starting to get out there and live your life!"

"Well, I don't know if I'm living my life, but I'm leaving the house at least, yes."

"Listen, you're a photographer, right? Show me a picture of yours and I'll read it—for free. Right here, right now."

"Oh no, that's okay—"

Betty sighed. "Do you have any idea how good I am at this? I have a *very* long waiting list. I'm booked solid for the next three months!"

"I'm sure you are."

"Any pictures in your wallet?"

"Of course not."

"What about that truck of yours? Anything under the seat?"

Well, yes, actually. In the glove box—

"Aha, I can see it on your face. Go out and get it. I'll wait here."

What the hell. She went out to the truck and opened the glove box. Shoved between the pages of an old guidebook was a slightly blurry picture of Mr. Disgusting standing on the fire escape of an abandoned mill in Lowell, taken around the time they first met. He looked sane and healthy and had a subtle tan.

Betty placed the photograph on the coffee table and stared at it without blinking for two full minutes. She seemed to be hypnotizing herself. Although, watching her, Mona felt hypnotized, too. She watched Betty pick up the picture, breathe on it, and then rub it against her angora sweater. She held it against her cleavage with her hand, breathing deeply through her nose.

"Cocaine," she said after several seconds.

Mona stared at the wall clock in a stupor, waiting for her to continue. Thirty seconds ticked by. She could feel her heart beating sluggishly in her chest. In the corner, one of the cats poked its head out of a carpeted cat condo and said, "Ouchy." She wanted to throw a pencil at its head like a dart.

"That's it?" she asked tiredly. "Cocaine?"

Betty didn't answer. Her eyes were closed but her head was moving as if she were looking around the room. "It's freezing in here," she whined. "I can't breathe, I can't see!" Her voice sounded like a five-year-old girl's. "I'm frozen! My eyes feel like glass." She fingered a fold in her sweater. "My dress is . . . stiff."

"What about the guy?"

"Dolls," Betty said. "I see dolls."

Ah, okay. This wasn't about the photograph at all. Last night Mona stuffed Carmen-Maria-Sofia into a plastic bag and buried her under some frozen peas in the freezer. Betty must have been peeking in through the kitchen window.

"Have you been spying on me, Betty? Is that what you do—spy on people?"

"Shh," she said, and held up a hand. "No talking." She looked away, shook her head. "Okay, I'm somewhere new." She winced suddenly and clutched her stomach. The photograph fell to the floor.

"Betty, you dropped—"

"I'm lying in bed. There's two dogs under the covers with me. They're breathing on my legs. I'm listening for footsteps in the hallway. I'm scared, very scared. My legs are hot—"

"Betty—"

"Shh! What's that noise? Something's beeping. Oh no, it's too late, it's too late. I can't stop it. I'm peeing!"

Mona's scalp tingled. Her feet were sweating in her sneakers. Bed, dogs, footsteps—whatever. But the bed-wetting alarm? How could she have known about that?

Diaries, that's how. Obviously, Betty had broken into her apartment and read one of her old diaries.

"Doggies," Betty said now in a weird monotone. "Angels."

In the corner, the cat jumped off the cat condo and darted out of the room.

"Dogs don't have cameras behind their eyes," Betty said evenly. "But dolls do. They watch and record, watch and record."

She felt the overwhelming urge to silence Betty. Something must be shoved into her mouth immediately. A sock, an apple, a fistful of dirt.

"If the dogs are on the bed you can't get me," Betty said in the little-girl voice. "Those are the rules. You can't see me. Stop looking!"

Mona slapped the coffee table with her hand. "Okay Betty, that's enough."

Betty shuddered. "Jesus Christ."

She frowned and looked away. "I don't know what your trick is, Betty, but it's working, whatever it is."

"Those were some really strong feelings," Betty said. "Really powerful. Something terrible happened to little Mona. Something really bad."

"It wasn't that bad, actually," Mona said. "What about the cocaine?"

Betty shrugged. "It was the first word that came to me. It doesn't always make sense."

Mona felt queasy. "Can't you just tell me about the guy in the picture? You know—facts."

Betty picked up the picture and fanned herself with it. "Fine," she said. "You want to know about this guy?"

Fuck, now she was scared. What if Disgusting was alive and well and living a few towns over? What if he was married? What if she ended up like Betty, engaged to herself and surrounded by cats?

"Well, you and this man were siblings in a past life," Betty said calmly. "I don't know if that interests you, but he was your sister. This was a long time ago. Two hundred years, maybe. He was a good older sister—he took care of you, looked after you, protected you. He loved you very much. And then you met again some hundred-odd years later, and that time he wasn't so good to you. Maybe you were lovers. He lied, cheated, abandoned you. And then this last time he had the chance to make it up to you, but I don't know if he did. I can't see much. You must not have been together for very long. But you've known each other a long time, and you'll meet again, perhaps sooner than you think." She shut her eyes briefly and then opened them. "Right now he's at the bottom of a body of water. Not the ocean. A lake somewhere, and not around here—I can tell by the trees." She studied Mona's face. "He's been dead for, oh, about a year, maybe more."

"What's his name?"

Betty let out a puff of air. "Is this a test?"

"Yeah."

She took a deep breath through her nose, let it out. "I don't know, but I can certainly hear his voice."

"What's it sound like?"

"Strange," she said. "Like a large, talking insect. I keep hearing a Polaroid camera taking pictures. He's telling me a name but I can't make it out. Rhymes with 'foreign'? He wants you to say it. I bet if you say it he'll stop haunting you."

"Don't be so dramatic," she said.

Betty looked at the carpet and tilted her head. "He says he's renting space in your brain, preventing you from moving on."

"Am I really supposed to believe you're chatting right now?"

She smiled. "He's making fun of me. He thinks my shoes are stupid. He's calling them 'poopy church shoes.' He doesn't want me to say his name because he doesn't want it in my mouth. He wants to hear you say it."

"Mr. Disgusting," she said.

Betty shook her head. "His real name."

"But that's what I call him."

"Names are powerful, Mona. If you utter his name out loud, you'll be able to move on and meet someone else. Aren't you ready for that?"

"Actually, I don't know his real name," she said. "He was adopted."

Betty closed her eyes again. "Werner."

"Really?"

"It's German. But he has another name."

"Ho, shit," Mona said. "I just got goose bumps."

Betty chuckled, clearly pleased with herself. "So say his name."

"Warren," she murmured.

"He can't hear you."

"Warren," she said again, louder.

Betty set the picture down and beamed at her. "You're glowing. How do you feel?"

How do I feel, how do I feel. "Uh, okay, I guess. A little lonely, maybe."

"Close your eyes," she said. "Now, I want you to picture a very specific shade of blue. It's called certainty blue. It's the color of a gas flame."

"It's the color of your eyes when you wear those crazy—"

"Do you have it?" Betty asked. "Can you see it?"

"Yeah, okay."

"Now keep the blue in your mind and go into your body," Betty instructed. "Focus on your spine. On the vertebrae."

"My spine?"

218

"Yes," Betty said impatiently. "Let the blue travel down your spine to the very bottom, just above your tailbone, and then hold it there and count to three."

Fuck, she was right. Something felt different.

"Stand up," Betty said. "Check it out."

She stood, walked to the kitchen and back, felt like she might cry. It was gone. That hard little knot to the right of her spine. Not merely loosened, but . . . gone. Like it had never been there.

"You've been released," Betty said.

"Holy shit."

"I never thought you were a Maura, by the way," she added.

WHEN SHE PULLED INTO THE DRIVEWAY AT HOME, SHE SAW Yoko and Yoko in the yard, standing in what they called the garden, which was really just a big patch of weeds. She got out of her truck and walked toward them. They were staring at one of the weeds they called burdock.

"Ghost moth larvae," Nigel said. "They're edible. They taste like almonds. We'll have to pick them off by hand. We can make something with them."

"Yikes," Mona said.

He bent over and examined the stalks. "Burdock is a blood purifier," he seemed to say to himself.

"Where are you coming from?" Shiori asked.

"The psychic's house," Mona said. "I tell you what, she said some spooky shit today that somehow fixed my back. I think she might actually be . . . psychic, goddamn it, which means I may only have a year to live. Fuck."

Nigel gave her a puzzled look.

"Are you okay?" Shiori asked.

"Totally fine, actually," Mona said, and walked away.

SHE WASN'T IN THE MOOD FOR THEIR COMPANY, BUT SHE also didn't want to be alone. Jesus's number was tacked to the wall near the phone. Maybe she'd call him tonight and invite him over. They could drink wine and she'd show him her life's work.

Instead, she found herself dialing Mickey's number. He didn't bother with hello.

"Remember that time we went to Vegas and got perms?"

"Yeah."

"I was just thinking about that the other day. The rest of my hair fell out after that. Do you still have that ring I bought you?"

"I lost it when I moved to Lowell," she said. "Listen, I want to ask you something."

"Uh-oh."

She stared at the Fat Fuck drawings on the wall in front of her.

> There was a house
> A little girl
> Two dogs
> One Fat Fuck
> It was a nice skirt
> Fat Fuck was found with no hands
> Fat Fuck is dead

Usually she focused on the captions rather than the actual drawings, but now she zeroed in on "Fat Fuck is dead," the drawing for which showed a man lying on the ground.

His hands were red. A girl stood over him, holding a knife.

"Why did you take pictures of me naked?"

He cleared his throat. "Well, people have been taking nude photographs since the camera was invented," he said. "It's called *art*. You love art."

"I thought it was pretty weird at the time. Still do. I think other people would agree with me."

"Most real art *is* weird. That's what makes it great."

"I didn't mind that much until I saw you showing them to your friends. That sort of ruined it for me."

"I was going through a divorce. I was ready to wake up in another solar system, and I'm not like that. I don't believe in suicide. So you know it had to be pretty bad for me to be thinking that."

"Remember our dogs, Spoon and Fork?"

He didn't answer.

"You sent them to a farm," she said. "True or false?"

"I loved you," he said suddenly.

"So, no farm?"

"I was the good guy," he said. "I was on your side."

"You gave me some really creepy dolls once. Remember? Spanish dolls. I was convinced they had cameras in their eyes, that they could see me, and I didn't even have to be in the same room with them. They held me hostage for an entire year. It was horrible. I couldn't even shower or take a shit without them watching."

"Cameras? In the doll's eyes? Are you hearing yourself?"

"You had a weird habit of watching me all the time. I'd be engrossed in some activity and I'd look up and see you there, *fucking staring* at me—"

"That was Fat Jim, dummy—not me! I caught him spying on you once and almost strangled him. Swear to God."

"You never own your part in anything," she said. "You ever notice that? You make everyone else wear your shit."

"Fat Fuck was found with no hands." No man in this one, just two severed red hands resembling maple leaves.

"This is your mother's fault," he said. "She ran off with that asshole and threw you in the garbage."

"You didn't do anything to stop her. I ended up with *your* cousin, not hers. Whose fault was that?"

"I thought you loved Sheila," he said.

"I did," she said. "I do."

"It's me you never loved," he said. "I used to call Sheila and she'd put you on the phone and I'd ask how things were going at school, and you'd tell me you were a lesbian. Or a communist. Or both." He snorted. "I never knew what the hell to say. Then I'd try to change the subject by asking if you still loved Bill Murray and you'd say, 'I only watch prison movies now.'"

"I was fifteen," she said.

"You were better off without me."

"That's sort of beside the point," she said. "Like, entirely."

What *was* the point? Why did she keep calling him? It was conditioning, partly. She thought she was supposed to call him. Wasn't it also biological? She felt a pull sometimes, on what she thought of as a cellular level. You were supposed to call your parents. You were supposed to have a relationship with them, even if it was shitty. But she didn't want a relationship. She wanted retribution. Verbal, emotional, monetary. And now she knew she would never get it. Perhaps it was best to give up, to get over it.

"Fat Fuck is dead," she murmured, and hung up.

JESUS HAD BEEN WANDERING AROUND HER APARTMENT FOR twenty minutes, picking up objects and putting them down again.

She loved nosy people. Her only regular guests were Yoko and Yoko, who barely moved, let alone touched anything.

"What's with all the throw pillows?" he asked. "You're like the Elephant Man."

"I'm relieved you know who that is," she said.

"Where's Carmen-Maria-Sofia?"

"I put her in the freezer," she said.

He didn't seem to think that was strange.

"Take a load off," she said. "Drink some wine."

They sat on the love seat in the living room with their feet up on the coffee table. His hands were flecked with white and yellow paint. She asked him what he was working on in his studio and he told her he was doing a reproduction of *The Ascension of the Virgin*, except Mary was rising up from the town dump and so she was standing on a pile of garbage instead of the usual heavenly clouds. "Hard to describe," he said. "You'll have to come by and see it."

"Why is your skin so perfect? Do you exfoliate?"

He laughed. "I'm not a chick."

"Well, you smell like one. Is that floral perfume you're wearing? I smell roses."

"Shut up and drink your wine." He examined his fingernails. "Do you have any shea butter?"

She laughed. In between the buttons of his shirt she spotted black ink. "Do you have a chest tattoo?"

He sighed and reluctantly unbuttoned his shirt with one hand. The names "Cathy & Danny" were tattooed in simple typewriter script across his chest.

"Who are they?" she asked, baffled. "Your dogs?"

"My parents."

"Did they pass away?"

"No," he said, and rolled his eyes. "I just love them."

"You know, it's not easy to surprise me," she said, "but, wow—surprised."

He set his wine on the coffee table and slid open the small drawer underneath it. He blinked at its contents for a few seconds before rummaging around. "Anything good in here?"

Before she could answer he pulled out a stack of papers and photographs. "What's this?"

"A barf bag from Korean Air," she said. "I don't know if you know this, but barf bags make pretty good stationery—"

"Jesus," he said. "Did you take these?"

He was shuffling through her last series of housekeeping pictures, all shot in grainy black and white. In each picture she wore a polyester housekeeping smock she'd ordered by mail and pretended to have been murdered.

"You shouldn't leave these lying around."

"Well, I don't," she said. "I keep them in a drawer."

He studied each photograph. "They're cool—very cool. Were you drunk?"

"No! I'm supposed to be working. And also dead."

"You don't look dead," he said. "You look passed out. You should let me do your makeup next time. I could make you look dead in five minutes."

"Well, this is just one series. There are other photographs. Many others."

"How many?"

"Four hundred and twelve," she said. "In my fantasies, my future biographer stumbles upon them after I'm dead, declares them a work of genius, and then Chronicle Books publishes them as a collection, and the book winds up on coffee tables everywhere, including those of my former clients."

"Sounds like you've given it some thought," he said.

"Daydreaming is part of my job."

"Well, I know a lot of people in the art world," he said. "I could probably get you a show while you're still alive."

"Where—at a bus stop?"

"This is good shit, Mona," he said. "Reminds me a little of Sophie Calle. In fact, it might be interesting if you wrote some text to accompany the photographs."

"Oh, I already do that," she said. "I mean, I keep written records. Actually, they're more like stories, because it's clearly . . . my own interpretation."

"What are you interpreting?"

"The lives of my clients," she said. "Based on the things I find in their houses."

"Who are these guys?" he asked.

He was looking at a picture of Spoon and Fork.

"My first loves," she said. "First and only, maybe. Unless I count Mr. Disgusting, who I'll tell you about another time, when I've had more to drink."

He cleared his throat. "Speaking of love." He set the photographs on the table and turned toward her.

"You're in love with me," she said. "Fuck. I knew this would happen."

"I have a boyfriend, Mona. His name's Colin."

"Okay," she said slowly.

"He's a general contractor. He builds solar homes. He's from Australia."

"Are you worried I'm going to fly into a jealous rage or something?"

He shook his head. "Listen, his dog bit the baby—"

"What baby?"

"The baby he has with his wife."

"He's married?"

"Separate issue," he said quickly. "Actually, a nonissue for me, since I don't believe in monogamy."

"I bet the wife believes in monogamy."

"Oh, she knows about me," he said breezily.

"Wow," she said.

"Back to the dog," he said. "His name is George, and he looks exactly like this guy." He tapped Forky's face with his finger. "He's an intense little dude. He's got, like, *presence*, you know? Charisma. He's like a circus dog. But he's bitten the baby twice—in the face, no less. Broke the skin both times. Poor baby has two black eyes right now. Anyway, long story short, the wife wants to get rid of George."

She poured herself more wine. "I'd get rid of the baby," she said. "If it were me."

Jesus didn't say anything, but he was beaming at her.

"Ah," she said. "I think I see where this is going. Why don't you take him?"

"I have two cats," he said. "George kills cats for fun."

"Hmm," she said. "Just my type."

He grinned. "You'd be great together. I already mentioned it to Colin as a possibility. He and the wife have been fighting about it constantly, and I just . . . want it resolved. Put to bed. I mean, not to put you in the middle of anything—"

"My middle name is Middle."

"So what do you think?"

"You must really trust me," she said, flattered.

"Of course," he said. "Don't you trust me?"

She nodded. She did in fact trust him, even though she suspected they had little in common at the core, as he wasn't destructive or prone to self-pity. He would never burn himself with a curling iron, for instance, or overdose on a stockpile of pills. He would never stockpile pills in the first place. She wondered why that was, what separated him from her, and realized it was right there, tattooed on his chest: "Cathy & Danny." He was one of the fortunate ones: he'd emerged from childhood a whole person, and his past wasn't some vast, immovable mass with its own weather system.

She thought of Mr. Disgusting's chest tattoo, the giant wooden ship, the sea, the words "Homeward Bound" written in a banner, and she remembered that thing Nigel had said about her, how she was no longer living among the lotus-eaters, how she was back on the boat, bound for home, and it was time she smote the gray sea with her oars and rowed hard—

"What are you thinking about?" Jesus asked.

"Oh, *The Odyssey*," she said. "Which I've never read. But apparently, according to Yoko and Yoko, I'm on a boat, so to speak, smiting the gray sea with my oars, and so on."

He laughed. "What the hell does 'smite' mean?"

"I think it means to strike something really hard," she said. "You can be smote by a stick, or a fist, or an umbrella. Or by a disease or illness. Or by your conscience. Or by a sudden, strong feeling. I'm pretty smitten by you, for instance."

He raised his eyebrows. "How's that?"

"Because you seem so . . . *at home*."

"Well, this couch is pretty comfortable," he said, and then shifted uncomfortably.

She laughed. "At home in your body, honey," she said. "At home in the world."

She watched his cheeks redden.

"Are you blushing?" she asked.

He looked at his watch. "Guess what time it is?"

She yawned. "Bedtime?"

"Hammer time."

"Oh, no," she said. "It's too late."

"I think you need to do it," he said seriously. "I think you need to smite that creepy doll. In the face. With a hammer."

"But we'll wake the dogs. Have you seen the dogs around here?"

"Get your fucking hammer, dude." She followed him into the kitchen and he opened the freezer. "You put her in a plastic bag?"

She shrugged. "I didn't want her to get frostbite."

He pulled the doll out and started opening kitchen drawers.

"Last drawer on the left," she said.

"Get your ass outside," he said. "We'll do it on the porch."

"If I had a porch," she said.

Outside, they stood on the concrete patio. He laid Carmen-Maria-Sofia on the ground and handed Mona the hammer. It was a clear, moonless night and all the stars were out.

"The sky would be perfect if it weren't for that weird cloud," she said, pointing with the hammer.

He laughed. "That's not a cloud, Mona. It's the Milky Way."

"Get out of here," she said.

"Quit stalling and *smite* this bitch," he said. "Or *smote*. Or whatever the hell."

She crouched over the doll. The hammer felt heavy in her hand, the handle far too long. She raised it in the air.

"Wait a minute," he said. "Your hand's too close to the head."

"Which head?"

"The hammerhead," he said. "Hold it farther down."

She repositioned her grip, raised the hammer again, and then hesitated.

"Do it!"

She let the hammer fall. The doll's face cracked but didn't shatter.

"Harder!"

She started giggling and then got a hold of herself and took a deep breath. "I'm sweating," she said. "And I have to pee."

"Mona, if you don't swing that hammer in two seconds, I'm going to start screaming. You don't want me to wake Yoko and Yoko, do you?"

She swung the hammer as if driving a nail, four, five, six times. The eyes were hard as marbles, but she kept pounding until Carmen-Maria-Sofia was just a body and a clump of hair. She moved onto the hands and feet and smashed them, too.

Then she dropped the hammer and looked at Jesus. He was smiling.

ACKNOWLEDGMENTS

I have my brilliant and generous friend Michelle Latiolais to thank for this book's new life, along with my agent, Binky Urban, my editor, Daniel Loedel, and the entire staff at Scribner. Many thanks to Courtney Hodell, Daniel Reid, Adina Applebaum, Whitney Peeling, Michael Taeckens, and the rest of the folks at the Whiting Foundation, for allowing me a break from waitressing and self-doubt, and for making my life feel less absurd in general. Thanks, also, to Ron Carlson, Bill Kittredge, and Mike Levine, and to my cohorts at the University of California, Irvine, especially Alan Grostephan, James Zwerneman, Ryan Ridge, Alberto Gullaba, and Ryan Hume. Thanks, also, to Franny Shaw, Kate Barrett, Shane Beagin, Maria Korol, Nicole Mullen, Sissy Onet, Kym Scott, Rebecca Goldman, Kat Dunn, Linnea and Vickie Rickard. To my family at Sophia's Grotto for cheering me on, to the Drexler family, particularly MaryLynne, and to my parents, Maureen Branch and Jim Beagin.